KRONOS

ONLINE

MITCHELL NELSON

TABLE OF CONTENTS

PROLOGUE

───◆◆───

"Are you sure about this Theodore? We have been treating you well, a few more years and you might even make management." sighed the reluctant shift manager.

Theo pushed the envelope back across the table and reiterated his point to his now former manager "I am formally resigning from my position Anthony, I appreciate the time here but I no longer have a reason to work here." after Theo finished talking and confirmed that the shift manager picked up the envelope, he got up and walked out the door. The fresh metallic air of the machine shop was in an odd way nostalgic to him as he left. Theo thought to himself 'well this is it, after this if things go right I won't have to work another day of machining again.' for Theo had just sold his stocks after some lucky breaks and bought himself a nice apartment to live in and commit completely to his new hobby slash career choice: *Kronos Online* The brand new enhanced reality MMORPG game. It had released only three months before and had become the top selling game of all time off presales alone.

The game offers state of the art immersion technology that allows the players to feel like they are in the game, the one catch is the machine to become immersed doesn't come cheap: $5,000 for the top of the line systems that let you lay back, connect the headset and "sleep" into the game. The science behind it took years of R&D but Theo was clever and took a leap of faith back when he graduated highschool and invested his savings into it by dropping out of college. Now that the company has taken off he can safely quit his job and if lucky he will be able to make a living off the game.

Kronos Online has the unique feature of an online marketplace where you can sell ingame items for real life currency depending on its rarity or power. There are hundreds of ways for people to make money within Kronos as advertisements, shows, tv spots and streaming are all popular ways to enrich oneself. Utilizing these parts of the game Theo plans to become rich off what every person dreams of; gaming.

Being 25 years old and technically jobless would press on normal people but Theo has no cares for outside opinions, he even brushed off his parents arguments when he told him he was moving out on his own after dropping out of college. Though he wasn't without any regret as his two younger siblings who usually brushed him off as a loner looked at him with even more contempt than usual seeing as he was literally quitting his job to play video games. But to Theo this would only be for a short while since as soon as he starts making the big bucks they will have to take back their stares and gossip.

The in-game marketplace from what he had researched was extremely profitable as many people sought to be the strongest and in their minds items equal power, But to Theo skill in a game is all that mattered regardless of equipment. He would be willing to sell off equipment others would never trade away if it meant he could pay rent for an extra month. There was even rumor that a sword had sold for $8,000 dollars to a top player in the game. That sort of spending power was commonplace among the elite of Kronos online and Theo planned to take advantage of that seemingly bottomless wallet used by the upper echelons of society. Theo is the opposite of that mentality and only spends money under absolute dire circumstances. If he had a choice his diet would consist of just chicken and water every day just to save the extra money on spices he would eat it dry or make a fire so he could save on electricity or gas. To Theodore spending money was like bleeding out and should be avoided at all cost.

After years of constant struggling and working at minimum two jobs since he had turned 16, Theodore had long dreamed of getting rid of the constant urge to save money and live minimally. He had needed to pay for most of the bills at home when he lived there as his parents did not care enough to help him or his siblings better themselves be it with clothes or proper diets. That all changed when Theodore said enough was enough and moved out at 20. Forcing them to take care of his two much younger siblings, 14 and 15 at the time. Since he lived alone in a wild economy he was forced to work the two jobs if he did not want to sell the stocks that were slowly accumulating value over the years. And once the game finally released, he knew it was time to move on to the next step of his life and go full force into this new hobby.

He placed a lease in a new neighborhood and moved to an apartment that could fit his new pod, the old one he lived in for the past 5 years had been run down and barely a studio apartment in comparison. His new place will cost almost double the amount but with how much he made after selling his stocks he can live there for one year at minimum before needing to make any real profit in the game. He would like to save up more though to pay for his little brother and sisters college since there is no way he is letting them work two jobs like he did and he knew damn well that his parents were not going to pay for it.

The waves of emotion crossed over him and his train of thought caught up to him as he finally made it out of the manufacturing house. Looking back one last time letting the wave of nostalgia pass he climbed into the moving vehicle waiting for him outside. It's time for his life to move onto its next step and let him move on from being a wage slave and into a warrior of a new world.

CHAPTER 1

Theodore looked around his brand new apartment with its tiny kitchen table and living room loveseat with a tiny flatscreen tv in front of it. This is his new home, and just delivered today was his new Kronos device, the system of everyones dreams that lets a person experience another world in the comfort of their own home. Theo just had it set up and was about to get into it when he saw the television running a segment on Kronos Online.

"There he is! Glass has just finished another raid with his guild today making him the highest level player in Kronos Online, he seems to be level 110 and managed to subdue the undead crypt outside of Plainsburrow in the Ferrow Kingdom. Lets see if we can get an interview" exasperatedly said the interviewer Chuck Carlson

The camera crew and interviewer hurriedly ran up to the party who had left the guild, "Hello Hello Glass we are with Y.O.K Gaming news could we have your advice to the newcomers trying to reach your level in Kronos?"

Glass looked at them, with his shining red longsword and enchanted armor glistening, then said

"Strength, they need strength and power. My guild The Entity will always be at the top and only the best can be with us, and if you aren't with us well you simply aren't going to be the best."

After Glass made his boast he raised the red longsword with a vibrant unique finish clearly showing it was a Legendary rated item and powerful enough to be given to the strongest player in Kronos then turned back to Chuck "Only the strong wield powerful weapons like these, This sword alone is level 110 and its attributes are fitting to someone of my standing. Only strength can answer strength." With an aggressive sigh he pushed past the interviewer and walked forward with his guild members not interested in Chuck's response. After catching himself from falling Chuck regained his composure then stared back at the camera

"Well you heard it here first folks, If you want to be the best you need to be in a guild! And the shining stars of those guilds today are obviously The Entity! Thanks for tuning in, catch us next time when we go over those adorable shepherd classes tonight at 7"

I turned off the tv, *who cares about guilds, I'm sure he didn't need anyone with him in that crypt and if he did he clearly isn't the best. I'll be different, I won't need anyone elses help.* With this resolute thought I went as fast as I could to the machine. It has a capsule-like appearance with an angled bed to lay in for longer immersion times. This is it, I may be behind a few months of game time but that won't stop me from taking the top spot- since the top spot would give sponsorships and sponsorships equal money. Time to kick in and start my story in Kronos!

I glanced at the clock before settling down and it read 4pm. I laid back into the capsule and put on the helmet, after some securing straps to keep me from falling off I pressed the on button on the helmet. The immersion was immediate and It felt like I was pulled into a different room, now standing. I felt weightless and in an empty space with options in front of me that I knew I could reach out and touch. Seemed like a basic character customization screen and name options, it was a reflection of myself and where I touched I could tweak the appearance however I see fit. I wanted to keep my appearance relatively close to what I normally look like, a slight increase in height here and there to put me at 6'3", I'll also make the red hair a little longer, 5 inches on the top and making it flow off the side is something I never would have been able to do at my old jobs, I already feel more free to be myself.

Then after making at least an hour of scrutinizing detail onto my character I get to the name. Something I want to stand out. I had been wanting to use this name since I heard of the game's release. My early subscription and investment allowed me to reserve a username of my choice for when I purchase the full setup. "Conquest" the blinking name in front of me filled me with some joy as the possibility of the name grows with time passing and the grinding I plan to do in this game. I hit confirm and then get to select the spawn location.

I did a lot of research on the different countries and so far only one country qualifies as an empire and that's the Hammerfall Empire. I do not want to spawn into a country that has no power gap for me to fill. Instead one of the smaller countries seems like the perfect opportunity to show my name as one of the few players in them. Though with nearly 500 million players it would be hard to find a city without at least a few players in them. "Stotonely of the Belfast Kingdom " Seems to be a perfect fit, the stats for the city shows that it is the second largest city of the Belfast kingdom and has only about 200 thousand citizens and maybe one thousand players. Belfast looks to be one of the smallest countries available to spawn in. That sort of formula feels like the perfect amount of challenge and adventure to make my name known. With that thought, I mentally selected *Start* and my vision went black, only floating in the top of my peripheral was the new notification and with a thought I opened it up.

<Player Character Conquest has been completed>
<Spawning you in Stotonely, enjoy your time in Kronos Online>

The first thing I see when I close and open my eyes again is a bustling city center with a majestic water fountain with a turtle statue on it. There were brick walkways spreading out in four cardinal directions around the fountain leading to different causeways surrounded by buildings and stores that are ripe with bartering and talking. I knew this game would look realistic based on the research the company was able to achieve with A.I. but this is ridiculous. If it wasn't for the different color hp bars below their names I would have no Idea who could be a player and who wouldn't be. After taking a few minutes to really grasp that i'm in the game taking a look at my hands and feet. Taking a glance at the fountain I walked towards it to look at my reflection. Sure enough there was my face staring back at me, it felt great to see and really solidified that this felt real. Immersion was important to the developers and they nailed it.

The freedom of movement was nice as well. The full range of motion is available to me as if it were real with tension pulling at me when I reach out to touch my hands together or feel the fountain's stone sidings. Once I finished admiring the craftsmanship and realistic texture of everything around me I started inspecting my inventory more closely. Turning my head towards the bag on my side and focusing my inventory pulls up with the thought, sure enough an entire inventory screen appears including my currently equipped items as well as anything else I have on me. Currently I am starting with a paltry amount of items since I am a new player this shouldn't be surprising but It still is sad to see. 15 copper coins to my name and a <Rusted shortsword> that deals a whopping 7 damage. Pair that with my mostly cloth clothes and I'm ready to die to goblins at this rate. From what I have been able to gather, movement in this game is extremely versatile and if I can use my movement from outside the game to give me even a small advantage I will take it.

Before I could delve deeper into my inventory and the stats of each item I noticed an older gentleman approach me with some worn armor with a metal shine to it.

"You there, young man, I see you have a sword. I am Talmor, an acting sergeant of the guard here in Stotonely. If you would like to learn the basics to combat you could join the militia in the training grounds. And if you have what it takes then you too can be part of the glorious Belfast Kingdom."

As soon as the older man finished talking, my first quest appeared in front of me.

<Training Grounds 1: Rank F>
Go to the training grounds and attempt training with the Militia
members
>Bonus objective: Swing Sword 1000 times
>Bonus objective: Block 250 weapon attacks
>Bonus objective: Win ??? Duels
<Reward: Experience and Reputation>

The quest seemed simple enough and with enough bonus objectives, I'm sure there would be a good reward for it.

"I would like to take you up on your offer. I'm Conquest. Nice to meet you, Talmor."

Talmor just waved his hand and turned and started walking down one of the causeways indicating for me to follow him. I kept close behind as we made our way through the town walking past shopkeepers and stores. We even walked past a church on the way. Talmor slowed down as we were walking past the church and spoke to me "I hear the god of creation Grisia is blessing its priests, if you ever became a pious man, this church would nurture you." and without giving me time to respond he kept walking forward. Not that I would have said anything since I have no drive to become a priestly man tied to a religion.

After walking for another five or so minutes, we make it to the second layer of walls and gates. With Talmor leading us, the guards let us in. Once the gate opened up, I was able to see a rectangular open field that had different training equipment and dummies strewn about across the fields. In the distance, I could see different sparing pits and stands overlooking them. Overlooking the training ground were the inner walls that separate the keep from the training area, towering over 20 feet of solid stone and the hint of an occasional archer making a patrol overtop. Over 20 young men were busy in a row taking commands from what seemed to be a knight with black hair and a chiseled face. Each of the young men seemed to be young militiamen just starting training and could barely keep up with each shout of "THRUST"

"SLASH"

"BLOCK" in rapid succession.

Talmor put a hand on my shoulder and while looking at the man in full knight armor shouted, "I've got one more trainee who needs some experience with a blade!"

The Knight stopped his shouts to the other trainees at the sighs of relief of each of them. And stepped down from his podium making his way towards Conquest and Talmor.

"Welcome new Trainee, I am Knight Captain Randall. I am the captain of the guards of this city and train the new recruits. It's always nice to see new faces of travelers here. If you are green behind the ears of combat, I would suggest practicing your strikes on the dummy over there, once you have that down go ahead and come join us." The Knight Captain finished his speech and pointed towards some training dummies at the edge of the walls. Afterward, he dropped a small salute back to Talmor and walked to his podium, all the other trainees snapping to attention at the return of their leader.

Talmor looked at me and with some unknown excitement in his voice said "Well this is where we part ways for a while, depending on how you do in the training I will see you later, give it your all and you will be fine if you leave these castle walls" and patted me on the back as he left the way we came.

Alone again, I made my way towards the training dummies. No one else was hitting them and there were 8 neatly made in a line for me to strike. I pull out the <Rusted shortsword> and with it firmly in one hand grasp an attempt to swing at the dummy. Of course I strike it, taking a form I had trained in reality. I was met with some positive feedback but I could feel the clear limitations that my mind couldn't make what I wanted to have happen appear. The game really feels like I'm swinging the sword but without a skill relevant to it, my balance feels lacking during this training. I still need to get used to the weight of a sword in virtual reality.

Somehow guiding the first strike, I stretch my arm a few ways and throw some more practice swings. As soon as the blade connected with the dummy, a little red 4 floats up from the point of contact. Showing I did even less than the damage the weapon has to this lifeless cloth doll. Not one to give up and eager to learn how striking in this game works, I begin my mindless assault on this dummy, its health never lowering to the point I can see red. The next strike was a stab in center mass, even if it glanced it did a 'whopping' 6 damage. The strike after that now with better footing, did 7. The fourth, a side slash at the dummies head did 10 damage with a purple color instead of red, indicating it was a weak spot that was struck. After striking the dummy another several dozen times, I noticed a green bar at the top of my limited hud, it was almost empty. I could feel myself being sluggish and the swings being slower than before. The damage seemed the same but I was having a harder time hitting the same place. Then after the bar was completely depleted, I received the notification.

<Depleted Stamina, Regenerate stamina to continue attacking>

I could no longer swing the sword and I could barely move. I was breathing hard and made it to a bench nearby. Seeing how this was a perfect time to look deeper into my inventory, I laid back on the bench and concentrated on the bag.

Inside other than the coins and sword, I had 10 meal packs, sticks and strings. Might as well see how these meal packs taste, cracking into one, I see it's just a box with bread, cheese and a strange chicken broth. I didn't expect the taste to be one of the senses I had in this system but sure enough, when I took a bite of the bread and cheese, it was just as underwhelming as it looked. Nothing special at all about the flavor but my stamina meter was steadily growing faster with every bite I took. As soon as I finished the mediocre meal, my stamina was just about topped off after 10 minutes. I went back to swing at the dummy with some renewed vigor.

I kept swinging until I hit it another 50 or so times until a notification popped up for me

<Skill Learned: Basic Swordsmanship 1>
All sword style attacks and skills will do 10% more damage

Sweet! My first skill. The uniqueness of Kronos is that you can learn skills from any simple tree as long as you practice it. Choosing a class only expedites it by giving you the basic skills and increased experience gained from those skills. Currently I don't have a class so all xp gained for skills is reduced to 70%. It will be further reduced to 50% when I choose a class, and only those skills for the class will be gained at the full rate. Simple enough, I plan to gain as many skills as possible before I choose a class. Then I won't need to be part of any guild or need to rely on anyone else as a jack of all trades.

Now when I swing at the head of the dummy, I do a whopping 11 damage. Not much more but it still is gaining over what I had. I kept at these strikes and until my stamina drained, I kept hitting the dummy. Once it was drained, I would take a break and eat one of my meal packs. I kept doing this until I hit the needed *1000* strikes on the dummy, but as soon as I hit that mark two notifications popped up for me.

<Bonus Objective: Swing Sword 1000 times COMPLETED>
You have gained 5 bonus stat points to allocate.
You have gained a level
You have gained 5 (Meal Pack)
<Skill Upgraded: Basic Swordsmanship 2>
All sword style attacks and skills will do 20% more damage

Now that is nice to see, I was given 5 bonus stats on top of my level up which is an additional 10. The extra meal packs bring me up to 8 meal packs left so not quite enough to make up for what I ate but still convenient to get at all. This was a very generous bonus objective and it only took me 6 hours in-game to get, though most players wouldn't spend 6 straight hours swinging at a practice dummy as soon as they enter a world like Kronos. but I am different. Any advantage I can take, I will do my best to grab. The extra skill upgrade is nice too, a true edge to receive when I'm still at such a low level.

With these new stats, I need to think about what will benefit me in both the long term and short term. As far as I know, there are no skill reset potions or any other way to reallocate these skills, so once they are dispensed, there is no way to unallocate them. Meaning I shouldn't put the points into things I would never need more than once. Dexterity gives me higher crafting speed and attack speed, but really focuses more on hand-eye coordination. Strength is very simple but still essential as it modifies my physical damage that I can do as well as the carry weight I would be capable of. Intelligence controls the time at which my mana is regenerated as well as the power of spells that I could cast. Charm handles the likability with NPC and their opinion of me as a traveler but bearing almost no combat benefits. Constitution handles my HP and stamina total as well as my hp regeneration, which is very important. Agility then has movement speed, stamina regeneration and even boosts attack speed when buffed depending on the type of weapon I would be using. Keeping this information in mind when making my skill choices, it seems obvious I focus on combat for easier experience grinding. Well, let's see what my character info looks like, if I think about stats, it should pull up my character sheet…

Name: Conquest	Class: None	Level: 2
Stat points to Allocate:	15	HP: 100+50 Mana: 50
Dexterity:	5	
crafting/attack speed		
Strength:	5	+5
physical DMG/ carry weight		
Intelligence:	5	
Mana total/regen and spell power		
Charm:	5	
Likability with NPC		
Constitution:	5	+10
hp/ stamina total		
Agility:	5	
movement speed/ stamina regen		

I am weaker than a fish out of water currently and the fact I will be in this training location for quite some time has to be considered. I think I would benefit from increasing my stamina as best I can to keep swinging at the dummy. I will put 5 points into strength and the rest into Constitution. The extra movement speed and stamina regen would be perfect for the long stretches of time spent here in the training ground.

Right as I hit accept on the stat allocation, I feel much more comfortable wielding my sword and taking a swing at the dummy, a solid uninterrupted slash to the head dealing a purple 15 damage. Significantly more than before and a rewarding feeling to go with it. Not wanting to stop, I kept swinging the sword to see how long my stamina would keep now that the regeneration had been increased.

One hour and 300 swings later, my stamina was depleted yet again but I was easily able to strike the dummy with much more precision and ease than I was before. Every once in a while I would get some strange stares from the other trainees since I have been doing nothing but swing at this practice dummy since I arrived. Well, I might as well ignore them for now and keep swinging my sword. After a few more hours, some rest and 1000 swings the sweet ding of:

<Skill Upgraded: Swordsmanship 3>
All sword style attacks are 30% stronger
You gain the ability: <Powered Slash>
<Powered Slash>
At the cost of 5% stamina deal 250% damage

Not bad! An increase in my damage, as well as flat-out damage-dealing ability, is great to have. But if this is what I get from 2000 swings, what would happen at 3000 or even 4000…

My mind is restless and the thought of free stats and strength driving me to keep swinging the dummy, rinse and repeat over and over again while some trainees look upon me with a dubious expression since I have been standing in front of these dummies for hours doing nothing but swing, swing, slash constantly. Though I was rewarded, every time I did 1000 strikes a pop-up would appear and my stats would go up by 1. Once I struck the dummy 5,000 times, I felt exhausted and my iron craved more than just strikes upon a dummy. The bonus of taking 12 free stat points from striking was definitely useful. I happily allocated them to Constitution. I am sure when I come back, I will see how far I can push the stat bonuses.

And I think with this I'll move on to the rest of the training even if it has been a few hours. Looking back at the trainees, I see they are currently doing sparring sessions under the supervision of the Knight Captain. How about I try to enter in about with some of them, test out how my swinging training and real-life acclimation has paid off.

I started to make my way towards the trainees and the knight captain spotted my approach, he walked from where he was observing a particularly aggressive set of cadets slashing their wooden swords at each other almost recklessly. He looked me up and down and could see the sweat I was giving off and maybe the glint in my eyes that I wanted to get in the ring with some of them and smiled. The knight captain then said

"7 whole hours swinging at the training dummy is some dedication I would not expect to find even among my most trusted knights. I'm sure that if you had proper guidance and training you would become a fine knight. Let's see how you fare against some other trainees that started today as well."

Then called out to one of the cadets, "Cadet Adrian come on over, I would like you both to fight in the ring here, this will be just a simple sparring match until the other person concedes or can no longer continue to fight."

The sparring system in Kronos online isn't unique in its simplicity, both opponents fight until one drops to 1hp and the duel ends, nothing is lost and no permanent damage is done except weapon durability. I was just drawn into my first sparring match against cadet Adrian, a younger-looking guy with dark skin and some stubble growing on his chin. He has about the same getup as me with simple trousers and a cloth shirt. The only true difference is he is an NPC or non-player character. This will be my first true combat against the A.I in this game. I took the wooden sword and shield from the rack next to the ring and started walking into the ring making eye contact with Adrian who was doing the same. Now that we are both wielding a wooden sword and a shield the sparring match can begin.

I had never used a shield up to this point but thankfully I have some extra agility and I can just imagine that you have to hold the shield up when he goes to swing. The shield feels light in my left arm as it's strapped to my forearm. As I make my way into the ring Adrian does the same. We both are limbered up and it's time for my first duel.

"I am Conquest, Let's have a good match," I said to the now flustered Adrian as he tried to get the shield properly latched onto his arm. As soon as he gets it strapped he looks back up towards me and responds like he wasn't quite paying attention "They can never get these shields on right, I'm Adrian let's fight Traveler" and as soon as he finished talking he lunged forward, all that flustered attitude and demeanor before flushed away and his wooden sword tip leading the charge was pointed straight at my chest.

Luckily I was able to bring the shield to block in time, but it seemed Adrian predicted this move and as soon as I brought the shield up to block the sword It was also blocking my vision of Adrians kick he was lashing out knocking my shield back. I didn't even conceive of the idea that you could kick in combat but here I am, with a little icon on the top right of my vision that says stunned and a little 2-second countdown. Right before the countdown ended Adrian was able to get a good slash off on my side, I could feel a little pain but luckily this game does not emulate that sort of feeling complete. Though the pain was there it was just dull and I could see my hp bar at the top of my vision be reduced by 6 points.

Now that I was no longer stunned I could fight back properly. Instead of letting him keep on the offensive since I could see his feet pivot to go for an overhead strike I used the same strategy he used and moved with more than just my sword as a weapon. I dodged to the side. He held his shield up and I bashed it with my own, using that bit of confusion to stab low with my sword towards his legs. I could feel the resistance in the blade as it cut into him followed by the little red number 7 float near his health, which was barely dropped. Knowing he was planning a counter-attack, I backed up as fast as I could and watched his sword as he came in again going for a sideways slash towards my right thigh. It was too far out of my shields range but if I could block it with My sword... I go to raise my sword and manage to parry his, causing half a second of stun on Adrian. Using that little bit of time, I knew what would work best for me.

I unstrapped my shield and tossed it at Adrian. He just raised his own shield when the stun finished and it harmlessly bounced off and fell to the ground. He did not expect me to charge in- sword first in a wide right swing to cut into his own sword hand. Unable to see the attack coming Adrian took another 8 damage as it cut into him. Adrian made a small yelp with surprise at the cunning attack but kept his stance firmly planted in the ground. I backed away just in time to intercept his counterattack with a parry of my own.

<gained 1 agility>

Interesting that it rewards me with stats when I come up with unique strategies. I'll keep that in mind, in the meantime, I need to keep blocking. Let's see how long I can parry him for without attacking. I still have that side objective to block a ton of attacks, why not try and maximize the effectiveness by parrying too. Shields are overrated anyway. All the while having these thoughts Adrian kept his advance thinking he had the advantage over me, every time he made a swing I put all my concentration on where he was swinging his sword and blocking it where I could, circling around him when he was stunned and rotating around him to avoid the edge of the ring. Though some of the attacks he made got through my novice defences and struck me three more times for 21 damage before I felt it would get out of hand. After blocking another 30 or so times, I went on the offensive, striking at his hands and legs when he overextended an attack or when I parried him.

Once the duel was turned to my advantage, it only took another minute of deliberate strikes to drop Adrian out of the duel. The final strike, utilizing the new ability <Powered

Slash> dealing a critical blow to his head with my training sword a whopping 23 damage. Though after the duel the effect of stamina drain was still very real and I was nearly depleted after the fight. I approached the now sitting Adrian who was rubbing his disheveled black hair where I struck him and outstretched my hand to pick him up "Thanks for the duel, it was a good fight".

Adrian took the offered hand and picked himself up with my help, responding in a pained voice "A good fight for you may be and I really thought I had you at the beginning too!"

Just as he finished talking, Knight Captain Randall came up to the both of us in the ring with even a little fire in his eyes staring at us. As soon as he arrived by our sides, he congratulated us "You both had an excellent duel and the foresight to conserve stamina in a drawn-out battle. Adrian, both of you started today and the battle prowess you both showed was impressive. You both would turn into excellent knights with proper training. Keep training and in two days I will have a minor tournament with all the trainees to see how they fare and who will be granted the honor of joining the expeditionary force led by a centurion in our nation's army in 3 days. You both would be welcome to participate regardless of your exploits in the tournament, but you would be joining as just a regular soldier instead of as my squire."

The offer was followed up by a new quest notification for me.

<Participate In the Trainee Tournament: Part 1>
Participate in the trainee tournament and place 1st to continue the quest
Participate in the trainee tournament and place in the top 4 to be rewarded

I eagerly hit accept since it would be my second *Linked quest* that I will be taking part in. Linked quests are special in the fact that if you meet the conditions for it and succeed, they will continue with greater and more powerful rewards the further you go. This would be great as my second quest in Kronos Online.

Looking at the expecting Knight Captain I smiled and responded with exactly what he wanted to hear "I will be looking forward to the tournament and I hope I will be exactly what you are looking for" the obvious confidence put Randall in a little bit of a bind as he thought it was conceited to talk with such boisterous attitude after winning a single duel against a trainee who had only fought for a single day as well. But since he was the one to make the offer and not one to skip out on watching a good fight, he nodded his head and looked to Adrian to hear his answer.

"I too would like to participate, I look forward to beating you in the ring next time we fight- Conquest" Adrians answer was humble but full of vigor as the light of a rival was made in his eyes. Having heard what he needed the Knight Captain shook both our hands and walked away making passing remarks to "get stronger, train harder, fight faster!"

I was excited and ready to take on some other trainees as soon as my stamina recharged. It was astounding how realistic they are able to capture the emotions on these A.I. Their actions in combat are realistic too, almost as if he was learning as the fight went on and was adapting. I would need to keep that in mind as I fight opponents, especially if I need to fight them again in the future since the same tricks most likely won't work twice.

Time in the game works differently than in reality, the pod makes it so we are able to experience the game at 4 times reality. So, 4 days in a game is only one day in reality. Meaning that the tournament will be tomorrow for me in reality but I have over 48 hours to accomplish proper leveling in-game. I had been in these training grounds for almost 12 in-game hours but in reality, it was only 4.

After about 10 minutes of resting and eating a meal pack, my stamina was recharged. It was time to find my next opponent. Taking a good look around the training ground I noticed a bench of other trainees all scanning the people around them most likely looking for a fight just like I am. Not one to pass up on a challenge I of course went up to them.

"Any of you fellow trainees looking for a sparring partner? I am Conquest and just started today" At the mention that I had just started training today most of them perked up to look at me with a slight glint of excitement and some evil glints. The middle of the four men got up, he had a straw hat on and was almost a full head taller than me looked me up and down and with some failed to hide the pride in his voice "I'll be your opponent *Conquest* I'm sure I can teach you a thing or two" and started walking towards the closest ring to duel in. The duel request gets sent to me and I accept.

He immediately pulled out a two-handed war hammer that seemed to have been made explicitly for training since it was made mostly out of wood. He brought that war hammer deftly above his head towering up and brought the beastly weapon down. I tried to block the heavy swing but my sword that I tried to block with was just thrown aside like it was just an annoying fly and it kept going down until it struck my left shoulder dealing a devastating 21 damage from a single strike. *Holy crap that stung* I thought to myself as I tried to regain my composure. I was hit with the stun penalty when he broke my defence which allowed him to deal such a heavy blow. Once, I fully grasped what was going on around me I spotted my opponent was taking another swing at me, same again straight from above but this time I knew better than to just wait and try and block it. I rolled to the left as he began to bring the hammer down and it barely missed me, striking the ground where I stood instead. Using the recoil he is experiencing from the overthrown missed strike, I took my sword in and jabbed out at him from his right, undefended and not wearing any armor he took 9 damage from the strike. Not enough to stun him or slow him down he just brought the hammer back from the ground and the aggressive game of back and forth was started.

Luckily this man wasn't nearly as proficient at fighting as Adrian and he wasn't trying anything new. Just overhead strike, dodge, get stabbed, side swing, dodge, gets stabbed. After about 4 minutes of excruciatingly repetitive combat with the brute of a man with a war hammer, he finally dropped to 1hp and the duel ended.

The smug grin of a guaranteed winner was no longer on his face as he stared at me with annoyance for winning. "I won't forget this, Conquest" as if I was at fault for him bolstering his own ego trying to beat a new recruit. I didn't want to let him off that easily though, so I had to ask him "I never got your name, but I won't remember it anyway" and walked towards the next man on the bench without hesitating and asked the next man to duel me. The brute of a man couldn't even comprehend that I ignored him and started getting all sorts of pissed off on the side while I continued to ignore him. The man I challenged, however sheepishly got up and pulled out a shortsword from his hilt, he was a lankier fellow with brushy brown hair and seemed to be barely in his twenties. He started walking towards the ring while trying to ignore the brute then said to me.

"I am new too at fighting, my name is Apollo, let's learn together" and as soon as he finished talking he sent the duel request. I accepted and with a smile began the duel with half of my stamina already depleted. Apollo immediately started swinging, while I attempted to parry. Trying to take advantage of the stunning effect from parrying the enemy's attack I kept blocking where I could and striking small blows towards the wrists that were exposed in his one-handed fighting style. A good note to have since I am fighting in the same style. Apollo didn't know his way around the sword that I was sure of and he didn't have the grace or charm that Adrian had nor did he have the strength the brute carried with him. The fight barely lasted 2 minutes as I kept him stunned and struck him as soon as I could. Once the fight was complete a new notification came up.

<Won duel against a higher-ranked opponent without taking damage>
You have gained 3 free attribute points

That is awesome! I didn't know he was a higher rank than me. And the fact that I didn't take any damage during the duel was impressive. I placed the free skill points into agility again to try and increase my reaction time in combat as I feel the stamina drain is too much when moving for strikes in creative ways. The bonus wasn't much but I could feel it may give me that added advantage if I need to fight someone better than the brutish man from earlier.

After I was done spacing out looking at my new statline, I shook the hand of my sparring partner Apollo as a gesture of a well-fought battle. It wasn't much but anything counts here especially if the A.I. is able to remember my actions at this level. The more friends the better in a small city like this. Before continuing my onslaught of the 4 benched men I took the seat of Apollo and ate one of my meal packs, these spars really did a number on my stamina.

One thing I noticed is that my stamina isn't recharging nearly as fast as it did before. I looked around my vision to notice a new icon of a bed. When I focused on it a new notification came into my sight.

<Sleep Deprivation: Minor>
To fight at full strength, you need to rest

It seemed this was enough for today's game and I needed a snack anyway. I walked myself over to the barracks near the training ground for trainees, paid a requested 5 copper and fell asleep on the bed inside. Once my character was asleep I logged him out and returned to reality.

One in-game day and I am already level 2 and far stronger than a similarly leveled NPC or player stat-wise. I am sure there will be players in the tournament so in the next few days I will need to train as hard as I can to get the advantage. I overheard some of the other trainee NPC saying they have been preparing for this tournament for the past three weeks. That means I will have a serious skill gap to overcome in this tournament. Well, it's starting to get night out and I better eat dinner and nap before a good gaming session tomorrow.

After logging out of Kronos, I meticulously took off the helmet and straps keeping me in the capsule and got up. I took a look at the clock and it was already 8 pm, what was 16 hours in-game time was only 4 hours in reality. I set an alarm to get me up at the crack of dawn in the game tomorrow morning and was about to head to bed when I decided to check the market on my PC. I set up a little desk with my outdated and pieced-together computer that barely ran. Once it finally booted up I went to the official global trade site, from

33

there I can see the going prices of items and the open auctions that people from around the world have put up.

I wanted to give myself an idea of what to expect at my low level and if there were any items worth selling If I were to get any. I sorted by level and set the cap at level 15 for items. Sure enough there were dozens of weapons, armor and accessories available which made the price lower than expected. Though as the rarity went up so did the scarcity of items. There was an epic sword for auction and even if it still had 14 hours left was at 500 dollars. Other rare and the like items sold for at least 100 dollars.

Weapons were selling for more than armor and accessories but there were still exceptions for the rule as the most expensive item being sold at this range was an epic-rated ring of self-healing it granted improved HP regeneration and the rate was almost noticeable in battle at low ranks. Its auction was almost over but the current price of it was 1200 dollars. Money was definitely there to be taken and I wanted a piece of it.

So with new found motivation and anticipation I turned off the pc and jumped into bed, ready to sleep and wake up gaming again.

Cora

Cora was an avid gamer who played Kronos since its release and was adamant about being the world's best assassin, coining the special name of Shadow to solidify her goal. She had barely been noticed in all her missions and even achieved level 90 with the amount of grinding and tasks she had completed thus far with almost no media notice. The tasks she had been given usually were to assassinate enemy mobs that were classified as elites or in some rare instances she even had to assassinate the boss mobs. Though recently she had been getting more politically affiliated assassinations, one was a captain for a patrol and another was for a raiding party leader that had been pushing too far into the wrong person's territory. Her Karma score would fluctuate wildly as her targets were never the same, some would be righteous as church leaders and others would be as vile as savages.

The target made no difference to her as long as the rewards were there and she was able to escape from reality in this virtual world.

Cora had just about finished another long day in Kronos when an NPC approached her who had robes that radiated an evil aura. Not one to shy away from any task regardless of alliances she waited in the empty alleyway waiting for the robed figure to make a move or give her a task. This time around the man was the latter and started to explain what her newest mission would be. Unlike her other tasks, it was one of capture, not murder and she had to think about taking it seriously, but when the reward was told to her she had to at least give it an attempt. A Unique grade weapon for a Count captured alive. The smile she gave was genuine as before she could log out she had to make some preparations for this new quest. The influence of a high-level player that has accumulated favours is about to be put to good use in obtaining this new weapon.

CHAPTER 2

Day two of my Kronos Online adventure has to wait until I eat breakfast and finish my morning routine. This new house isn't bad but I *should definitely buy more furniture, I* thought to myself. Eating cereal while sitting on my bed is hardly sanitary. Glancing at the time I see my alarm was punctual at waking me up again at 6 am, I plan to be in the game every day at 8 am in order to get the optimum amount of time online. Of course, I was cut short yesterday because of the move but that will not stop me today. Once I finished my hearty meal, I got into my workout clothes and decided to go back to a dojo I went to when I was younger. Conveniently I had moved only a mile away from the place and the cardio of running to it in the morning greatly improved my stamina.

As soon as I left my new home in the brisk morning air I already felt better than the day before, I could still see some stares from people across the street since my posture was still terrible and I had an unkempt face full of scraggly hair and clothes that didn't match, but that didn't stop me. I don't care what they think and I was going to the dojo to get some of this pent-up aggression out as well as train my body to be better again.

I ran for about 10 minutes before I came up on the dojo with an old red sign hanging above the door, *Rocky's Kali Martial Arts Dojo*. This place has a unique form of martial arts trained here called Kali. Kali is a form of martial arts that specializes in not just one form of combat but multiple, being able to use any weapon to defend oneself is tantamount in combat and it was drilled into me since I was a child. Before even entering the place I could hear the shouts of trainees and clangs of wood sticks striking one another. nostalgia-filled my mind at the sounds. It was refreshing to hear and I took my first step in through the door.

———————◆———————

Rocky

Rocky was a diligent man who dedicated his life to martial arts, through decades of focused will and training he had reached the apex of strength and dexterity when it came to combat. He had become world champion in multiple fields of martial arts and after a time formed his own dojo. There was always a drive to find more disciples to take on the path of Kali Martial arts but the path was always strict and though many can navigate the roads very few can see the end like he had. This morning was the same, he had a few other teachers below him that he had assigned to other branches but even after 5 years, he hasn't met a student that had the drive to learn and the passion to fight through the pain that comes with this training. Almost 7 years ago he met a student that seemed more promising than any other he had met, at the time he did not realize his potential but on his last day at the dojo he sparred for 5 hours straight before leaving, his hands bleeding, and body bruised he did not stop sparring until the dojo was closing. Rocky saw those eyes, ones of what could have been seen as despair or perhaps rage but in any case, they were ones that had ferocity in them. When he left he had never returned, his contact information that was there when he signed up didn't work and he failed to contact him again. Ever since then he regretted not going out to stop the lad before he went and ask him what drove him to this point of fervor.

While Rocky was lost in his thoughts an older teacher came into his office and roused him from his contemplation "sir I think you might want to see this, I have a new student here today" which to rocky wasn't that big of a deal dozens of people applied to start training at his gyms every day but even then taking on a student from those applicants wasn't something special to him.

"What kind of student have you worked up, James?" The question was met with a grin that spread from ear to ear on James' face and his shiny teeth showed when he said the next words. "This young man had passed the trial tests perfectly, I almost thought he was a student of a rival dojo, then when he went to spar he had a stance similar to your fathers."

This made Rocky sit up instantly, the only two people to train directly with his father was himself and the student he had met years ago. Before his late father passed he had given some special attention to one of the students at his gym, not really sure why he was so special until it was too late. He had seen it before and there was no way he was going to let it slide this time.

"Bring me to him" Rocky immediately stood from his desk, and walked towards the exit.

"Theodore, you said your name was right? What reason have you come to this dojo?" a burly man in a gi that had a distinct black belt on and was escorted to Theo by two other built men with black belts as well. They were all professionals and had an extremely imposing view on them when standing over theo by almost a full head. The one in the center asking the questions had black hair and a chiseled double chin and it seemed like every inch of the man had muscle on it. Not wanting to delay the men anymore I answered.

"Yes, you can call me Theo Sirs, I used to come to this dojo when I was younger and I wish to learn more from here again." I said with resolute expression and a slight bow, typically when a student leaves a dojo they are not allowed to return, I bowed in hopes they would listen to my pleas but I would accept if they refused me without complaint.

The man in the middle face brightened and stood up straight, placing a hand on my shoulder and guiding me to stand up straight. "Of course you can train here Theo, you can call me Rocky and I will be your trainer here." After the words left his mouth the faces of the two other men with black belts turned and looked at him with shock on their faces. Their expressions gave me a bit of a chill looking back at the man called Rocky as if a tiger hand-laid its eyes on me but that didn't change my thought. What was on my mind currently was the cost of this dojo as I remember it was expensive enough that I couldn't afford it and my sister's hospital bills so I had to stop coming. I hope it was cheaper because a personal trainer sounds like more harm to my wallet than good.

"Sensei, how much is it going to cost me to train here every month?"

The man on the left spoke first "Our cost is 150 dollars befo-"

Then Rocky's side cut him in the gut with a jab and spoke over him "he meant 15 dollars Theodore, 15 dollars a month to train here." again after he spoke the two other men stared at him in disbelief but neither had come up to counter his words.

This put a huge smile on my face and I happily bowed again, "Then where should I start!"

Rocky smiled back at me and pointed at the course he had in the room for training. It consisted of a three-minute timer and multiple training bags/blocks/equipment. Every time the timer would go off you would switch to the next piece of equipment and train on it until the timer went off again for an unsaid moment of time. Rocky then received a gi from one of the other two black belts next to him and tossed me it, along with a white sash. "Put this on and then start in the training block for today, once you are able to stand it for three hours we can put you in sparring for technique." It seemed extreme but I remember when the old man last taught me how to train, it was similar and I was glad I took the time to build my physical fitness like I had in the past.

After I changed I took my attempt at the blocks and had my charge at them, after an hour I was exhausted and felt like puking. But I kept going even though I would be late to get on Kronos. I know that this first impression would be beneficial in the long term to be healthy. After two hours my muscles were sore and I felt pain everywhere ignoring the strain and focusing entirely on the training, but before I started my third hour Rocky had come up to me stopping me from my training. Just then I had just noticed I was being watched by other men in the dojo who had black belts on. He put one hand on my shoulder and spoke softly "Theo when I said work to get three hours I meant over the course of a few weeks, not on your first day. I can tell your muscles are hurting and if you don't stop now you will pull something and be gone for weeks. Take a breather, go home and come back at the same time tomorrow and try again. You did good"

You did good.

It was a phrase I hadn't heard since I was here last. Hearing the praise I raised my head and bowed again but I damn near fell over. "Thank you sensei" and wobbled my way back home, though I had a sinking feeling I was being followed but I was too tired to care anyway.

As soon as I made it home I closed and locked my door, took a shower and drank some water. It was a bit later than I wanted but the workout was worth it and I would have time to rest inside the kronos machine. I stretched for a few minutes so I wouldn't cramp up too badly and laid down in the capsule ready for an intense day of grinding in Kronos online.

————◆————

Rocky

"I told you he was the one," said Rocky to a questioning James. "I have to admit, his will is tenacious and you could see he would have easily worked himself to the bone if you didn't step in. Though why did you lower the cost of our services to him, especially if you are going to be taking time out of your own schedule to be training him?"

At the question, it seemed to make Rocky bolster up in pride at the remark "Because My father saw the same thing I see in him now, and if he left because of money problems. I will not jeopardize his training because he can't afford to come in. I think he can be my successor if we train him right. Think of him as your little brother from now on. That is an order from your sensei. He is part of the Rocky family." Each of the black belts listening all stood up straight at the weight of his words and took it extremely seriously. Before everyone dispersed two more extremely built men came into the dojo and shared their findings "We followed Theodore home, he only lives a mile away in a decent apartment complex

44

uptown. Here is his address and contact information" after handing over the sheet of paper and photos a smile crept on Rocky's face.

"We won't lose him this time."

———◆———

<Login Successful>

I woke up where I went to rest in the bunks, becoming corporeal again and getting out of bed for the second time today. I was excited for some training. I didn't get too good of a look of this barracks before I logged out and I missed the dreariness of it with all the cobwebs and dust floating around. It was clear not many trainees used this place. But that isn't something for me to worry about. I left the barracks with spirits high and stamina full out on the look for XP.

Leaving the comfort of the shabby barracks I was met with a bustling training field in front of me, trainees from yesterday and even more assorted fighters some players among them, were doing all sorts of training exercises from running laps around the enclosure, swinging at dummies, shooting arrows and even duels amongst themselves. According to my side objectives I need to win a certain

45

amount of duels as well as block attacks in order to complete my first quest. So it seems sparring will be my best choice for getting stronger.

Having a plan sorted out I started my determined march towards the men in the training grounds having sparring matches. Seeing a few of them off on the side looking like they are waiting their turn, I got in line behind them and asked

"Is this where I go to test my metal?"

"You may, let us pair you with someone your skill level new recruit" said the burlier of the group. He then pointed at another young man in the line who couldn't have been older than 19 with his helmet covering almost all his facial features except his narrow chin. His helmet barely fit on his head clearly holding back a full set of blonde hair and I was nearly a foot taller than he was. But the burly man insisted he would be my opponent.

Relenting, I followed the younger man into the ring. He bowed and withdrew a longsword from his hilt, its ornate design should have been a clue to me he wasn't just some trainee testing his skills. That and the crest he wore on his chest piece - which was clearly shiny compared to anything anyone else was wearing here. In a higher pitch than I expected he said the first words since meeting him, or her now that I heard the voice

"I am Isabel von Torez and I shall be your opponent."

It was like a slap in the face as the armor she wore completely hid the fact she was a woman. Most of the time you can tell in rpg games depending on their armor but hers was just plate mail and her posture was that of a knight. I shook my head and gave the proper respects she is due as a fellow trainee.

Seeing her resolve I returned the kind greeting "I am Conquest, let us learn together" and accepted the duel.

She immediately swung the sword down but stopped as I went to raise my own to intercept, she knew I would block and feinted her swing to the side for a jabbing blow instead. It caught me off guard and dealt 12 damage. Her stature may be short but her power with the longsword is more than I expected and she has the skill to back it up. I tried to think of a way out as quickly as possible against an opponent who clearly knew what she was doing. The first thought I came up with was going on the offensive with the shortsword, going low and on her non dominant side. But to my surprise when I swung my sword all she did was change her stance to be that side instead and blocked effortlessly. Instead of trying the offensive strategy then I need to play opportunistically against her assault. The gap that gets opened when blocking the strike is what I need to aim for.

Isabels assault was relentless, feints, swings, jabs, kicks and even a spinning slash over and over again she was able to get through my defences and I was only able to block a single time and doing so didn't even stun her for the opportunity I was looking for. She was the most skilled opponent I had fought till now. Eventually she brought me down to 1 hp and I lost the duel. Though she did not act arrogantly when she leaned down to pull me from the ground.

Her voice was soothing, "That was a good duel Conquest, you lasted longer than any I had faced until now among the new recruits and even managed to glance at my armor. Thank you for the fight and I look forward to seeing your results in the tournament" with a smile that could only be gleaned at through her helmet.

<Plus 10 relationship with Isabel>

I made a simple bow to her skill and then noticed the laughter from the men before who sent me to be her opponent. They knew she was above my skill level and led me to fight her anyway. In a sense I was grateful but I still was ashamed of losing a fight so early on in my career basically as a trainee gladiator.

"And thank you Isabel for teaching me" I remembered to respond but was still in a little bit of shock from the ordeal. Looking closer at her armor I could now tell she was indeed a *she* with armor that had bent on it to add space and armored leggings that had thinner plate than typical but gave the impression it was just as strong or stronger than the normal. She was at a much higher level than me and her equipment would have made it impossible to beat her with my current stats and weapon skills. Though this did make me even more interested in knowing who she was, a uniquely named NPC in a training ground for soldiers, equipped with shining armor and a crest of a turtle clearly from a noble clan almost screams questline to me. I followed her off the dueling circle and attempted to open a dialogue with her,

"So what does your crest represent?" I asked with willful ignorance of its significance that she seemed to notice.

"It represents the von Torez household with the crossing swords and turtle shell shield. I am Count Rodriguez von Torez's daughter. My father is the man who maintains this region and rules this city. The fact that you are staying here and fighting in the training ground without even knowing that is astoundingly ignorant."

<Minus 5 relationship with Isabel>

"I didn't mean any offence to Lady Isabel. I hope you can forgive me as I am a traveler new to these parts and unaccustomed to the traditions of where I travel."

This time Isabel looked amused at my confusion. And even gave a slight smile at my quick attempt to recoup my dignity from her remarks. I could feel my cheeks turning red from the implied insult but held fast with my comment. Once she finished her contemplation she responded with a much lighter tone than the one she started with. right after I received another notification.

"Well you are the first traveler I have met, I did not expect to meet one training with my fathers guard either. So it was nice to get a bit of practice to compare the travelers' skills to my own. I'm glad to know I can still handle myself!" she said with pride in her voice before one of the burly men poured water on her self proclaimed greatness.

<Plus 1 Charisma>
<Plus 7 relationship with Isabel>

"Well your ladyship this traveler is brand new to the training grounds, I saw him be brought in by Knight Captain Randall just yesterday. As a traveler he is surely one of the weakest of them at least in strength if not in skill."

As soon as I heard the man's comment I started looking with greater interest at their outfits. The 6 men who were waiting in line weren't looking for a duel, they were standing at attention to keep Lady Isabel safe and I am only now noticing the same crest on each of their leather and plate armors as well as the glint of actual metal on the weapons in their sheaths. Me running up and challenging them to a duel was reckless and stupid but it seemed to have paid off. This realization seemed to have been clear to see on my face as the man started laughing even more than he did before now that I had given them a look once over.

"Ha - Conquest do not look down on your skills as the Lady here has been trained to fight since she could wield a sword and her stubbornness has led her to be a blessedly skilled fighter indeed. Feel no shame in losing to her," he said with no more mockery in his voice.

"Well thank you for the attempt to learn, and If possible I would like to spar again one day." I felt like throwing the olive branch out in hopes that the connection to the royal family of this city could deepen.

"If you manage to win the tournament then perhaps we will speak again traveler. In the meantime hone your skills and grow stronger so you can better serve my father."

As soon as she finished talking she turned and with her entourage, she walked away towards the castle at the end of the training ground.

<Secondary objective added: Win the tournament to gain lady Isabels favor>

With a long-winded sigh and rubbing my wounds, I gathered myself, ate a meal pack and headed towards the next group of actual trainees. My motive was clear and I knew I had to increase my skill and level before the tournament.

The next 3 game hours were a blur of duels with new trainees that had no reason to wield a sword. I took my time blocking each of their attacks and as soon as I won my 13th duel today a new notification popped into my view.

<You have succeeded in blocking 250 strikes>
You have gained 5 stat points and 1 level
<You have leveled up>
You have gained 10 additional stat points
<You won 15 duels in training>
You have gained 5 additional stat points
See Knight Captain Randall for further rewards

Wow! What a treat now the <training ground part 1> quest only has one thing left to do, see Randall. The first thing though Is I need to allocate those new points.

Name: Conquest	Class: None	Level: 4
Stat points to Allocate:	20	HP: 150+50 Mana: 50
Dexterity:	5	+5
crafting/attack speed		
Strength:	10	
physical DMG/ carry weight		
Intelligence:	5	
Mana total/regen and spell power		
Charm:	5	
Likability with NPC		
Constitution:	15	+5
hp/ stamina total		
Agility:	17	+10
movement speed/ stamina regen		

The new stat points aren't a joke. Doubling my agility and increasing my dexterity will significantly increase my attack speed and ability to dodge attacks. The added constitution will increase the time I can grind for XP later on as well as my survivability in battles. Now that I have my stat points allocated I should go find Randall. It luckily did not take long, he was talking with a few other trainees on the other side of the training ground next to the dummies. I took a slight jog up to him since he was just finished talking to one trainee I made sure to hop in next trying to pop a similar stance as the other recruits I saluted the Knight Captain and said

"Sir Randall, I have completed the training request for me and wanted to report to you."

He gave me a good once over looking at my stance as well as my weapon on the hip.

"You have been training hard, and I saw your duel with the lady earlier. I was surprised you lasted as long as you did and I'm sure she was just as flustered at the fact you gave her any problems at all. Since you have completed the basic training of a recruit I wanted to give you a little something I give to all recruits, but since you managed to go far above and beyond what is normally expected here I would also like to offer you the choice of weapon you feel fits you best." After he finished his speech he pulled out a bundle of different weapons and placed the bundle on a nearby bench. I eagerly watched him as he unfurled the assortment and was earnestly impressed by the quality of this starting gear. Each one had a blue hue to its metal gleam meaning it was a *Rare* item and for it to be given to me this early on is incredible.

The rarity system in Kronos online goes like this. White colored items are basic and common, there are no magical properties and they have no unique characteristics at all. Green represents a slight magic to the item or some sort of effect that the item carries with it but still just an uncommon item. Blue hue shows a rare item, one that is only able to be obtained either through trials or hard earned quest items. Purple goes beyond that and shows Epic rarity items that can only be obtained through true feats of unparalleled skill or achievement. Yellow is the color of a unique item, given to chosen elites in a country or from extremely difficult bosses. Orange rarity means it is Legendary and typically a country would only have a few of these items in its borders and would be considered national treasures to have. The last rarity I have only seen in forum posts is Red, or mythic in rarity something that no man would normally have in any circumstances unless it is a world scale quest as stated on the official Kronos Website.

Knowing this, the blue hue coming from each of these weapons shows that my achievement must have meant something to Knight Captain Randall. Through analysing the various assortment of weapons ranging from a spear, another shortsword, greatsword, longsword, bow, warhammer, battleaxe and even a dagger. They each had traits to them that would be invaluable but I could not inspect them until I made my choice. Looking back at how I was fighting I enjoyed the mobility of the one handed sword but the defence was lacking with its lower reach. As much as I wanted the bow I never attempted to use one yet in this game so it would be foolish to choose a weapon I have no skill in, same goes for the hammers and axes. Thus that brings me down to a greatsword and a longsword. The nice thing about the greatsword is its abundant power behind each of the swings that would be made with it. The biggest downside however is I would be forced to use it with two hands, something that would limit my battle prowess and flexibility that I am trying to take advantage of. The last logical choice would be the longsword, the ability to use it with just one hand but still have the versatility to swing it with both shows as a very powerful weapon. Especially having tasted the skill that Isabel used against me it has to be my weapon of choice.

"I've made my decision, the Longsword." while pointing at the longsword.

<You have chosen (Sharpened Longsword of Bleeding) as your reward>
<You have completed Training Grounds 1>
You have gained 1200 experience
Relationship with Randall plus 25

"You made a good choice, this used to be my blade when I fought as a squire. Cherish it well and it will guide you through many challenges. Hone your skill and fight hard in the tournament, Conquest. I do wish to give you this bit of advice before you run off again. I would suggest training in the forest outside the city, perhaps gaining strength through life or death battles would benefit someone with a grandiose name of conquest."

"Thank you for all you have taught me and the opportunity to learn more. I will keep hold of this sword as a memento to your teachings. I will see you at the tournament, keep an eye out for me in the finals"

After my decree that I would make it to the finals, I received yet another prompt

<Training Grounds 2: The Forest>
You have been given a task to fight in the forest to grow your level and hone your fighting skills. Head to the forest and gain 3 levels before the tournament.
Bonus Objective: Kill 15 wolves
Bonus Objective: Kill the (Old Bear)

The quest seemed to have continued into its second part, not one to deny it. I started to walk towards the edge of town, passing by all the different stalls and the church yet again. I have two in-game days until the tournament and I can't waste any time. While I'm on my warpath towards the edge of the city I took some time to analyze my weapon and its characteristics to better plan my range of attack later.

<Sharpened Longsword of Bleeding>
Damage: 11~15+5 from sharpened
Slashing attacks deal bleeding effect
Level requirement: 4

Not bad for a sword at level 4, seems like a weapon geared for dealing lasting damage. The sharpened effect makes it so it deals extra damage flatly towards foes. The bleeding effect is huge as it will deal an extra 50% of the damage dealt over the course of 6 seconds and it stacks for each injury. So hypothetically each slash I can deliver almost 30 damage not even including critical strikes or hits on delicate areas. It seems an extremely aggressive playstyle will be opened to me when I just have to strike the opponent a dozen times to eliminate them.

I took some time to stop near some shops and pick up some extra meal packs. One of the clerks gave me a funny look when I wanted to eat the bare minimum in quality items but I was used to it in real life so not much could get worse. I purchased as many as I could with my remaining money and then started to notice groups of guards jogging down the causeways back towards the training grounds and zigzagging throughout the town. The town square I started in had both players and NPC talking with each other trying to haggle and sell items to one another, be it from crafters or merchant class users but even among them, some soldiers had eyes trying to analyze all those who set foot in their line of sight. The salesman all had an energy of people wanting to make money off of others, so I kept my distance and my money strings closed- even though there was no money to be taken, the sight of all the guards nearby had me unnecessarily guarded. After about an hour of walking around town and getting more accustomed to how to find the exit from some NPC shopkeepers I finally had to head towards the forest.

Now that I'm making it to the edge of the city I approach the first line of defence to civilization which is a 15 foot stone wall around the perimeter, the outer gate here was guarded by some overly alert foot soldiers, as I approached they eyeballed my belongings and looked me up and down. After their scrutiny, they asked with an inquisitively aggressive tone,

"Where are you headed?"

"Out to the forest to fight the Old Bear".

They looked me over again when I said that and looked at each other. Then they laughed and waved their hands letting me pass and I exited the city on my way towards the forest. Wolves and a beast called the <Old Bear> have to be killed in the span of today just to keep up with the leveling schedule. Seems like a steep order but I have enough meal packs to keep me through the day for continuous combat. With a full stamina and health bar, I made my way into the forest from the gates.

As soon as I took my first step into the open forest I knew I was no longer safe. Combat here is real and failure to fight would mean death. I readied my new longsword in my right hand and started walking my way deeper in the forest, crouched and squinting to try and spot enemies before they spotted me. Sure enough not even five minutes later there was my first target, a wolf eating its last prey- a helpless bunny. Not trying to leave this golden opportunity to sneak up on the wolf, I became thankful of the additional dexterity I added, letting me walk even a little more coordinated amongst the underbrush. What felt like a few minutes I finally was 10 feet away from the beast before its snout came out from the meal. The wolf sniffed a few times and it's teeth flared as its head snapped to my direction. I had been spotted. Abandoning my crouched pose I readied myself for the wolf's charge, from what I had been reading in the forums wolves are level 3~6 and vary depending on their color and size. This one's name above it just says Wolf level 4 and is a typical grey colored wolf- a fair test to my battle abilities here.

The wolf, not waiting any longer and aggressive in nature, charged my position. All four legs pumping in motion to tear my throat out with a maw of jagged teeth. As the wolf approached I prepared my heavy blow skill and struck it as hard as I could in the head with my sword. The wolf as it tried to regain its footing when I stepped to the side was met with a longsword to the face for a purple 39 damage and immediately started bleeding for more. I backed away from the wolf as I watched the remaining fifth of its life drain away from bleed damage alone.

<Wolf has been slain gained 250 experience>

A true one-hit kill on my first mob. This is going to be a breeze if I'm reading this, I only need 2250 experience left to level up to 5. I barely used any stamina dodging and swinging as well. I picked up the wolf drops, which was just some animal hide of low quality and feeling optimistic if not a bit cocky yelled as loud as I could to attempt to provoke any wolves that could hear me.

"Come and get me you damn furballs!"

<You have awoken the Old Bear>

"Well shit. That's not a wolf" I muttered to myself as I immediately heard the tearing of the forest and crumbling of small trees to my left.

"Shit shit shit" I was prepared for maybe a few wolves but it sounded like this bear was meant to be a final boss to this mission, not the second encounter! I peered into the forest in the sound of the coming destruction to try and get a glimpse of my opponent. Sure enough a giant brown bear emerged from the trees with a scar near its eye. The thing was massive and its paws were easily a foot across. I didn't even have an idea of how to dodge those massive arms especially when it was barreling at me faster than I could do a complete sprint. With only seconds remaining until the beast was upon me I readied myself, firmly planted my legs in the ground and awaited the charge. As soon as the bear was upon me it stood on its hind legs towering over me with its stature that would surely make a child cry. That's when I saw the name above its head.

<Old Bear Level 23>

Its first monolith of an arm swung at me, I tried to block but much like fighting the man with the warhammer, it smashed through my defences with its mass alone. It tossed me aside like I was a ragdoll and I bounced off the ground once before coming back to my feet just in time for it to approach and swing again. This time I jumped out of the way to try and save some health since I lost nearly a quarter with the first strike. As soon as I made it out of the bear's claws I did a full two-handed spinning swing with my longsword and sliced into the side of its hide. 28 damage. All of that effort just to inflict less than a twentieth of the beast's health.

Feeling no form of hopelessness I made sure to let this beast know the name of the man that will kill it.

"I am Conquest you old bear and I'm here to claim your hide!"

After my valiant shout, which was to intimidate it as much as it was to pump up my own falling morale. I promptly had the fight of my life. The bear kept swinging its giant arms and every time I would lunge out of the way just in time while giving a retaliatory swing back at the bear. This repeated for nearly five minutes from what felt like hours in my mind as the stress of this beast nearly crushed me every time it swung its arms. But finally, the health of the bear was at a reasonable level for me to deal a final blow. Both the bear and I were haggard and breathing heavily covered in wounds. I know I had barely a tenth of my health left and so did the bear. The final blow would be dealt and whoever got the strike first would be the victor.

One of the strikes the bear landed was on my face, my left eye covered in blood and my vision similarly impaired. I only had one strike and the bear thought the same. It jumped at me and I did the only thing I thought I could do. A <heavy blow attack> combined with a stab, both arms outstretched and crouched below to strike the belly of the beast it connected and showed a wondrous purple number and 78 damage. The follow-up strike of the bear never happened as it slumped next to me and dissolved into loot. I gathered the bear pelts and ignored the notifications for when I would be more conscious and safe to read them. Struggling to my feet I started pushing my way out of the ruined shrubs and marked trees towards the only safe place I know.

After most likely half an hour of slow hobbling and sneaking to avoid wolves that would most likely kill me if they caught my scent I spotted natural light. Headings towards the tree line where I finally made it out and could sit to heal up and regenerate my stamina again. The shock of combat was intense and I wasn't expecting to get out of there alive, I could feel my heart pumping in my chest causing my hands to shake with excitement and adrenaline. I was sure I would discover how the respawn mechanics work in real-time. Luckily for me the longsword did a critical strike on a vital point and defeated the beast at the perfect moment.

After what felt like hours of walking- which in fact was only 20 minutes of hobbling. I made it out of the tree line into relative safety. Once there I sat down against a tree that seemed relatively comfortable in the plains and started to look at all the notifications I received after combat.

<You have slain Old Bear LvL 23 gained 3400xp>
-you have obtained Bear Leather
-You have obtained Bear bones
<You have leveled up>
You have gained 10 additional stat points
<Skill Upgraded: Swordsmanship 4>
All sword style attacks are 40% stronger

<Secondary objective completed Slay Old Bear>
Gain 1 point in each stat for slaying Solo
Obtained skill <Makeshift Bandage 1>
<Makeshift Bandage 1>
Ability to heal wounds with makeshift bandages
Can stop bleeding effects

That was a huge amount of different abilities to utilize and a hefty skill boost to go with it. First thing to do was to allocate the 10 new skill points into stats that would be helpful to me. I dropped them evenly into dexterity and strength as the damage increases and attack speed buffs would be incredibly helpful if I run into another bear-type monster. The extra one stat in everything was incredible. It was as much as leveling up again but without the extra level. In addition to that I was urgent to test the self-bandage skill out so I came back to my feet and looked around for some spare leaves that could be fashioned into a bandage. Once I found some decent-sized leaves and string from my pack I activated the new skill.

<Self Bandage: Crude>
You have healed for 4%HP
Bleeding effect stopped

That was an incredible heal rate for something that didn't require any stamina or mana. I found some more items laying around and repeated the self bandage, an interesting thing to note is that when I was healing only when I hit 100% did I obtain proper vision in my eye that was clawed out. Once the HP problem was solved I consumed a meal pack to regenerate my stamina. Now that I was fit as a fiddle I started my march back into the forest on the route for wolves. My Longsword and I were thirsty for the experience points. Just as my march began I ran into my first set of players in the wild. There were two of them, one seemed to be a druid class while wearing green garments with ordain flowers and leaves and the name of *Sylvain* she was level 12 while the other was a warrior by his obvious hammer and shield combination, his name was *Horus* and was level 14 the confidence he had when he walked was pompous in a way. They seemed to have spotted me at the same time and approached with a surprised look on their face. The armored warrior spoke first in what I could only assume was a condescending attitude.

"What is a level 5 doing here? The wolves will eat you alive. And what's with that name? Conquest? Really have an ego going to name yourself something so almighty."

I immediately did not like this man. But before I could shoot back any sort of retort the appearing druid Sylvain interjected though I could see her eyes more focused on the sword at my waist than anything I had to say.

"Stop it Horus, we all had to start at a low level anyway. Who knows he could help us hunt, an extra frontline fighter would go well with me supporting since my buff skills work on more than one person-"

"We don't need a noob to pull us down, otherwise we will have to save him every time we run into trouble. How else are we going to hunt the old bear if we don't get to a higher level first? We need at least 3 level 10 party members to take it on according to the forum."

Finally, something I can interject on I made sure to put my two cents in.

"I already fought and killed the <Old Bear> I'm sure you both could do it if your control is high enough to fight him."

They both looked at me with a small hint of pity as a new player spouting nonsense and they proceeded to ignore me, even though the druid no longer had the air of grace about her.

"See Sylvie, this guy has no idea what he is talking about, he probably couldn't tell the difference between a rabbit and a wolf if he fought one. Lets go"

After Horus's insult to me, they both turned and walked deeper into the forest, in the wrong direction if they were to be fighting the bear. But after their rude remarks, I wasn't about to correct their path even if they would believe me when I told them. So back onto my warpath I started marching again to the same place I fought the bear.

CHAPTER 3

———◆◆———

Once I made the 10-minute walk; far away from those two players I was again alone in the forest surrounded by who knows what. I started the crude attempt at sneaking the entire time while going from brush to brush avoiding the trails set by other adventurers or hunters. It was a silly feeling as I knew I wasn't sneaky in any way shape or form, but I could tell my sneak skill was slowly being made as I kept up the crawl. Eventually I heard the rustling and tearing of wolves in their habitat, then soon enough the sight of them 30 meters ahead was revealed. Below a small cliffside covered in large rocks and possibly a cave sat sixteen wolves in a pack, one with a white matted fur much larger than the rest. A majority of them were the same size as the ones I fought earlier and most likely weren't higher than level 6, though the big white wolf was surely the alpha the way the other wolves cleared out of the way when it walked. I took my time to observe them for a while since I was undetected to see if I could spot any weaknesses but none were forthcoming. Near what seemed to be an opening of a cave at the cliff face was a campsite that was recently destroyed. The wolves must have ambushed the poor people camping here. Though that would explain the chewing.

I kept hidden and so slowly a turtle could pass me I made my way closer to the wolves. Then while I was making my approach a new notification appeared

<Sneak skill acquired>
<Sneak 1>
You are able to conceal yourself partially in brush

Nice! I let the new skill fill the bar while I kept my approach to a steady snails pace. Soon after I found myself only 15 feet to the nearest wolf but I knew I couldn't make it any closer without them spotting me so I set my plan of attack. Using the rocks towards the side of the cliff I will reveal myself and draw them in to only attack me from the front. No chance of getting ambushed or flanked when my back is literally to the wall. Though this will mean it will only be a one-way attack and I cannot retreat if I become overwhelmed. But the comments Horus made earlier made it clear to me I need to earn my name of *Conquest* and I will prove it to at least myself with this act. I have done more than enough combat training in real life to fight well in this complete virtual world.

Now that I had my resolve I stood up and sprinted in one successive motion towards the cliffside, I could hear the wolves scrambling up as they were all startled at the sudden noise. Just as I ran into the cliff I spun around on my heels longsword in both hands as I turned towards my soon-to-be assailants and prepared for the assault. The wolves all started to howl as what they thought was easy prey landed in their midst. The smallest of the wolves were the first greedy and hungry beasts that decided to take the first bite into the said meal. Unluckily for them, I was waiting for a quick sidestep and slash brought the first wolf into a fine digitized mess that signified its death. The other of the two wolves that made the jump landed to my left as I brought the sword back to its side and impaled it with a downward stab. The same fate befell it and the experience was mine.

The older and more experienced wolves now saw the danger that I could bring to them once the younger ones were slain. They started to circle and surround me while the white wolf just sat back and watched while the others made their display of intimidation. I readied my sword again as the wolves started to strike, these ones all took more than a single strike and I was pushed back. One by one they would come to bite at my legs when I swung at another, After I hit one it would fall back before I could strike it again and another would take its place. I kept repeating this motion and my health kept dropping but soon every wolf but the white one had been struck at least once and some twice. They had a hint of fear in their doggish eyes but the drive for hunger was stronger than the glint of my bloodied sword. They launched yet another assault on me and my longsword met it with grim resolve. One by one the wolves were cut down until there was only the white wolf and me with less than a quarter of my health remaining. Finally after the rest of its pack was annihilated the white wolf made a move.

It growled with ferocity and sprang at me with speed, unlike the others. I was barely able to get out of the way and when I tried to counter it by swinging my sword it was already out of the way. The blade harmlessly hit the ground where it had been and the wolf was circling around pushing me away from the cliff face without biting into my skin. Now that I was no longer against the cliff the wolf was circling me trying to find an opening just as I was. I kept my sword extended and pointed at the wolf while rotating left and right to keep my eyes on him. Eventually, the wolf must have spotted what he wanted since It dove forward towards my left leg and took a large chunk into it, snapping its mighty jaws onto it. It brought me down to 10hp and I already felt it crunch down into my bones. The situation was dire, my stamina was already running on fumes and I had a penalty making me slower. I one handed the longsword while grabbing the scruff of the wolf's neck and started to repeatedly stab and cut the wolf that was latched to my shin.

8hp.

The wolf yelped in pain but refused to let go, so I stabbed it again.

5hp.

The wolf's jaw loosed but still kept gnawing and I kept sawing.

3hp.

Finally, the wolf turned to pixels and I immediately started to wrap my wounds with some premade bandages. My stamina was drained completely at this point so my mind was anything but clear during all of this and the damage I sustained was immense. The bandage made it so I could walk again but the pain still is present even though it was dulled by a huge amount. I kept bandaging myself as soon as the 15 second cooldown was over and once I reached 50% HP I started picking up all the loot from the slain wolves. 15 grey adult wolves and a white alpha yielded a ton of hiding and teeth that could be given to the adventurers' hall later on. Once I searched for all the loot I was about to check out my notifications when a lulled yell for help resonated across the cliffside and trees around me. At first, I thought it was a side effect of my stamina loss, then I heard it again.

"Help me" I was instantly back into battle mode and looking around for the call for aid. The high-pitched scream happened again and seemed to be coming from inside the cliff, upon closer inspection there was an opening to the cave I saw earlier and with my longsword at the front, I started my way inside.

Luckily the cave wasn't too deep and there I could see the source of the screaming. It was a little kid, he was an NPC by the color of his hp above his head but his fear felt genuine. He was hiding behind some broken-down tents and a campsite that was most likely attacked by those wolves. At Least I thought he was hiding but when I came around the corner the kid was tied up and covered in scratches. I immediately helped him out, cutting his restraints and trying to calm the young boy down. I talked to him.

"It's going to be okay, my name is Conquest and I'm here to help you. What happened here?"

The little boy, barely 10 from his appearance, could barely stifle the tears as he tried to respond.

"I'm... I'm... Ben, I was kidnapped and they brought me out here, the men left the cave but didn't come back, all I heard was them yelling then nothing... Please save me mister Conquest"

<Bonus Objective added: Save Ben>
Ben was captured by a mysterious group
Save Ben and bring him back to his family in the city
Rewards depend on Bens health

"Of course I will help you, Ben. Let's get you back to Stotonely and reunite you with your family. What is your family's name?"

"I am Benjamin Von Torez, my sister must be worried sick about me. Just bring me home please mister Conquest".

Well, that will complicate things. Of course, this kid is related to royalty... What kind of beginner mission is this? I helped the kid up off the ground but he had a very clear gash on his leg that was looking obviously infected. Upon closer inspection, Ben could not walk at all on the leg. So the only option was to hoist him up on my back and walk him back to town. Once I got him up I started my slow dredge back. My stamina was slowly being eaten away even though I was walking leaving the tiny amount I regenerated to dust. While I was walking I started noticing movement out of the corner of my eye, I pulled out my Longsword with one hand and held onto Ben with the other. Out of the brush came another wolf, thankfully it wasn't an alpha but in my condition, It would still be a tough fight especially while protecting Ben.

The wolf pounced and to my absolute horror launched straight at Ben without a second thought of the sword in its way. I turned my body to block the jumping predator and its teeth sunk into my right shoulder. My arm locked up with its teeth embedded into me. I tried to shake it off but the thing didn't waver. it considered me a free meal and started to rake at me with its legs since I was defenceless. I wanted to set Ben down but who knows if there were more wolves in the area that saw Ben as a quick snack. Since I couldn't shake the wolf off I found the nearest tree and with all my force bashed the beast into it. Its teeth finally relented and I used a powerful strike to crush its face with my sword. The beast pixelated and I grabbed the pelt and put it into my inventory. Ben was crying and when the fighting finally stopped he held even tighter, worried that the second he let go he would be consumed by the flesh-hungry wolves.

While Ben was glued to me, I kept on walking towards the exit of the forest. As soon as the light of the plains was visible I started to increase my pace. Sure my stamina was being eaten but as long as it wasn't Ben or myself I don't care. Either way, I shouldn't need it when in the safe zone. The strain on my legs was unusually high and I could tell I was overburdened with the load of both Ben and the pelts. Once I made it to the gate the guards that scrutinized me earlier both noticed my approach and ran out of the castle, weapons drawn and pointed at me before I could even react.

"Drop Sir Benjamin this instant."

Their spears were angled at my throat and without making any sort of sudden moves I began to let him go but was stopped as he held me tighter and shouted at the guards -

"No! Conquest saved me and he has to bring me to my Sister! I want to see my sister, let us through!" Though the kid had a large wound and was still a child his shout was less of a temper tantrum and more of an order than I expected. The guards seemingly realized they misread the situation and started to step aside for me.

"Thank you for saving Sir Benjamin, Lady Isabel will be most grateful for bringing him back here. She should be".

"Don't worry I know she is in the training area, and I am glad I could help the Torez family." I had to interrupt them otherwise I'm sure my legs would give out while in front of them or young Ben would lose too much blood. I brushed past their spears and started walking into town. I bandaged Ben as best I could but the wound was too much for my bandages and prevented me from healing him further. I kept carrying him all the way to the training area where word must have come that I was bringing her brother because as soon as I walked through the gates of the training zone she came running with all her guards. Though to my surprise and fear she and her guards were completely armored up unlike last time and had a grizzled unlaughing demeanor compared to when I fought them earlier.

Though Ben was smart and saw the situation coming, and shouted first before their blades were drawn at me.

"Sister wait! Conquest here saved me from the kidnappers, please don't hurt him!"

Isabel slowed when she heard the words of her brother but then realized what he said.

"Conquest? You are the man I spared with earlier are you not? How have you come to be the savior of my brother only half a day after our first meeting?"

I was stunned by her comments but she is not wrong to be suspicious especially with a time discrepancy that small between events. It would be hard to believe it is all coincidence.

"Yes I found him in the forest, I believe the kidnappers were killed by wolves outside a cave, I slew the wolves and found your brother tied up. I brought him here as soon as I could."

"For a reward, I'm guessing..." said the hesitant and untrusting overprotective sister who was still approaching, sword in one hand and the other extended toward Ben to get him away from me.

"How could I ask for a reward when this boy was brave enough to ask for help in a cave full of unknown dangers?"

She slowed after hearing this and started to drop her guard.

"You seem to be a good man, you are still new here and there is proof enough of your skill to defeat the wolves when we were sparring earlier today... Thank you Conquest for saving my brother, please give him here." and reached out with both her arms towards Benjamin. I felt like holding him longer would only put me in more danger so I handed him over. He muttered one more time "Thank you mister" until reaching out and grabbing his sister and hugging her dearly he finally started to cry and then so too did Isabel. They started to walk away when the guards approached me. The one who laughed the loudest at Isabels and I's fight earlier now had a dark expression on his face but reached out with his hand for a shake. I took his hand and he pulled me close.

"You did a great service to the Von Torez family, and even if you did it without greed in your heart you should still be rewarded. My name is Alan and I am the leader of these knights, we didn't properly introduce ourselves before and I believe that to be a mistake. It is good to make your acquaintance Conquest."

I returned his happy gesture and nodded "Likewise Sir Alan."

Alan continued "I understand you are to be in the tournament tomorrow. Take this ring, it may help you cross the gap some of the other competitors will have over you."

He handed me a ring and I gratefully took it, the magical item radiated with mana and I could easily tell it was at least a rare rating.

"Thank you, I only wish to help those in need. I will prove myself tomorrow at the tournament." The burly man smiled at me then, the grim attitude seemingly fleeting at my words.

"I am sure you will do great, we will be watching your progress with great interest. And I wish you luck." After his farewell words, he left to regroup with the rest of the guards around the young lord and lady.

I finally took this time to sit down and read all of the notifications that I suppressed during combat and the heightened awareness I needed to have during the escape from the forest.

<You have slain 15 Grey Adult Wolves>
Awarded 4500 experience
<You have Slain Alpha White Wolf>
Awarded 1300 experience
<Skill Upgraded: Swordsmanship 5>
All sword style attacks are 50% stronger
<You have Leveled Up>
You have gained 10 additional stat points
<Completed Quest: Save Ben>
You brought Ben back to his sister safely
Awarded 8000 Experience
Awarded 6 free stat points for no damage to Ben
<You have Leveled Up>
You have gained 10 additional stat points
<Training Grounds 2: The Forest>
Talk to Knight Captain Randall for reward
Bonus Objective: Kill 15 wolves <Complete>
Bonus Objective: Kill the (Old Bear) <Complete>

Holy shit. I may have been wounded fairly significantly but man those bites were worth it. The risk/reward was high for this battle for sure. Now there is only one thing left before I get my reward and that is to talk to Captain Randall. If the item is going to be on the same level as the sword I would be extremely happy. From what I had read on the forums, magical weapons and rare items are exactly as their rating would imply, rare. Typically people do not get their first rare Item until they are level 25 or higher. I have a very strong rare longsword at that as well to add to it. Not all rare items are good in any way and I'm sure that if I sold these in the online market I could get a few dollars. It makes me wonder where this chain quest will go!

Now that I was more relaxed and the guards were dropping their inquisition like glares I was prepared to talk with Randall. Looking around the dulling training field since it was almost sunset now I found him in his usual spot on the podium overlooking the grounds. His appearance was no less intimidating while standing there. This time there were no trainees around him but I did spot those two players from earlier walking near him. I approached Randall and gave him a skirt wave before saying.

"Randall, I have returned and completed the quest to become stronger. I have also slain both the bear and the wolves."

"I heard you did a great more than that, Conquest. You even managed to save the little lord from the hands of wicked kidnappers. Impressive handiwork. You need a reward befitting your talent, and you seem to be needing a reason to stay in this country, I have to have you in my knights." Randall explained, and towards the end was practically shouting at me with excitement. He clearly thought highly of me and that filled me with a sense of pride.

Though like before, I was unable to respond in time before the two approaching players interjected rudely in the middle of our conversation. Horus shouted at Randall

"You can't really believe this little... Level 7 now? Can be responsible for defeating the bear we were hunting all day and couldn't find it. It only spawns once a week! There is no way..."

For the first time I could see true frustration in Randall, he was not used to being interrupted especially by someone he does not seem to respect. "Who do you think you are to pass judgment on Conquest? He ALONE fought the old beast of the forest and slayed the wolf pack with their leader in tow then after that CARRIED young lord Benjamin all the way back to the castle into the hands of Lady Isabel. All you accomplished today was slaying a dozen wolves and wasting my time. Leave and do not come back until you have completed the task I had given you." And with a resounding clap, he pointed towards the gate while looking at both Horus and Sylvain. Sylvain looked back at me with some eyes of greed disguised as a regret as if I would say something to sway Randall's mind, but there was no reason for me to do that especially with how they treated me earlier.

"Thank you, Knight Captain Randall, I appreciate the vote of confidence and I will not disappoint you. I do wish to further prove myself in the tournament tomorrow if possible."

"Of course, Conquest, I cannot have my top recruit be talked down to by ruffians. Though the Item I wanted to give you just does not suit you in my mind and I feel like it justifies me looking for something that would be more befitting you. How about you meet me for dinner at my home, where we can discuss your reward from me." After he finished talking, the quest was updated on my screen.

<You have completed the quest Training Grounds 2: The Forest>
You have been awarded 9000 experience
To continue this quest, follow Knight Captain Randall
<You have Leveled Up>
You have gained 10 additional stat points

"Thank you Captain, I would gladly join you for a meal." and followed him back to his home, which was conveniently right outside the gate into the training grounds. He brought me to the front door to his home and knocked before opening it. He angled himself to fit through the door even though his armor was still on and the bulkiness of the shoulderpads seemed like they would catch. I followed him in and inside the house, there were moderate furnishings that radiated a warm feeling and clearly had been kept clean. While looking throughout the room as I entered I looked down the main hallway past the stairs and there was a woman with auburn hair and brown eyes. She must have been in her early thirties and had a smile that exudes warmth when looking at Randall; she wore a yellow sundress with complex sewing patterns that would be hard to purchase from any shopkeep.

"Conquest, this is my wife Teresa. Teresa this is Conquest, a promising trainee that I wanted to treat to a meal."

And with a voice extremely soothing to hear she said "It is a pleasure to meet you conquest, welcome to our home I have some food being cooked and it will be ready in about an hour you are welcome to sit at the dining table until then"

I bowed to them both since that seemed to be the traditional requirement here and responded with "I am grateful for the hospitality." Randall left the room to change out of his armor but guided me to the dinner table first before leaving. I took a seat at the spacious table in the well-lit medieval-style home and was impressed at how cozy this sort of life could be. The fact that these were artificial intelligence is still surprising to me as they are so lifelike that it is hard to tell the difference sometimes. If it wasn't for the fact that the hp bars had different colors depending if they were player or NPC then I would be convinced this is just an elaborate ruse made by the game developers and a group of players. It was off-putting in a way but I was all for the extra immersion. It made it feel truly like another world.

Teresa was in the kitchen finishing up cooking when Randall returned from his room, he came back with a tan tunic and basic cloth pants. The only thing he still had from his knight captain garb is the sword he still had fastened to his belt.

"Conquest"

After he had sat down he began staring at me with a much more serious expression on his face than before.

"You are a talented traveler, and I believe you have a good heart. So I wanted to share with you a story of one of this kingdom's founders- Grend Amear. The man who was side by side with Randell Belfast the first king of the country known for his red hair and his self-proclaimed title of 'The Ginger King'. Grend was the hand of the king, he made this country stronger and though it was over 400 years ago his legend is still talked about today but sadly only in a hushed secret like we are having now."

While Teresa was still in the kitchen, Randall made sure to have my attention while he retold a story passed through his family.

"Grend had a unique ability that seemed to have been scrubbed from history, only my family and a few others know about it. His class was that of both a warlord and a fighter. He blended his skills between fighting and commanding his troops, and they weren't normal troops; they were an unending tide to those they fought against and had an unyielding servitude towards Grend alone. One day he stopped fighting for Belfast and left the country, the only thing rumored is that he is said to have left behind a path for his successor to take up his mantle. I want you to find more about this ancient history and I feel that pursuing this will greatly increase your strength"

<Training grounds 3 has changed>
<New quest, history of Grend Amear>
Obtain clues about the forgotten class and legendary leader
Grend Amear

I was stunned that the quest chain had changed, it must have met a secret objective that altered its path. And learning about the lore for this country was good to have since even though all the forums I was reading I never heard mention of the name Grend. I chose the Belfast kingdom because the leadership of its old kings was notable even amongst other kingdoms of similar size. Though it may seem to have all been attributed to this man, Grend, instead of the actual kings.

"I will of course try and find more hints to this legend, do you have any idea where to start looking?"

"One place you could try is the citadel of Haral that is one of the oldest cities on the Kronos Continent and the Belfast

Kingdom. Someone there is sure to have an older family lineage. The only better place to think of would be this cities nobles, the Count would surely have some information but he could take it as hostile thought if brought up the wrong way"

I did not care to leave the city but it would be easier than trying to gain an audience with the Count of this territory. Though as much as I want to immediately start hunting down all traces of this legendary figure I do still have the tournament tomorrow and need to place highly.

"I will start looking for Grend Amears history as soon as I fight in the tournament tomorrow."

"Then it will be a glorious tournament I know for sure. If you need any pointers do let me know and I will do my best to guide you."

"Thank you Captain"

Just then Teresa had finished cooking and broke the tight mood that had been twining together in the dining room. It seemed to be a complete chicken and mashed potatoes with a hearty steak on the side. The two Tbone steaks looked delicious and Teresa saw the eyes both Randall and I were making towards them and placed one on each of our plates.

Randall had a happy expression and said "Thanks hun, looks delicious"

After an hour we finished our meal and I thanked him before leaving. During the meal, I had gotten the <Sleep Deprivation: Mild> status effect and I was eager to get rid of that. Once I had left I found a nice guild to sell my loot to, was able to get 3 copper for each basic hide, 15 for the alpha and finally a whopping 50 for the bear's pelt. After all, the money was sorted and haggling finished I had gotten 1 silver and 10 copper. I went to the inn close by and spent the 15 copper it cost to stay for the night as well as a meal in the morning. I did not need to sleep in an inn, just log out and I would still gain the benefit of removing the sleep deprivation status effect. The true bonus to sleeping in an inn was the increased stamina and HP regen for the day after sleeping in one. It was a minor buff, but any buff would be nice when I had to do a possible Player Vs Player tournament the next day. And from what it looked like the competition would all be a higher rank than me. Though with all these extra skill points it may not make too much of a difference. Before I log out though for the day I should allocate all the skill points I had acquired which was a lot.

Name: Conquest	Class: None	Level: 8
Stat points to Allocate:	46	HP: 200+100 Mana: 60
Dexterity:	11	+10
Strength:	11	+16
Intelligence:	6	
Charm:	6	
Constitution:	21	+10
Agility:	24	+10

An absolute plethora of skill points; I nearly doubled my stats with them. My fighting potential had become significantly stronger. I decided that my strength is what was holding me back in the previous fights, the power I needed to kill some of these basic mobs like the wolves was laughable. I should be able to kill them in just one or two hits with the specs on the weapon I have currently. Though true to my original purpose I wanted to be as versatile as I could instead of diving 100% into the same stat. Sure I could have made myself have 56 strength but would it matter if my enemy just dodged the strike? Instead I allocated them between my different stats. Agility and Dex will increase my attack speed and reaction time as well as improve my ability to improvise in combat. The constitution is a no-brainer when I keep having duels that almost kill me. I almost forgot the ring I received earlier, I took out the magical item and put it on to see its stats when I was met with. . .

<you have equipped (Ring of Restoration: Epic)>
You are Bound to this item
<Ring of Restoration: Epic>
Regenerate 3% hp every second at the cost of 1% mana

I logged out in a rage. A two-hour break should be enough before hopping back in for the tournament. After I took off my headset and sat up from my pod and nearly screamed. It was a stupid idiotic mistake and I did it. I equipped the ring to see its effects instead of bringing it to a seer to analyze it. Now, I'm *Bound* to the item and will not be able to sell it. It was the ring I saw on auction for $1200 and I now am screwed since I equipped it. That was an entire month's rent here. Gone. just like that. Well, I am sure I will fester over that for the foreseeable future. Some items come with the *Bound* characteristic and you can usually see it or even remove it if you scan it with a seer or wizard first. It has been a long morning for me. I guess I will be the type of player to rely on this item during the tournament. Who would have guessed a trainee coming into combat with a ring that cost a month's rent? Talk about overkill.

I threw a freezer pizza into the oven and set a timer, in the meantime I turned on the tv and sat on my depressingly small loveseat. As always I had it set to the game news channel that featured current events. I flicked through the different channels to find something valuable to me.

"... The mines of Mordal opened for the first time today..." Switch

"... The food shortage in the Kor Republic continues...." boring

"... Royal families kidnapped..." Nope.

"... Thousands of troops on the march towards the Jorgan Principality" *Hold on now.* That country is bordering Belfast and that could spiral into me if I don't pay attention. I turned up the volume of the tv and leaned in to listen to the broadcast.

Chuck

The news Anchor Chuck Carlson was accustomed to doing video game broadcasts but as it was the most requested subject from the network he did not have much choice in the matter. Chuck was a level 34 warrior that specialized in dual-wielding combat but if he was compared to any true ranker, those that are in the top 5% of players on Kronos he would be poorly matched against them. He was forced to go here and there sacrificing his leveling time for his job capturing live-action footage of different battles that happened around the continent in Kronos. This time around he was on the border of the Jorgan Principality and the Raynor Kingdom. The Raynor Kingdom had recently mobilized its forces seemingly out of nowhere and were moving into the Jorgan Principality with the goal of total war. Chuck's goal was to show the world about these movements and stir up as much of a buzz about this fight for the highest ratings possible.

That is where it leaves him, standing only 100 yards away from an army 10,000 strong with easily 500 cavalrymen and knights to support marching in amazing unison. The grass plains they were on had a dingy sky that had the feeling of gloom and doom to it as the soldiers went on their path of war. Unsurprisingly players were part of the army in mercenary guilds as some of the best experience in the game is done through war. War gives added experience to all kills to both players and A.I. It also gives Guilds and strong players the opportunity to earn reputation or nobility through feats during the war. Some guilds may even be granted pieces of the taken territory so whenever a war occurs it becomes a huge topic among the players.

Chuck was able to flag down a man in silver armor marching on a horse at the outskirts of the armies line. Men surrounding him held the banner of a lion striking the sky, the man of obvious noble upbringing made his way towards Chuck with a somewhat sour look on his face and a silver hp bar above his head indicating it was an A.I.

"What have you flagged me down for? Are you not part of the march?"

The soldier clearly did not care for the interruption to his busy marching schedule so Chuck had to think fast to keep his attention.

"Well good sir I was hoping to know what your name was and perhaps your role in this upcoming conflict."

"It will barely be considered a conflict, our soldiers will be quick and efficient when dealing with their meager defences. I am Duke Yularan and I am leading these men to combat. And if you do not move out of our war path you may be considered a target."

One thing Chuck was good at was keeping up with world events and he knew that the prince of the Raynor kingdom was almost always the one to lead any major assault and the fact that the Duke was leading instead sounded like a good talking point.

"One more question Sir Duke Yularan, Where is the Prince? Should he not be leading this assault into enemy territory?"

Those words clearly struck a chord with the duke and the flash of anger that showed on his face would have been the first sign to back away and apologize. Unlucky enough for Chuck, this NPC was a unique grade and had a far higher level than those of the current players. Instead, the second sign he was angry met Chuck first in the form of a sword that was unsheathed and decapitated Chuck for the question about his liege. The man holding the fantasy-style wisp that acted as a camera for live broadcasts to the real world was stunned looking at the enraged duke who had just beheaded his news anchor. Then the Duke turned his gaze full of rage towards the wisp and said in both an angry and distraught tone

"Dogs of the principality will be hunted down for what they did to the prince. It will not be forgiven."

The last thing the wisp saw was the charge made by the duke. It then changed the view to two more news anchors in a normal news-style broadcasting room.

"Well, that did not seem good at all for our poor on the scene news crew! But the drama continues as the attack perpetrated by the Raynor Kingdom seems to be a retaliatory one instead of a first assault. Everyone should keep an eye out, when you see the sigils of the Lion striking the sky you are bearing witness to the Raynor Kingdom! But vise versa the accused country Jorgan Principality has the symbol of a

Medusa with many snake heads. If you see either of these sigils you are in for a treat as war is an opportunity! We will return after a few brief messages from our sponsors. This was your host Cameron Leavly and you've been watching Y.O.K News network!"

Habeas

Elsewhere unseen from cameras and prying eyes. A man with no battle gear stood in front of a dungeon in the Farrow Kingdom. The only items he had equipped were some thin leather makeshift armor and a cowl-like cape. Standing like a statue in front of the dungeon facing outwards, a group of adventurers made their approach, one wearing shiny red armor and wielding a shiny red sword. The name Glass above his head showed he was indeed the number one player in the official rankings, and on his sides were almost a dozen members from his guild the Entity. Glass, in his cocky attitude and annoyed expression, stalled in front of the man at the door to the dungeon and called out to him before wielding the sword towards the man.

"I don't know who you are but you are standing in Entity Territory, rid this place or die trash." In truth, it was just territory that the Entity bullied other players to avoid so they could monopolize all the loot to be gained here.

Finally, the man stood, unfurled his cowl and a deep red name appeared above his head indicating he was a player killer with a large list of sins. The dark name above the players' head showed 'Habeas' and when he stood he too withdrew a sword, blue and slim but radiating its own shade of dangerous energy seemingly able to cut someone by just looking at it. For the first time, Habeas spoke.

"Are you supposed to be someone important? Well, I never heard of you" this statement caught Glass and his guild members back as each of them had been interviewed at least once and Glass himself has a special dedication to him on the news. They all realized he was making fun of them and they each started casting buffs and preparing to slaughter this intruder Habeas. Seeing this, Habeas decided to goad them more "Ah are you some sort of PvE-ers? Nothing in this place but low-level loot" referring to them as players who only fight common mobs but him talking down about the dungeon at his back was infuriating as it was a dungeon a team of level 100 players needed to raid together in order to be safe. This struck a nerve in Glass and he thought enough was enough. The fight had begun.

Theodore muted the TV when the commercials started to run to truly grasp what this revelation of invasion has and how it may affect him... Earlier on the news, there was a glimpse of someone saying royal families were being kidnapped. And the fact that he had saved Benjamin from would-be attackers cannot be a coincidence. For now, he was powerless and had no way of interfering with the actions of a great country so his only option was to be diligent and become strong enough to do something.

From what Theo was able to research on the topic any quest involving the history of the game world usually yielded greater rewards than average and he was about the founder of a country. After obtaining both rare and epic rated items so early on in his gaming career he had nothing but confidence. Now that his pizza for lunch was eaten and his legs stretched, still sore from working out in the morning at Rocky's dojo. He decided it was time to hop back into the pod and get ready for the tournament.

CHAPTER 4

Once Theo connected he was rewarded with the buffs related to sleeping in an Inn.

<Well Rested: Increased HP/Mana/Stamina 10% for 6 hours>

It was well worth the extra coin to sleep here. In this tournament, I will need every advantage in order to win. Shortly after stretching again I went towards the door and was met with a slight knock. It startled me but I opened the door and a young girl, maybe 16, was carrying a plate of food that I had paid for the night before.

"Here is your morning meal sir, I hope you have enjoyed your stay. Feel free to leave the dishes in the room when you leave." she had turned away and left before I could say thank you, perhaps I startled her too when I answered the door as soon as she knocked.

After taking the plate of food back into my room, I was delighted to taste actual food, it felt just as good eating this as it did the steaks. I had the other night even though it was just some fresher bread and unidentifiable meat cubes floating in some soup. The cheese on the side was delectable and hit the spot though. Once, I scar fed down my food I left the inn and headed towards the training grounds where the showdowns would be taking place.

Though one thing I noticed leaving the inn was the increased troop presence up and down the roads, it seemed every guard was on duty today and there was no drop in security as tensions must have been high after the kidnapping. Every once in a while I was offered a passing head nod by some guards as if they knew who I was, though maybe my reputation had spread since it is a hidden stat until you either hit level 25 or enter a guild. Reputation is affected by any interaction done with A.I. as depending on how high it is could mean you are known in more than just the starting city perhaps even starting country if it is high enough. Though I will not know what my reputation level is until that point. I nodded back at most of the guards until I made it to the gate leading into the training grounds. Even though security had increased, I had luckily seen a familiar face.

"Sergeant Talmor!"

"Conquest! It is a pleasure to see you again, I heard what you had accomplished, thank you. Are you here for the tournament?"

"Yes I am hopeful, I am able to show the skills I have learned here"

"I am sure you will, good luck conquest. I do wish to warn you, some of the travelers I have seen are quite impressive themselves, there is a man named Horus who was unrivaled in his skills with the hammer. Be diligent."

"Thank you Talmor I will."

After that brief exchange, Talmor waved to the other guards and the gate opened up for me to enter. As soon as the gate opened the sound of fighting and sparring could be heard from inside, swords crashing against shields and arrows striking their targets- people were warming up.

The combination of buffs and extra skill points should make me fight with the same start line as a level 16. With the supplement of my skills and strategy, I feel confident that as long as no one too overleveled joins I should be able to make the top 8. I started making my way towards the makeshift arena with stands that were hastily put up overnight around the previous sparring grounds that I had used the day prior. I came around the corner of the benches and saw a man with glasses with paper in front of him.

"Participating or spectating?" he said with a bored expression.

"Participating, my name is Conquest" I informed the disinterested attendant.

"Ok, Conquest. You will be fighting in 2 rounds. Once you finish the preliminaries you will be in a bracket of 32 participants. Win 6 matches and you will be the victor." every word that passed through his lips seemed to take more and more energy from the man.

"Thanks" eager to wave him off and find my opponent. I went past him and found a few sets of benches labeled 'Participants' and took a seat there next to what I could only assume were my other opponents.

Sure enough I could see some players as well as A.I. on the benches. Horus was there as well as some player with a shining metal helmet. His name was Pond and honestly, it made me want to laugh until I saw his weapon. A giant Greatsword easily as tall as I was resting next to him and it was more iron than the sword. The amount of strength he must have needed to allocate to equip that behemoth of a weapon would be staggering. Turning my head towards the rings in the middle it looks like there are 8 "stages" which are just squares marked out by rocks. Each one had a pair of fighters that were attempting to best one another.

I took a seat at the far end of the bench and let myself relax and breathe before the match I would be participating in. Sure enough, after the set of matches going on in the center were done, a man I recognized, Knight Captain Randall, walked to the center and with a voice louder than expected was able to calm the crowd and he announced the start of the last round of preliminaries. He started calling out names of those on the list, once he arrived at the last ring he looked up from the sheet of paper and made eye contact with me and stated-

"Conquest versus Cane" I had gotten up and the summons and I noticed an A.I. behind me had gotten up as well. We both made our way towards the ring and I finally had a good look at my opponent. He was a lanky man with robes and a dagger, his appearance was that of a rogue style of combat and his stance was loose and uncaring as he made his way to the other side of the circle. Randall gave me a nod and announced with a big shout.

"Let the Battles BEGIN"

Immediately the form of the man Cane that I was fighting started to shimmer. It must have been a class unique skill as it started to become harder to target him. Faster than I could expect he appeared behind me and jabbed me with his dagger in my lower ribs. The bite from his blade was rough on my unarmored skin and I could feel the HP draining from me. His attack came with a bleed status effect and as soon as I tried to swing my sword to counterattack he had already left his spot doing the same blur effect as before. I focused my stance and edged towards the center of the ring trying to keep my blade between his unfocused appearance and my vulnerable back. Cane made some quick dashes and the blur effect faded as he approached, I went to block the strike that was upfront but was surprised again as the dagger bit into my wrist instead. The wound isn't bleeding but the strike made a dent in my health. This time instead of letting him pull back I charged him, tossing my longsword to my left and striking him before he could run. The blade struck deep into his shoulder and his health visibly declined. He may be fast but his health is abysmal. It seemed he had hoped to strike me down in those two first blows as he didn't blur again and his face was haggard like when I ran out of stamina. I cornered him and struck him down to 1hp and the duel was over. I have qualified for the tournament and will be in the 16 contestants both A.I. and players that will test their mettle.

I moved back towards my seat proud of victory against a different style of opponent. It was haggaring to adapt to his quick strikes, I will need to think of a better way to combat stronger opponents that utilize that class tree. I am at a distinct disadvantage with my lack of class features and titles when facing opponents as I am right now. As I took a seat before I could even turn back around the bell had already rung and the opponent on stage was defeated. There stood a woman wearing black armor that covered her from her head to toes, wielding a large black sword to boot. She must have been right at the height of the level cut off for the tournament and funded by someone as that gear looked expensive, at least rare or better for each piece and part of a set. Her opponent was an A.I. that seemed to be another assassin-type class based on the weapon he was wielding when he got back up. The beautiful armored woman turned her head away from the ring and walked back to her seat before they could even announce the end of the fight. She won no contest and the next fight came up. These fights were nothing to gawk at but none were as fascinating as the armored women.

The player Pond had struck some serious blows and fought another player named Skittles, taking him out in the first set of rounds. I spotted Skittles as he was leaving the arena in a huff clearly sour that he was eliminated with no chance to prove himself.

After another half an hour it came to the next set and my turn came around. Luckily, I would not be facing the armored woman or Pond, instead, it was a slightly built man in leather armor, bow in hand and what looked to be a shortsword on his hip. Not to take him any less seriously as I hadn't been able to see his fight since it was before I had come up to the ring. No hesitation I prepared myself for the arrows.

The announcer Randall gave a hearty shout "Conquest VS Raiden, FIGHT" And the battle began.

I immediately caught an arrow to the shoulder as I started to push his side of the field. I did not notice my health had dropped by a third and inflicted the bleeding effect off the bat. Dropping the shield that had no help stopping this high-level bow skill I instead opted to use that hand to apply a bandage mid-fight while pushing my opponent. No rules said I couldn't heal and this is a skill I had taken myself to learn. With one arm reaching out with a longsword and the other padding down a bandage I tried to strike Raiden. It was hard to tell so far if he was an A.I. or a Player because of his leather helm so predicting him became difficult, right as I thought he was about to let loose an arrow this close he dropped his bow and pulled out the shortsword in an extremely fast fashion catching me off guard. I was able to reduce the blow to that of a glance but it still struck me in the same shoulder that was cut, stopping my bandaging skill from completing. Grunting with annoyance I wielded the sword with two hands and decided to blunt force my way through. It struck him again, parried, struck, parried, shoved and soon overpowered the man only wielding a shortsword. His health dropped to one and the battle was over.

I had barely noticed that the bleed effect still didn't stop until the duel ended and status effects were forcefully removed, that was one strong effect as I'm sure it would have taken some serious time to go away on its own. His strategy must have been to try and time me out and have me bleed out on the battlefield. Clever strategy, I helped Raiden up from the ground and he spoke to me as I grabbed his arm "You have some insane control being able to strike exactly where I left my guard down, If it wasn't for the fact I can see you are a player then I would be surely convinced you were some special class A.I. Good fight Conquest!" He said that last part with some cheer in his voice even though he had lost. He was a good sport and I was going to make sure to keep that name in mind in the future. "That bleeding skill was intense, bypassing my shield and staying in effect the entire fight would have been a sure win if I didn't spec so much into HP."

After we both nodded I went back to my seat and hurriedly turned back to watch the upcoming fight between Pond and the beautiful woman. They both made their way up to the stage and Randall announced the fighter's name. "Catalina Versus Pond! FIGHT" and the battle began, it was unusual for someone to have their username be a direct name so I am almost convinced it was an A.I. but the armor was too unique for it to be some random A.I. The fight started off intense right off the bat, the giant sword from Pond struck wildly with the speed that was unexpected from the heft that had to accompany the sword. He landed strike after strike on Catalina but instead of slowing down, it seemed she was speeding up and letting the strikes through, though reducing them to mostly glances because of the armor and some proper footwork none of the strikes landed anywhere critical. The situation started to change when a faint red hue started to illuminate Catalinas armor, that is when it hit me. She was a berserker class, specializing in dealing with insane amounts of damage after she is in critical condition. I have read about it in the forums. It is a rare class that is hard to come by even by rare standards. The quest lines for them are typically brutal and require a huge amount of skill to make it through the constant combats with low hp to qualify for the class. I can see how she was letting Pond get her health low while also preventing any status effects from critical strikes. This is when she activated her first skill since the fight started. Raising her sword in the air with both hands she brought it down with the power of a falling star, Pond could barely resist even with the weight of his sword between him and her. He was pushed straight into the ground and since he wasn't wearing any armor he was immediately brought to 1 hp ending the duel. The strike was by no means weak either as I am sure Pond has similar health as I do. The pond was clearly frustrated by this loss, smacking his fist on the ground before standing back up again. But by the time he had stood up Catalina had already left to take a seat in the stands. The crowd was going wild from this show of power. I couldn't blame them. Even I had my breath taken away at the sheer weight of the strike.

The semi-finals are what was in front of me. If I beat my next opponent I most likely will have to face Catalina in the finals. My attention gets pulled away from the arena and over to one of the larger more decorated observation booths at the end of the training field, sitting on a raised platform sat what seemed to be the royalty including Lady Isabel watching over the fights. I seemed to have made eye contact with her and she gave a curt wave before turning to the arena again. She was stunning in a dress that seemed plated for combat that truly befitted her attitude. I was caught staring as the person to my right hit me on the shoulder, it was Randall "You have done well to catch her attention with your performance, be sure to keep up your skills for these remaining fights since from what I can tell you will be sorely outmatched in more than just gear. But regardless I wish you the best of luck Conquest." He gave me a firm handshake and made his way up to the observation stand with Isabel.

I could see him preparing to call my name and who my next opponent was. I started to stand and was surprised to hear "Horus Versus Conquest!" We made our way into the arena and stood on our respective sides, the entire time Horus was staring me down with a glare that felt like it was seeping into my skin with spite. "You stole my kill in the forest Conquest, I plan to humiliate you in this ring so you can feel the same shame I did at a missed opportunity" and before I could retort him Randall gave the starting shout "Fight!"

Unlike his boasting, he clearly took me seriously as his stance was a mix of both defensive and offensive wielding his hammer with both hands in a trained manner to deal with swords. He started to circle to my left, his eyes floating between my sword hands and my face trying to predict my next move. It was a good sign that he had some experience fighting outside the game as these sorts of tells can only be spotted by truly skillful fighters. Nodding with a bit more respect for the fighter I'm about to face, I took a more aggressive stance to try and fool him, wielding my longsword up in front of my shield in an unusual stance that gave my next actions a bit of unpredictability. Horus in turn changed his footwork to reflect my change, deciding he was more of an action fighter he went on the offense and took one wide clean swing on the side of my sword hoping I wouldn't be able to defend it with my shield in time because of my sword arm. He was right and I took the bash in my elbow as I was withdrawing the arm, Horus just had more speed stats than I do and it showed the difference in stats in moments like these. I braced the strike but a status effect message came up in the corner of my vision.

<Sprain(left arm): Movement speed with Left Arm reduced 25%>

It was a crucial mistake to take my eyes off the fight however to inspect the message as it gave Horus the time to bring the hammer back again and get ready for another swing. I immediately adjusted my stance to bring the shield to the forefront in hopes to brush off the next attack. What I didn't expect was Horus kicking my shield outright with his leg and bringing the hammer down on my now exposed chest. I was momentarily stunned when he brought the hammer down and took another strike. My health was teetering at 2/3rds now and I have yet to even inflict a single blow on Horus. All I could think was I am getting rusty and tomorrow I am going to go back to my old dojo. Focusing back on the here and now I look back at my opponent Horus and come up with another clever idea.

Horus has a shit-eating grin on his face because he thinks he has the upper hand in this fight, which by all rights he does at the moment, but I won't let him keep it. Not letting him think out the next move I dash into him using my skill <Powered Slash> and rack my sword against his hammer, then as he was blocking I smashed his leg that kicked me before with my shield and pushed him back. I pulled my sword back and pushed up on his hammer with my shield as I went for a stab with the sword, putting a clean cut into his stomach but to my dismay, it only did about 15% of his health even with what showed as a critical. This wasn't going to be an easy fight. Tooth and nail, inch by inch we fought for every advantage every time one of us made a mistake the other would make full use of it to go on the offensive. His level was just higher than mine but his skill was only barely below leaving a dangerous power gap between us.

After what felt like five minutes of back and forth, we both were at half health staring at each other like we just insulted the others parents and were out for blood. That's when I noticed something, he was limping. The leg I hit before with the shield had a hobble, I must have inflicted a status effect on him when I smacked it. Thinking for only a moment I came up with an idea. I came at him with the same strike that gave me the initial advantage on his leg and he knew it was coming so performed a counter, which I was hoping for. As I went to bring down my <Powered Slash> strike on him I canceled the attack by dropping my sword and instead bashed him in the leg again with my shield since his arm was up and out of position to guard. It went perfectly as I heard a crack and saw a red critical show above the strike.

That hit alone brought him down to quarter health but he could still move and now all I had was a shield and no sword. With my left hand being sprained I was already at a disadvantage with the weapon so now I could focus more on martial arts and see if I could get in close to deal final blows. Switching my shield to the sprained arm so I wouldn't have to move it as much and because In real life I was a harder hitter with the right fist.

Horus was confused for a moment and thought I had blundered by dropping my sword so he pursued his perceived upper hand and lifted the hammer for a quick strike on my weakened arm. Though he didn't expect me to tank the strike with the shield even if it still lowered my HP I came in with a quick uppercut with my right followed by two quick jabs on his jaw. The strikes did abysmal damage but they still lowered his health and caused him to stagger back. The crowd was going insane at this but I had no time to turn around as this only made Horus more pissed off. He came at me with abandon, striking over and over with the hammer and because of the sprained state of my arm I was unable to block correctly so some damage still went through my defences. It was a battle of attrition as every time he struck I put a jab or two into his face. It was no longer a calculated match of professionals, it was a brawl to the finish. I don't exactly know how long it took but I was impressed when he fell to his knees, his leg had given out when I kicked the weakest one. Using my shield arm to hold back the hammer I pummeled into his face until his HP dropped to 1 and the duel was over.

I checked my own health at 11. One more strike and I would have been toast. Horus, who had taken my strikes these past few minutes looked up at me with no longer a face of spite but in fact one of eagerness. I decided to reach out a hand and to my surprise, he actually grabbed it, followed up with a "You know Conquest you may be a low level but that was some impressive fighting. I have to ask you, what class do you have to specialize in both hand to hand, sword fighting and I even saw you attempt to heal yourself in an earlier round. It must be at least rare."

I looked at him and was for a moment stunned at the direct question but it was an honest one of admiration more so than malice, so I answered honestly.

"I still have yet to choose my class."

As soon as I mentioned this his face contorted to that of a scowl and after getting up he quickly pulled his hand away. "Fine then keep your secrets" and stormed off back to the stage.

Making my way back to my seat as well I wasn't met with some congratulations from the other fighters and observers and instead, I finally noticed that the crowd around had grown to an actual audience and they were all shouting. During those fights I never had time to look at my skills, sure enough most of them were leveled up or close to leveling. My XP hasn't changed but that makes sense since there aren't any enemies killed and I haven't gotten a quest clear reward. While I was looking through my notifications I noticed the crowd's yelling had changed to something else. Reverting my focus to the people around me I noticed they were all looking up at the raised observation stand and screaming! Up there I was able to see Isabel and Captain Randall fending off over 5 assassins. Other guards were trying to make their way up the stands but were blocked by some overly large men in black robes.

Thinking fast I ran as quickly as I could through the crowd that was taking the opposite action and ran straight towards Isabel and Randall. The notification was too chilling.

<Save Isabel: Rank B>
Reward: Improved relations with Isabel
Reward: Improved relations with Kingdom Nobles
Reward:???

Having these rewards dangled in my face as well as the fact Isabel was a very pretty woman I ran with haste towards the assassins. Instead of taking the stairs, I climbed up the side of the observation area instead. Making my way up the wooden buttresses I came over the edge almost to get stepped on by Randall's armored boots. He was being pushed back badly as he was taking on an extreme amount of opponents. Dodging his heavy feet I stand myself up only to barely block an assassin's dagger with my shield. Making myself a little harder to hit, I took up a defensive pose next to Randall and looked around at the situation on the stands. It was a small observatory with three chairs, Randall and I were on the front edge in the center while Isabel was isolated on the side. Even though she was only 8 feet away from us there were still 2 assassins between us both. I looked over at Randall "I am going to take a break for Isabel, can you give me cover?" like a father looking towards his son that finally took up the family business he brightened and nodded his head "I will buy you some time".

I wasn't expecting what came next, Randall lifted his shield and sword and shouted loudly initiating a taunt skill "Come at me you cloaked Cowards!" and with it, he managed to pull the attention of the two assassins blocking my path. They cut to the side to get a better strike on Randall as I slid my way towards Lady Isabel's side. "Conquest! What are you doing here?" she said frantically as she blocked a dagger aimed at her throat.

"Saving you hopefully, please come with me my Lady" using some words I heard in old medieval movies to try and get her moving she turned and only with a few moments of reluctance before following close behind.

"I am going to jump down, I need you to follow, I will catch you"

Isabel was shocked. I took the first leap and jumped 10 feet down to the ground floor that had cleared out of civilians. I turned back just in time to see Isabel's feet first crashing into me, that armor was heavier than it looked and I took some damage dampening her fall. Looking back up I could see Randall was surrounded on all sides by almost 9 assassins as he prevented them from following us off the ledge. "GO Conquest! Take the young Lady out of here!" Though from what I could see on Randall he had not taken too much damage from these assassins he just lacked the speed and damage to take on so many at once when they constantly blocked his attacks together. Looking over at Isabel who was looking back at Randall as well with the same amount of apprehension to leave I understood why he addressed me instead. He knew she wouldn't leave unless she was dragged. I grabbed her hand and she with a startled look on her face turned towards me. "It is time to go, we need to get you back to the keep." withdrawing her feelings to run and save Randall she swallowed it back and nodded at me "Thank you" in a near whisper, then turned to follow.

We ran from the fighting straight through the now empty arena where all that was left were guards and assassins. Picking a careful course to keep us out of harm's way we made our way past the stands and past the training grounds where I saw Talmor running towards me with sword out and at the ready. "Follow the dirt path laced with yellow flowers, they will lead you to the side entrance of the keep. I will help hold them off." I thanked him and pulled harder on Isabel's hand in the direction he pointed. I could see the peaks of the towers to the gate mentioned by Talmor just ahead.

Looking up the walls I noticed they were empty and no archers were making their march back and forth as I saw earlier. The night was starting to fall over us and the sun was setting on the other side of the castle casting a deep shadow over us. Right as there was a bend next to the wall I had a chill run down my spine and stopped in my tracks. I pushed Isabel in front of me and turned around. I witnessed the shadows move and out emerged a shape revealing itself. There was a woman who was tracking us, mask up and hood covering her face. She wielded a sickly purple dagger that seemed like I would die from a flesh wound. Knowing she could strike at any time I didn't take my eyes off of her and pushed Isabel who was behind me to keep going. "Isabel makes it to the gate, the guards will be waiting for you there."

She reluctantly let go of my hand and with what sounded like she was crying she said "please don't die" and I could hear her run towards the gate. She was an A.I. and if she died she was gone for good. If I died I would just have to log in after 24 hours. Their lives had a certain amount of precious nature to them that I respected. I wasn't going to let this assassin get her way. I dropped my shield on my right and prepared for the fight putting the sword in both of my hands.

Cora

Cora was annoyed at the initial setback of her mission, she hired some decent-level assassins using her hard-earned gold coins to put on this show. Sneaking them into the crowd and attacking when they were at their loudest to have a perfect surprise. But flaws started to step in at some random player's intervention. One of the participants in the arena decided to be a goody two-shoe and climb his way onto the observation deck saving my target before I could deal my final blow. I was then stopped by that damned knight captain having to leave my assassins behind while I pursued the pair alone. There he was once again standing in front of me blocking my way to my prize. His gear was abysmal and I clearly had a level advantage over this noob. I took my stance and rushed the guy, his name showed over his head <Conquest> and frankly, it was ironic that he was going to be toppled with a single knick with my blade.

Taking a view at his stance I noticed he kept his right arm out of view while holding the longsword with both hands. Assuming it was wounded from a previous conflict I activated my <<Shadow Step>> ability to teleport on that side but I almost lost my footing as I had stepped on a damned shield on the ground.

As soon as I caught myself the imposing sword from this low-level player came thundering down with a whistle behind it but glancing the blow away with my dagger he seemed prepared for it and struck at me with a low kick after loosening his grip on the sword as a counterbalance. These were high-skill moves but thankfully I had armor that didn't care and his kick did practically nothing to my shin guards. I could see the frustration on his face as I used a flash movement skill to get on his other side, he saw me coming but couldn't stop the dagger from getting a gash on his shoulder. The timer for this player was beginning as the bleed effect is one of the best effects possible with this Epic grade dagger. I grinned with a victory behind my mask and could see a focus on Conquests face but then his eyes widened and I could see it shift to a site behind me, immediately on alert myself I swiveled around in time to see a woman clad in black armor and a giant sword bearing down on me. Her first swing immediately took away a quarter of my health and I almost let the second one though if I didn't pop my emergency skill to teleport back into the shadows. This mission today was a failure for me but I know the attack is coming that would make it impossible for me to capture her later, I can only hope she survives so I can capture her later...

Theo

As soon as I saw Catalina running up with that red hue and sword raised high I felt both fear and happiness that I was being saved. She struck the assassin with insane amounts of damage and she still lived but was pushed back, indicating a very high level. Then before Catalina could run the second strike through her a black veil surrounded her and she disappeared in an instant. It gave me a bit of a chill that as soon as the assassin arrived she had vanished. I watched as Catalina strode up to me and handed me a thin vial with red liquid in it. Then with what seemed to be a soft voice, she said "drink this, thanks for saving my friend"

I drank the potion and the bleeding stopped and my health went back to nearly full. "Thank you, you saved my butt back there. What should I call you?" I asked Catalina.

"You can just call me Cat, let us go check up on Lady Isabel" Her response only led me to have more questions whether she was a player or an A.I. Without being able to see her Health bar I can't tell the difference. Not many players care for the A.I. and even when they do they seldom take the time to learn their names or verbiage. With almost a wary walk I followed behind the armored woman towards the gate around the bend. Sure enough, there was over 20 guards standing firm with spears and shields pointed outward. Isabel was waiting at the gate looking back to see who would continue to pursue her, whether to confirm if her savior had died. Both Cat and I walked forward to the line of guards and they stopped bringing their spears to bear on us when Isabel waved her hand at them. As we approached I started to have a sinking feeling because my quest is still not over even after bringing her back to the castle entrance.

When it comes to the ranking of quests, they start at F and move up to E, D, C, B, A, S, SS and finally SSS. Kronos online has guidelines on their site for recommended party members for each rank of the quest, E-C can be done solo or in pairs, while B requires a large team, A at minimum requires a guild to complete. S is a national event while SS and SSS have not even been leaked by the creators. Thinking on this difficulty system, the fact that bringing her back to the castle did not qualify as saving her meant there was more to this quest than meets the eye. B ranked would mean I should have a team of at least 20 members balanced and ready for combat and seeing how it started off with a ton of high-level assassins taking shots at Isabel right off the bat I can only imagine where it may go from here...

Reuniting with Isabel and the guards surrounding her, with Cat at my side we both approach her and bow. I spoke first however as I couldn't get the crawling feeling out of my skin that entering this castle may be worse than dealing with the assassins at our back. Thinking on the fact that there were no archers on the walls but instead an entire squad of guards at this hidden gate waiting for us instead of coming to help fight the assassins? It was too suspicious for me, and I already have a hard time trusting people.

I started scrutinizing the guards surrounding Isabel then reached forward to grab her hand to start pulling her out of the center of them. She resisted but I was insistent. Cat started to notice my intention then nodded at Isabel and she relented, letting me take her outside the circle of guards. I could see Catalina unsheath her sword and walk between Isabel and the guards.

She wasn't as careful as I would have been however and asked Isabel without any hint of keeping the question quiet "Lady Isabel do you recognize any of these guards? This entrance is supposed to be a secret for just the royal family.`` As soon as she said the words, shock appeared on her face and her head abruptly turned to look behind her at the guards who swung their spears in her direction. Unluckily for them, however, Catalina was expecting this reaction and rewarded their betrayal with a cold heft of steel shattering their wooden spears mid-thrust.

Pulling the lady out of harm's way again and behind me, I pulled out the spare sword I picked up earlier and shoved it into her hands. I remember how skilled she was before and I know that if she is to survive she has to pull her own weight in escaping. "Where are the 6 royal guards you had with you earlier? Could they be of any help?" I asked with honest curiosity, I immediately regretted asking as I could see her beautiful face scrunched up and eyes plastic wrap over with tears at the mention of her colleagues. With a soft voice barely able to be heard over the traitors being chopped apart by the berserker in the background she said with sadness dripping along with her tears "they. . . were cut down by that assassin from earlier. They saved my life at the cost of their own." I nodded, and replied with a grim expression "Something dark is happening here, where is your brother? I believe your castle is compromised and we need to rescue you both"

At the mention of her brother, some of the tears in her eyes dried and a look of concern replaced it. Turning her face up and looking past the gate I realized what she was going to say before she said it. Cursing in my mind I heard her speak and the notification of the quest updating. "Thank you for your concern, my brother... he should be inside the keep in his room, he is a smart boy if he heard what was going on he must have hidden in our old hide and seek spot, he would be safe there if we can get to him first."

<Save Isabel and Benjamin: Rank B+>
Reward: Improved relations with Isabel and Benjamin
Reward: Improved relations with Kingdom Nobles
Reward: History book of Von Torez household

I nodded at her and gave her the best smile I could muster, even though it was fake and said in as positive of a tone possible "Of course we will save him, once we deal with these traitors please guide the way in."

<Plus 15 relationship with Isabel>

Her pretty face solidified a smile for the first time since he saw her with her brother and it almost made it worth it. Turning back his attention he could see that half the guards were already defeated by Catalina and he rushed to back her up against the remaining ten guards. They had started to surround her seeing that they wouldn't be able to get to Isabel until they finished her off. But their plans had backfired now that both myself and Isabel joined the fray. With their backs to us, we struck with rage in our blades and decimated the first guards caught unsuspecting. Some turned to fight back but the advantage was already turned away from them as they were caught off guard. Catalina must have been at least level 50 and these guards were only in the '20s. A little higher than I was but my stats brought me to be on par with them. Isabel had skill levels that shut down any basic attacks they tried to make against her and after a few minutes we finished them off. To my dismay, the quest wasn't over and I knew that the sinking feeling I had earlier was correct.

Cat finally raised her face shield and revealed her stunning black hair and eyes, she had a pointed nose and thin lips across a blemish-free face. It was breathtaking, but then after being lost for a moment heard her words "let's join a party so we can see where to go" I didn't want to agree in case she stole some good gear but I was sure that if I didn't take her help I would have no chance of completing this mission. The pop-up for the party invite was sent and we both accepted it. Isabel had most of her information hidden and had a silver name indicating she was an AI, Catalina however showed she was level 49 and with a gold name, she was an actual player and a berserker class. I took special care to limit what I shared with them as I didn't want her to think I was too low level or to reveal I haven't selected a class yet.

Now that we had that established both Catalina and I turned to Isabel wondering where we had to go next. She pointed to the right side of the small gate and behind some yellow flowers was a lever she revealed and when she placed her hand on it, it glowed and allowed her to move it. Soon the gate started to lift slowly and once completely raised we made our way inside as quietly as we could. I luckily had the stealth skill but it became abundantly clear that neither of my companions had it with the battle dress of Isabel and the bulky heavy plate that Catalina wore. It would be hard to imagine no one heard us, but it became clear soon enough. No one could be found inside the compound. There were no guards and no lights to be seen, but I know that since corpses disappear in grey light after being killed then there would be nobodies to be seen. This left an eerie sound on the inside of the wall where every shuffle of armor and every step on uneven rocks could be heard in the grunges of the night.

Isabel whispered to us that there should be guards all over the place and the lights should have been on, which was obvious but she was panicking. Though what she said after almost made me groan "Ben's hiding spot is the bottom floor of the keep, we can go into it using the back cellar entrance." and with that, she pointed towards the rear of the castle on the right side. Catalina knew her strengths better than I did and was taking point in our march towards the side of the castle's keep, she could withstand a sneak attack from an assassin while we most likely could not. The march forward felt like it was drawing on, I kept having a terrible feeling after every step we took. Sure enough, as soon as we made it to the cellar door it burst open and two masked men came out, one holding a bag on his back that was massive and obviously full of stolen goods. In each of their hands, they held a scimitar and without hesitating rushed Catalina before she could even react and managed two swift blows on her. Unluckily for them however is that she is a berserker and from the health bar I could see on my HUD she barely lost 5% of her health from their strikes.

Both Isabel and I concentrated on the man holding the stolen goods while Catalina unleashed her unrelenting assault on the other. After trading a few blows and parries we managed to take out the intruders. Being a person who leaves nothing to waste I wasted no time inspecting the bag on the man, but to both my joy and dismay it wasn't some pieces of fine china or royal jewelry it was instead Benjamin. Ben was unconscious and had a status effect sign on his health bar so from what I can assume he won't be waking up any time soon. Isabel was almost in tears seeing her brother again hugging him and brushing his hair but also holding onto a sense of horror looking into the cellar doors with the connotations of all that is occurring. Something big was going on here and we have to get out of the city walls if we are to keep these two alive.

CHAPTER 5

———◆◆———

Thinking of how to transport the unconscious noble left me with one option- I had to carry him. Picking up Ben forced me to holster my sword and make me a noncombatant but I couldn't make Catalina or Isabel carry him. Isabel didn't have the strength to do it and we needed Cat to defend us in case more assassins showed up. This didn't mean I was useless, the bandage skill still had its merits and since I was attempting to hide while carrying Ben my sneak skill was leveling at a good pace. Following Isabel's directions, she started guiding us to the gate where we entered. I couldn't blame her train of thought as it is the only known information about this situation and who knows what else is going on at the main gate. Finally, the sounds of conflict broke out in my ears. I can hear swords upon swords in the distance towards the other side of the building. Now we have to make a choice, head towards the fighting and assist our allies or attempt to flee secretly out the rear entrance.

"What if my father is back from the front lines, he could be here to save us!" Isabel nearly pleaded to us to go in that direction. Catalina was quick to pour water on the hopeful thought "No, if he was here now you would hear his call to arms and he would have his army at his back to take back the castle. It sounds like just a small skirmish of what is most likely the last remaining guards inside the keep. We have to use their sacrifice to get you out of here." The cold words rang in Isabel's ears and I could see her face droop in understanding. The situation was grim and she had to escape, even though she knew most of the guards were putting their lives on the line. She came to a decision and brought her head up high.

"We will leave through the gate we came in, and take as many trusted guards as we can to escape. Hopefully, Knight Captain Randall and some of his knights are still alive and we can regroup with them. Thank you both for getting me this far, let us all get out of here alive."

It filled me with a bit of hope after hearing her words, they were the first solid bits of planning this A.I. had been able to do on her own and it's hard to think that she is not a real person behind that face. The emotions captured on everyone I have met so far can be extremely unsettling especially in this dire situation. Coming back to my senses I kept up and followed them towards the gate, no guards to be seen, no traitors or intruders either. The gate was still open from when we entered it and we made our way back through it, walls covered in darkness and the sounds of swords clashing from the arena grounds still covering the air. The dust was still unable to settle as combat was still running rampant and there was chaos across the field. As we approached the stands we could see the pockets of combat were now even more isolated than before. There were no longer assassins anywhere to be seen but instead enemy soldiers with a segil of a face surrounded by snakes covering their shields. It now came to me that this was not a petty assassination attempt but a full-scale invasion and first strike by an enemy country with a clear objective to take out their leadership. I could hear the town's bells ringing now, as they had been alerted to enemy soldiers being able to infiltrate the walls and even more approaching from the west. The Medusa surrounded by snakes represented their neighbor country, The Jorgan Principality.

This was significant news as just earlier today he had heard the news that the Raynor kingdom had mobilized to suppress the Jorgan Principality. The three countries shared a border and Stotonely was the gateway city between them. The mountains that kept the border between each country were opened by this border city, if any army were to assault the Belfast kingdom from those two neighbors they would have to make the choice to suffer casualties in the mountains or fight their way through the high walls of Stotonely. I had to think quickly, the coordination of these strikes was too great and Stotonely only had 200,000 citizens.

Now taking point to get a better grasp on the situation in the arena I could see there that our side had equal numbers of soldiers inside the walls. Each of their soldiers was elites to have infiltrated the city before the main assault was alerted. "Cat, Isabel, if we are to have any chance whatsoever we need to free up some of our soldiers from combat otherwise we will have no chance of escaping the city." At the mention of fleeing the entire city, this drew some alarm from both Isabel and Cat but hearing the blaring sound of the alarm bells shook them back to their senses. Both of them nodded and charged into the guards closest to winning against the intruders. The more that are freed up for combat the easier we will have to take advantage against other groups.

The battle went fiercely, but I was stuck as an observer holding Benjamin. Every time I saw an opening I made sure to let them know about it and give orders to strike. They trusted my words as every time they listened it resulted in a small victory and more spared troops. This went on until we were in the final group in conflict, having saved about 40 soldiers I noticed two men standing back to back fighting a horde of enemy soldiers. One was knight captain Randall and the other was a player. His armor was that of this nation's officers, no shield to be seen and on his shoulder showed the turtle shell emboldened there. I could see the soldiers around me itching to rush and save the man they clearly respected. The rank insignia on his chest showed the gold fist signifying a centurion. Being separate from the city guard the army of Belfast held ancient roman ranks as their standard. A centurion would be the equivalent of a modern captain, commanding multiple lieutenants, or Denarians in Kronos who in turn command multiple squads of men led by Sergeants also known as Veterans here. The unique status of this player meant that he rose to the rank of the centurion in a country's official military which is a rare occurrence as there aren't too many benefits to limiting oneself to a kingdom. Instead most players opt to operate out of a mercenary guild and get hired for gold.

His name, Silvax was clear above his head and displayed almost like a badge even when surrounded by enemies. The two were in a precarious position as every time they lashed out to strike their opponents they would be struck from behind by another enemy in the gap. The soldiers, impatient and unable to wait any longer, rushed the troops surrounding their centurion and cleared the way. I noticed as soon as the troops were shoulder to shoulder with Silvax they attacked faster, stronger and with more purpose than when I gave them commands. They made short work of the remaining soldiers Silvax and Randall walked up to our party with wounds covering their bodies. Randall spoke first though he seemed winded as he did so

"You really came to our rescue back there Conquest, I see you have the young lords with you as well. We have been fighting non-stop since the tournament was interrupted, do you have any news as to our situation?"

Weighing my options and thinking of a solution I came up with one on the spot.

"Catalina and I rescued Benjamin and we have been escorting Lady Isabel since then. From what I can see is that Stotonely may not have fallen yet but It will soon. We have to retreat from here and fall back to the next closest city, do you have any ideas?"

After giving my piece and assigning credit to Catalina as well for the rescue, Silvax approached next. In my mind, he was going to hoard the glory so I immediately fell into a guarded state not wanting to yield any of the rewards we fought hard to achieve.

"The Citadel of Haral is the next closest city with fortifications. It is north of here, about half a day's journey. It is where we kept most of our standing armies. If it wasn't for the fact I was going to do dungeon training with my men I would not have been here to defend my hometown." said Silvax in an honorific tone. It was strange he had associated with this country so close and from the close relationship with the other soldiers which all seem to be NPCs. An impressive feat as from what I have read on the forums it is incredibly hard to maintain positive relations with A.I.

"What is the status of the army? Should they not have been here for this?" Randall interrupted inquisically to Silvax. Silvax heard the question but without even changing expression turned to the knight captain and answered

"They were dispatched, led by Count Rodriguez Von Torez to handle the Dungeon outbreaks in the east mountains. Word that a dungeon calamity was released had sent the kingdom into a tizzy. I was tasked with training up these new soldiers up to speed in preparation for the clean-up efforts.-"

The mention of both a dungeon outbreak and a dungeon calamity is a shock. A dungeon outbreak is when a dungeon isn't raided enough and the monsters surge forth onto the lands around them. This can be cause of celebration if prepared for or disaster if left to fester. In this instance, he had mentioned a Dungeon Calamity which is a way for the A.I. to reference a raid boss. They are extremely rare disasters with legs, or whatever appendage helps them navigate. If it was indeed a raid boss then it makes complete sense that they dispatched the army to handle it. Raid bosses are one of the strongest classes of bosses that typically require upwards of

500 high-level coordinated players to handle both the raid boss and its minions that guard it.

Every time a raid boss shows up it typically is broadcast and widely shown around the world. So far only 3 have been seen and each time it required the nation they appeared in to quell their rise. It's simply that players are just not strong enough yet to deal with them even though Glass and his guild The Entity have stated their goal to fight one.

"-The appearance of the calamity and this invasion is poorly timed. We are spread too thin. Let us gather our forces and escape to the Citadel then we can plan further but our priority is to get the nobles out of here safely." Silvax continued.

Silvax stood straighter and pointed at three men from the survivors and with a shout gave them orders.

"Denarian William, gather your swordsman and become our shield then send a squad to scout out the northern gate. Denarian Sagen, I need your bowmen to keep an eye on the walls and shadows for assassins when we make our break out of here. Denarian Davis, keep a lid on that mouth of yours and bring your men to the center, you will be the keeping close guard on our VIPs" They were clean and concise orders and as soon as he spoke them his troops began to move. Denarian William almost looked like a miniature version of Silvax with less bulk, Davis wasn't wearing a helmet and let his blond hair hang loose to his shoulders and had a wide grin at the comment Silvax gave him. Sagen kept silent but with some simple hand gestures, the green archers that had experienced true life or death combat for the first time moved in an organized pattern. It was almost art seeing the forces move in such a calm fashion compared to when they were running rampant alone or even when I was commanding them. Silvax became a leader for a reason I can tell now with a growing respect for the Centurion.

Knight Captain Randall spoke next "I have a duty to this city to guard it well, I will organize the defences and try and buy you as much time as I can. The remaining city guard will hold a final stand here at the keep and attempt to lure them here." he turned to Isabel with a sad expression for what he wanted to say next "Lady Isabel, it has been an honor to serve you and your father. Please escape from this place, Live and reunite with old 'Rodriguez for me." and after saying so, gave a crisp salute to her. He patted me on the back and left towards the southern gates where the loudest bits of combat remained. None of his guards or his knights were still alive by the time we returned to the training yard. Talmor was nowhere to be seen and I felt a pang of sadness at this. It was at this moment I truly came to understand that the lives of A.I. in this game were unique, and when they died they were gone for good.

After Randall left, Isabel almost started crying again but brought her chin back up looking at Catalina, "We can't let his sacrifice be in vain. We must escape from here," and standing up straight turned her head to the Centurion. "Centurion Silvax as the Lady of the Von Torez household I command you to escort us out of this city and to the Citadel of Haral" The order was given and Silvax heeded it. He bent to one knee and stated in his official-sounding tone "You will be done my Lady"

That was it, once the command was given the rush began to escape the city. Silvax masterfully commanded his men to scout ahead and clear the paths. From what we had seen the assassins were gone after they accomplished what they needed - taking out most of the city guard and their remaining knights. Every time they encountered any remaining enemy infiltrators, Silvax ordered his men to surround and destroy them with extreme prejudice. In the distance we could hear battle horns and drums being played, then in the distance fireballs from catapults and magicians were thrown at the city. Things were getting desperate as hell rained from the sky. Isabel, Catalina and I were at the center of the formation surrounded by Denarion Davis and his troops. Silvax was taking the point this time around and crushing the enemy at every step. He took special care to prevent any civilians from being harmed.

The fear was genuine in most of the citizens' eyes as the war brought pillaging which was a real fear to any who had been in this situation in the past. As much as we all wanted to start saving as many people as we could, we knew that if we brought them all with us we would be spotted by the enemy and our escape would be foiled. So, with a heavy heart, we gave them the best chance we could by slaying any rogue enemies and ushering the citizens back into their homes as we made our way north. As soon as we caught a glimpse of the northern gate we each had a sigh of relief at the reassuring sight of guards on the walls. None had their arms pulled back and we made our way to the large wooden doors that separated the city from the outside. Men were stationed behind the gate but it was clear to see they were just militiamen with words picked up from any which place. Most were panicking as they had never had combat before thus they knew their situation had grim hopes.

Scanning the faces I saw one that I recognized, it was Adrian who I had sparred with earlier. He held his head high and his face was bitter. I could see his knuckles were white as they held the longsword with an iron grip. I waved at him to gain his attention and it seemed to have broken his resolute expression and his grip loosened. "Conquest? What are you doing here? Bringing reinforcements I hope?" and a glimmer of hope shone on his face as he eyed the troops around me.

Seeing his eyes I knew what he wanted to hear but I almost didn't have the heart to shatter those hopes.

But then, looking around at the rest of the militiamen, almost 50 of them surrounding the gate unorganized and without discipline I got an idea. "Silvax, escort the lady into the forest and wait for an hour, if I don't return in that time, leave me. I have an idea that could save some lives." He looked at me and nodded, then commanded the gate be opened for him at the shock of the militia around us. Isabel saw this and misunderstood my intentions coming up as I handed Ben off to her. "Conquest why do you have to sacrifice your life too? Aren't there enough dead heroes in this conflict?"

The question stung me at the thought of Talnor and Randall going into the grey ash but kept a hold on my idea. "My lady I have to save as many lives as I can, tell them to listen to me and I can rescue Randall." This last part caught her off guard but with the idea that I can save Randall she nodded and shouted to the Militiamen "Brave warriors of Stotonely, Conquest will be your Sergeant, listen well to him and you will survive!" she shook my hand and allowed herself to be escorted out of the city. As soon as the last of Silvaxs men made it through the gate it was closed behind them.

My mind started to work overtime as I formulated a plan to get Knight Captain Randall, I refuse to let that man's good graces go to waste and for my linked quest to fail. When the gate made its resounding thud an eerie silence came over everyone with only the faint sound of combat in the far distance. Adrian came up to me and with the eyes of all the militiamen on me, they looked at me with expectation. Adrian spoke first, "What are we to do Conquest?"

The gears turning I looked back at all the expecting eyes and replied as confidently as I could, mimicking the leadership talents of Silvax as best I could. "You are all Men, warriors of Stotonely not by choice but because you have to. Your families are counting on you, those at your side are counting on you." The militia started to perk up, and the guards on the wall started to look down at my speech.

"You all have a purpose today, and we have to stand strong against these invaders. You militiamen, I ask you, do you want to save this city?"

The fire started to enter their hopeless eyes, a hoarse cheer started to rise from their throats.

"The opportunity is here, you, my soldiers, have it in you to save this city if you follow me. Follow me and your families can live on, this city can live on!"

They were closer now and the hoarse cheer became a roaring OOHHH. Seeing their attention fully focused I pointed my sword towards the southern gate where Randall would be holding the line and continued my speech. "To the front! If we demoralize them now we can survive!" and without prompting or ordering I started marching south, but not quite in the direction of the gate, but instead towards a quaint home I had dinner with 40 brave militiamen at my back.

CHAPTER 6

My goal was in the process of forming but If I manage to get Captain Randall to see that he has more to lose than his walls he will fight with more fervor and try to escape. We made it through the city and the men were still following as I stopped in front of a quaint villa in the center of town. I knocked on the door and an arrow split through the wood only inches from my face. In a panic, I shouted to gain her attention "Teresa it's me, Conquest, I am here to bring you to Randall" at the mention of her husband's name the door slowly creaked open to reveal the homebody Teresa in leather armor and a bow in her hand. She was ready to kill whomever came through that door if it wasn't her husband that was certain to me.

Teresa followed in step at my side and we were followed by the militiamen including Adrian. As we came closer to the walls the constant firing of magic and siege weapons was clear in the sky. It was imposing as the night sky glittered with the jarring sight of war. As we made it past the shopping district and church we rounded a causeway that leads straight to the southern gate. In the distance, I could see it still closed and organized guards behind it standing with spears at the ready. As our force approached they became aware of our movement and some turned spears raised until they saw that we had no formal sigil or outfits on and the fact we were mostly just a group of militia. They turned back to the gate.

I approached the man in the center with the closest thing to armor on and talked to him as clearly as I could over the sounds of war "Where is Knight Captain Randall, His wife is with us and we need to speak with him urgently" the guard who I now recognize is an official sergeant like Telnor was turned back to heed what I was saying but shook his head "Knight Captain Randall is extremely busy right now leading the defences of the city, Unless you have some key information that can stop an army of 20,000 soldiers then I don't see a use with you bothering him- even if you have his wife with you."

Well, he has a point I thought, but I needed to be persistent since this could be our only way to keep the city from being sacked. "I am telling you right now that this is that kind of information. Where is he?" The sergeant saw the seriousness in my tone and expression and yielded finally, pointing up the wall towards the top of the gatehouse. "He has gone up there to lead the men. Be quick if you truly can save my home." I nodded and started running towards the gatehouse stairs.

The rooms were stone and covered in guards, the higher up I went they started to become more concentrated and higher leveled based on the gear they had equipped but even then it was paltry compared to what I saw when I made it to the top. I was met with the sight of thousands of soldiers and siege engines in the distance that seemed to cover the dark plains I was hunting in just a day before. Every time a fireball or other attack magic was cast and sent up at the walls I could see a few magicians on the walls cast shields to deflect them. It was a terrible battle of attrition and I could see they were forming ranks in the distance for a final push. It took everything I had to rip my eyes from the mesmerizing sight of soldiers at war to look at the rest of the entourage on the top of this gatehouse. There stood Randall giving commands to other men and I noticed he had stopped talking as his eyes glanced back at our posse at the top of the stairs. He had locked eyes with Teresa who was close behind me and ran to her. "I'm so glad you are alright, but why…" his voice trailed off as he turned to me, his previous face of happy relief had turned to a wicked scowl. Then in a gruff voice full of threat, he said "Conquest. Why have you brought my wife from the safety of the city to the front lines when I am trying to lead the defences?"

For a moment I was concerned with my choices but I knew I only had one shot to save Randall, and that was to leave Stotonely for another day. "Knight Captain Randall" I started with as serious a tone as I could muster, "I have a plan to save as many people as possible, but I need your help." Randall looked at me with eyes full of scrutiny, we may have had a high relationship bonus but I am still an outsider to him. But after he looked back and forth between Teresa and me, I realized my forethought had worked. "What is it you have in mind Conquest? I am running out of options as I am the only man above the rank of sergeant left in the city after the assassins made their attack. I have about 2000 men at my disposal and a few magicians who I have focused on targeting down their siege weapons. But as you can see-" he makes a gesture out into the plains "- we are still outnumbered nearly 10 to 1. The fate of our city is almost set in stone, so if you have any way to keep this from being a bloodbath I am all ears."

This is where my scheming mind came into play. "I need some form of noble clothing, I want to go out there and Parlay with our enemy. While I buy the time, I want you to spread your men to all corners of the city and gather everyone except those on the walls to the north gate. Then as soon as I return we will escape through the north and leave the southern gates completely open. We may lose the city but what is a city without its citizens."

It was a radical approach and I could see the faces of those around me, I could read their expressions and all of them but Randall thought I was crazy. He nodded his head after a minute of deliberation.

"I can get you those clothes, but who will you be impersonating? I know not of any nobles with your stature or... lack of power," he questioned me but I was prepared for it.

"Leave that to me, If I can buy us an hour with stalling, then even at the cost of my life I will get the innocent people out of this city alive."

Finally, Randall saw my reasoning and gave some orders to the men around him. Nearly 10 agonizing minutes later I was dressed in some aristocratic robes and a white flag on a pole. Leaving my men behind I made my way to the ground in front of the gate.

Strengthening my resolve I nodded my head at the surrounding gate guards and they opened the wooden portcullis. When I took my first step outside I almost got the urge to turn back inside and run but resisted the urge. Thousands of soldiers were lined up and many held the medusa banner of the Jorgan Principality, they held their line about 500 feet away from the wall. Scattered among their men were towering trebuchets and magicians. One thing I noticed as soon as I started to make my walk forward, the spells and rocks that were being launched at the city stopped, my plan was working. When I had made it about halfway to their lines I saw a group of what seemed to be knights on horseback making their way towards me. Four of them in total had unique colors to their armor and shields. One sat in the center of their formation and his armor was the most impressive, shining and green. His helmet made his face imperceptible but I could tell by the way he strode his horse towards me there was a smug look behind it. Not trying to blow my cover I kept as straight a back as I could even when they surrounded me pointing both spears and swords at my face. I wanted to show I had the air of a noble and that I would not be threatened by lessers. To complete the act I made sure to be the first to speak.

"Is this how you treat a Viscount coming to discuss terms of surrender? Am I not owed the respect of knowing the victors of this valiant siege?" being sure to toss in some pleasantries to keep my head on my shoulders, the riders looked at me and nodded. They lowered their weapons and the one in green armor raised his faceplate revealing the name above his head. "I am Duke Stanely Freneferd of the Jorgan Principality. I am the victor of this siege as you have said, what terms could you possibly hope to have as you are in no position to bargain. Total surrender is the only term I will accept." I could tell he had no respect for me, and I can see why with the title of Duke it was a title that represents one right next to the noble lineage in power. I had to get him to talk to me more otherwise he would kill Randall. "Your honorable Dukeship, I humbly request we parlay the terms of this surrender, I wish to ensure the safety of my citizens and that they will be treated humanely when under new leadership. Is there a place we can sit and talk about these formalities?"

The duke considered it, I was sure he wanted to just chop my head off and be done with it. Eventually, after a few more seconds of drawn-out silence, he nodded "Very well Viscount. Follow us back into our camp and we will have our discussions. What is your name? From what I understood the ruler of this city was Count Von Torez, I see after his death you have taken command? I was sure it would have been his daughter and I would need to raze this city to the ground knowing her stubborn nature."

This caught me off guard, I had no idea the Count had died, was he assassinated I am not sure but I couldn't let this man know of it. "Opportunistic leaders often rise to power in times of strife. Though it seems my reign over this city is nearly over, I, Viscount Conquest, have done my best for the people." hearing my name he nodded as if understanding some truth and spoke back "Of course it all makes sense now, Well Viscount Conquest, let us have our meeting and depending on these terms maybe it does not have to be the end of your reign. As you said, opportunistic leaders are made in these times of strife. As a viscount, I am sure you had plenty of hard times to obtain your rank. . ." The duke started to take on a more calm tone, as we made it to a tent on the far side of his army. I made sure to keep my eyes peeled at all those in the forces around me. I saw lines upon lines of trained soldiers in the center column, knights were scattered across each platoon of troops. It was a hopeless scenario for Stotonely and for my bluff to work I needed to hold off these forces using words instead of violence. One of these days I will have the strength to do it myself but for now, this is my only course of action.

I then spotted a familiar face, It was Chuck Carlson. I had seen him on the news before. I gave him a wave as if I were noble and the knights around me noticed this. They must have got the wrong idea and figured him out as a spy as what happened next almost made me feel sorry for him. One of the riders pointed at him and troops went into motion to drag him away. It was quick but before I could see what happened I was ushered into the tent with the Duke.

The room inside the tent was clean, in the middle sat a war table with 8 chairs around it. Duke Stanley made his way to the far side of the table and sat down in the largest of the chairs, then looked back at me and gestured to the one opposite of him. The rest of the riders stayed outside leaving only the Duke and I in the tent. Leaving no hesitation on my face but internally sweating bullets I sat down in the chair and crossed my arms. Stanley started first with a harumph and a cold, expecting tone "Well you are taking my time Viscount, what terms are you seeking to fill with this meeting. You can't truly be here for just your citizens' safety. What can you offer me to stay alive and serve my country?"

What. It took everything I had to keep my jaw from dropping open in shock. He had read too far into my intentions but I wasn't going to let this opportunity slide, thinking fast and improvising a new plan I put on as shocked face as I could and with awe in my voice replied "I should have known the Great Duke Stanely would see through my offer as soon as I approached. Let us get to the point then, I want to keep ownership of this city that is true. And what I have to offer you is great indeed Sir Duke. I have information on the Raynor Kingdom and its intentions to invade your country, the Jorgan Principality, with my country's aid."

This idea started to swirl in Stanelys mind I could tell and he finally wore a serious expression. "I know of the invasion of the Raynor Kingdom, we struck down their army on our way here. How could this information be important to me? And besides, the Belfast kingdom's army is caught up in a dungeon outbreak. There are no chances for a joint invasion."

The Duke sat back in his chair having come up with his own reasoning and flaws in my story. I cursed to myself and altered my lie to have a hint of truth in it. The best ploys always have equal parts truth as they do lies in order to convince another party. "You would be right to assume that some of our army was held up during the outbreak but wrong to consider that you destroyed the Raynor kingdom's army. As a viscount I was in the meeting during their plans, Count Rodriguez was to march through the mountains and attack your country through the north while the Raynor kingdom bought time through a fake siege near our joint border, but instead sending their armies to your southwest territory. You besieging Stotonely was all part of their plan, they knew you would press forth and were content with you razing this city to the ground if it meant they struck your castle without you to defend it. The leadership of this country has heard of your prowess in battle and determined any battle needed to have you out of the picture in order to win." At this point, I was completely off the rails with my story and saying it with as utmost confidence as I could. The added compliments were to bring his guard down. As soon as I finished my statement however, he stood up immediately and placed both hands on the table. His face was covered in rage and he stared at me with glaring eyes.

"If what you say is true, then you are right about this paltry city being a sacrifice for them to lure me out of position. It is genius. That explains there is no standing army or magicians on the walls. It was a complete distraction. Viscount Conquest, you have won your life today and a deal is to be struck between us. I will take my army and retreat back to my capital to fend off their counterattack, afterwards when I return if you open the gates upon my arrival you shall keep your city under my rule and no razing will take place. However, If I return and you block my movements in any way I will reduce this city to rubble and kill every person living here without mercy. This is my deal, do you accept?" I let loose a huge grin, stood up and reached out my hand for a shake "Of course, My duke. These terms are harsh but I cannot complain. Thank you." then bowed my head to him. Looking up at the duke from my stooped position I could see a smug face looking down on me full of superiority. I made sure to have him take the upper hand in the deal as if he was the one in control, that is the secret to fooling power-hungry people, even in this world. The A.I. duke then ushered me out of the tent and had one of the knights escort me back to the city. Only one hour had passed and I had no idea if it was enough time or not for the citizens to get ready to escape. Glancing around I could not see Chuck anywhere and slowly saw messengers get sent out to all stretches of the army, from what I could tell it was the order to pack up and leave. As I was making my way back to the walls I noticed a glowing notification that was brighter than the others I had been ignoring. Curious, I clicked it and was rewarded with a new Title.

Title Earned <Savior of the City>
Plus 10 to all stats

Titles in Kronos online were rare to come across, and when you received one typically you were rewarded in kind with many different types of boons. Some were stat increases like this one but others also increased relations or gave specific skills unique to the title. In any case, getting this title was the equivalent of ranking up six times. I was happy and kept walking towards the wall.

As soon as I made it to the front line with the escorting knight he nodded to me and without a word turned around going back to his camp. Turning back to the city I looked up at the top of the gatehouse, sure enough, I could still see Knight Captain Randall looking at me with eyes as round as plates. The gates opened by the time I made it to them and Randall was there waiting for me.

"What on earth did you say to them? Why are they packing up and leaving?" His expression was that of awe but also suspicion. It was an understandable reaction, all I told him was that I would buy some time for them to leave, not that I would make their entire army retreat. So I told him the truth, I told him that I was acting like a viscount and had revealed I was in control of the city and that the army was secretly attacking the Raynor kingdom at their capital. This made Randall guffaw and howl with laughter and the pure insanity and prideful assumption that the enemy duke had made. But he soon calmed down when I raised my hand to get his attention. "According to him, Count Rodriguez is dead. And he knew about the dungeon outbreak and the fact that he was dispatched to handle it. I don't know what this means for the kingdom but it can't be good. We still have to evacuate since as soon as he returns here he will raze it to the ground."

The cool bucket of water was poured on Randall and he lost his happy expression. The current predicament was still extremely serious and he had to act now in order to save people's lives. He knew though that he could not have done it without my help. "Thank you, Conquest. You gave the people here a chance, and even if we have to flee the city, any lives saved will be because of you."

Hearing him I smiled, "Then I will leave leading the evacuation efforts to you Randall. I need to rendezvous with Lady Isabel and let her know what has happened here." Randall nodded at my words and shook my hand before sending me off.

Before I could get away I noticed the militiamen were standing behind the gate waiting for me, eyes just as wide as Randall's as they had seen me return from their army and them retreating. "Conquest, did you really cause them to retreat? What do we do now?" They had sparkling eyes and new hope written all over them. "We escaped. Gather your families and everyone you can and follow Randall to the north. I only bought time for this city, nothing more."

Then giving me a salute for the first, and possibly last time Adrian turned and left to help Randall evacuate as many civilians as they could. With one final glance at everyone I smiled and started running for the north gate. It wouldn't be long until they would leave without him to the citadel of Haral.

Having rushed as fast as I could through the city, yelling for the guards I had met earlier to open the gates for me, I sprinted through expending my stamina to travel ground faster. Right as I made it to the tree line a kilometer away I was met with 4 arrows at my feet and a group of figures moving from the trees around me. Thankfully I recognized them and they recognized me. It was Silvax's men, "Denarian Sagan was it? Thank you for not skewering me." he nodded his head and gestured for me to follow him. Soon enough I was brought to Silvax, Isabel and Catalina who after seeing me all came to my side to hear what news I had. Once I had their attention I started my explanation and told them everything that happened. When I was about to deliver the bad news I set one hand on the smiling Isabel's shoulder and told her. "I'm Sorry Isabel, according to the enemies' leader, your father was killed." after delivering the grim news her previous smile was struck from her face and it looked like a ton of metal had landed on her shoulders. She almost fell to her knees but Catalina caught her with my help and she held Isabel close. Silvax winced after hearing the news and turned to Lady Isabel and dropped to one knee in front of her "It will be an honor to serve you, Count Isabel Von Torez."

CHAPTER 7

After delivering the grim news and the proclamation of Silvax, we continued our procession towards the citadel. I kept pace at the front of the pack with Denarian Sagan while Catalina consoled the now Count Isabel. I could see the grim weight of losing her father and possibly her city is a lot to be thrust upon someone so young. I could only imagine how Benjamin feels, every now and again I would look back and see him sulking, walking slowly behind the pair with his head down staring at their trailing steps. It took a lot to not go and try and comfort him, he reminded me too much of my own little brother.

Many years ago, I remember how my brother looked at me when we had just got done buying ramen, potatoes and eggs from the grocery store and on our way out we spotted someone with an entire cart of steaks of all different varieties. It was something we have only eaten once before when our father still had his accounting job. After the recession hit, he lost it and our family was plunged into poverty. It hurts me still watching his face as we both knew we wouldn't be enjoying those niceties for a long time. There were many days where I went to bed hungry just to make sure my little siblings could eat.

After a few more minutes of debate with myself, I couldn't stand it anymore and moved back towards Benjamin. As I approached, I could see the tears that were trailing down his cheeks. He could only be twelve or thirteen, barely old enough to comprehend death but he was forced to understand today that he will never see his father again. When I approached, he looked up at me, eyes red and glossy with a mix of sadness but also a hint of rage in his little face. I knelt next to the young noble and put a hand on his shoulder in an attempt to comfort him. Before I could get my words out he hugged me. And as soon as he did his waterworks started all over again. I returned the hug towards him and told him

"It's going to be okay, we are going to get you and your sister somewhere safe. Uncle Conquests got you."

Through labored tears and hard breathing Benjamin muttered out between sobs "My daddy's gone. I want to see my dad again. . ."

And Benjamin continued to cry while I continued to comfort him, I picked him up and continued walking with the group. Slowing down only gave us more risks so I held him tightly and moved closely behind Catalina and Isabel who was now looking at me holding her brother with a bittersweet smile and some tears of her own.

She could barely grasp on her own that her father was gone, she was not able to comfort someone else when she herself did not have the answers.

It was a familiar feeling. Once again I am reminded of the realism of this game as it feels like my past. When my father fell into his depression after the loss of his job our mom didn't know what to do. Taking care of three kids while being the only person earning money in the household was extracting a heavy toll on her. I could see that look in Isabel's eyes, one of defeat and indignation. I won't let what happened to my mother happen to Isabel in this virtual reality if I have any way of preventing it. I smiled at her and nodded in the only way I knew how to comfort her. In a way saying that I would take care of Benjamin while we made our travels to the citadel.

After four more hours of tirelessly walking, we came upon the imposing metal gates of Haral. This Citadel was responsible for the defence of the south, all trade made its way within a mile of this place so any armies would be forced to come near in order to advance further into the country. Our group of soldiers and nobles made its way towards the gate as it was closed ahead of us. I watched as archers drew their bows above us and we waved them off showing the flag of

Von Torrez. A few moments passed and the gate opened to us.

Silvax, Catalina and I escorted Countess Isabel to the center castle. Isabel was treated as a lady of the court but was not recognized as a count yet as we made our way in and requested an audience with this city's ruler; Earl Jefferies Claycoax. Fortunately for us all, he did not make us wait long and came into the room. The Earl had interesting purple robes that had feted golden lining surrounding the edging with valuable material clearly making up his outfit. He was skinny but easily two meters tall, his face had a mix of annoyance and inconsideration on it as he approached the countess. And in a snobby voice full of contempt he looked down on the countess that was standing now at his approach and looked straight back up to him in as serious of a face she could muster in this situation. The earl was the first to speak between them just as tension in the room began to rise to an uncomfortable level.

"What brings Count Rods' children to my citadel without prior notification?" his nose practically pointed at the sky as he spoke.

"My father Count Rodriguez Von Torrez is dead and I, his eldest daughter, has taken his countship. I have come with news of an invasion from the south and request aid."

These two sentences threw Earl Jefferies through a series of shocks as his previous expression of contempt now had a surprise as his nose finally dipped a bit and he looked down towards the new countess.

"I am sorry Countess Isabel. I was unaware of your circumstances. Do you have an accurate number of the forces that have invaded? Have they overrun your city which is why you have fled to here? Should I be expecting an army at your back threatening to run rampant through my citadel?"

As the Earl went through his speech he went from a sweet forgiving tone to that again of annoyance and contempt. As if she was more of a bother to respect her than her title demanded. Silvax heard this tone however and was not about to sit idle while his new ward was insulted. Standing up from the cush seating he had been resting in and with a hand on his sword he approached on the left of The countess. His approach was also noticed by all the guards present in the room, all of which lowered their spears and halberds at our party. Isabel brought a hand to her side and stopped Silvax from withdrawing his sword. She then spoke first in an attempt to both calm the nerves of the room but also to show her rejection of the way she had been treated up until that point.

"I am a Countess- Earl Jefferies. If you continue treating me with a lack of decorum and respect I deserve then I will be forced to act."

"To be frank your countess-ness" The earl started in an extremely rude tone "What exactly are you a countess of? Your city is most likely in ruins, you have no troops except the ones you brought with you, your father's army is most likely gone if what you say is to be believed. And frankly, I do not take kindly to threats in my own home after you came to ME for help. What exactly can you offer me that I would be interested in?" When the Earl finished speaking he still did not call for his guards to stop showing their weapons to us but instead was intent to hear what Isabel had to say.

"I have the mining rights to the Drandall Mountain range to the east of my city, which is still under my command. The enemy army had retreated before I had come here for the request for aid. I would speak more carefully to me Earl as I only came here as a consideration for the relationship between you and my father in the past. I have plenty of other political allies I could rely upon" without a falter or stutter in her words Isabel delivered some confident words and promises that even peaked the greedy Earl's attention.

With eyes shining with a glint of green he now looked completely at Isabel and waved off the guards' weapons. "You would trade me the mining rights to the entirety of the

Drandall Mountain range? Of course, I could save your city if that is the case, I will mobilize my-"

Isabel cut him off before he could solidify what would be an insanely good deal.

"I need more than just your army to help my city. I need you to get word to the Duke of the South to send his men. The warden needs to be aware of this invasion otherwise our whole nation could be at risk."

The earl bit his lip and had a glimmer of fear in his expression, I caught the sight clearly from my comfy chair across the room. The second the 'Duke of the South' was mentioned he became quieter. As if the name alone would summon him.

"You see about the Duke... Are you sure the severity of this invasion warrants calling him? You know how he can get in combat. I could only imagine if this turns into a war. . ."

"That is exactly why we need him. We need his knights and mages and the strength of the Red" as soon as the word red left her mouth, the earl backed up a step.

"I understand, I will do this as long as the entirety of the Drandall Mountain range is left to me at the end of this conflict."

"You have my word as the Countess of the Von Torrez Household."

After she spoke they both reached out their palms, grasped and cut the back of their hands after shaking. "The oath is sworn and we will be done for the kingdom"

After they shook hands she turned away and started walking towards the exit, Silvax silently followed and so did Catalina, then finally myself and Benjamin, still clinging to me, now sound asleep in my arms.

We promised to regroup in the morning, I left Benjamin with Isabel and bid all of them a good night and went to the closest inn to sleep. I had leveled up over 15 times during that ordeal and had constant notifications throughout it. My stats are looking pretty decent especially with the skill level increase from my new title *'Savior of the City'*. My head was killing me however as I had been online almost all afternoon and night in-game. I paid the fee at the inn, laid down and logged off from Kronos online.

As I got up from the pod, I turned on the TV to check up on the latest news while I grabbed my food. And sure enough, I tuned into the Y.O.K. News network and there was Chuck Carlson, the news anchor I saw outside Stotonely. It seems this recording is from when the army first arrived at the city.

Chuck Carlson

Chuck Carlson was standing in the middle of an impressive thousand-man formation. Sweat was beading on his forehead as he made his way through the lineup of soldiers wielding a flag with the Medusa sigil. As he made it more towards the front of the lines, he could get a good visual of Stotonelys walls under siege by this impressive army. As he made it to the front of the line Chuck witnessed a single man in noble robes and attire waltzing alone towards the army from the now closing gate.

"Folks you can see here that Stotonley has sent out a diplomat in the form of most likely a noble who owns the city or at least a relative of them. Seeing as he is wielding a white flag I can only assume the capitulation of this city is already assured. Ah here comes the welcoming committee" as Chuck said this the camera swivels towards the men on horseback in fancy armor charging towards the lone man, almost like they were going to kill him on site, but they halted right before arriving in front of him.

"It seems they are deliberating now, Ah it seems they are bringing him back towards the center of this formation, let's see if I can get a few words!"

Chuck then started making his way towards the marching procession, as he came closer to the marching group Chuck noticed the noble in the center of the group was looking right back at him with a grin on his face and waved! He saw the name 'Conquest' above his head and realized it was a player! But as soon as Conquest waved at him the men on horseback gave a signal to the men around Chuck. The men acted immediately and grabbed onto Chuck Carlson, dragging the man out of the ranks of soldiers. That is where Chuck was unceremoniously slain for being a spy.

Theo

Cutting back to the newsroom of the Y.O.K. News network the two reporters were staring at each other with a mix of surprise and humor at the sight of both a player lord and their news anchor being killed. The man and woman pair then finally started talking, the news anchorman Jeff Rogers spoke first, "You know Chuck, always able to get them up-close shots of things others could never imagine, and it does not disappoint! Even more shocking news today is to figure out there is a noble player in the Belfast Kingdom. This makes three players hold Noble titles. The world of Kronos seems to have endless opportunities no matter where you go!"

The anchorwoman Jessica Polinska continued Jeff's speech "-It may be full of opportunities but you have to be aware of the dangers as well! Especially since the entirety of the raiding party formed by Glass and the Entity guild was wiped out during an accorded raid. The battle was said to last an entire hour against a boss monster they refuse to comment on. The dungeon they raided was one they had claimed a few weeks ago when Glass became the first Noble ever in Kronos Online. This discovery was made possible by you the viewers! We had heard they were going on a raid and then they just started respawning at their headquarters. Glass had this to say. . ."

The TV cut to a fancy red building with an ornate exterior with the ENTITY logo in bold letters above the gate-sized door. Glass and a few other members of his guild were standing outside it as countless news anchors attempted to get their attention.

"Is it true you fought a demon in the dungeon?"

"Is this a dungeon outbreak?"

"Can we expect to see more of you respawning in the future?"

"What happened to your sword you showed off the other day?"

This last comment manages to make Glass look at the reporter with a red face full of spite and say "The sword I had yesterday was weak, so I needed a new one. No more questions, I have business with the Empires nobles now" and as best as he could pull his face back into a calm look pulling out a purple-hued sword with interesting engravings upon it. Though the average user can tell the previous sword was much more illustrious and of a higher ranking. . .

The camera cut back to the newsroom and Jeff stated the obvious, "Looks like he lost his sword in that fight, dying in Kronos is definitely brutal, any death makes you lose a level and an equipped item at random guaranteed. Just bad luck he lost his prized sword so soon after his boast on the news before. But that's life when you play Kronos."

I turned off the TV after finishing my food. I thought to myself, *If even Entity gets wiped after a raid then I will take any advantage I can get.* Any levels they lose means I have more time to catch up. Looking at my current circumstances I start to realize they thought I was a noble. It was an impressive misunderstanding that I will take full advantage of. My goal at the moment was to ensure that Isabel was safe. After that, I am assured I can collect on all my quest rewards from before all the events that occurred. I will be able to continue my linked quest that ran into the history of Belfast. Since the quest was to obtain an inheritance I would love to obtain it all for myself.

It was a long day and I needed to get some rest. I went to my shabby room and laid down for the night dreaming of the riches that lay in wait behind a certain inheritance. In the morning I did my routine, ate breakfast, went to Rocky's dojo for an hour and then jumped back into the pod to enter Kronos for a fresh day of adventure.

CHAPTER 8

—◆—

Leaving the inn and meeting the others at the designated place I found Catalina was still with Isabel and Ben. Silvax was pointing at different troops in his regiment giving orders this early in the morning, it was impressive as usual to see them unflinchingly follow Silvax. The sun began to crest the horizon and the birds were singing their musical tunes, it was a pleasant way to start the day. Though that peaceful illusion was shattered when Isabel met my approach with a book in her hands.

"Conquest" she began "I believe I can trust you. You have saved both my little brother's life as well as everyone in my city. I think you of all people, one who has no obligation to our people or our safety, who has risked everything to keep us alive. You deserve this."

Finishing her soft-spoken speech she handed me the book, the cover was simple. It was a brown leather hardcopy book with a symbol of a creature with many legs and the title in red font 'Grend Amear'. Isabel went on to explain what the book was.

"Grend Amear, he was a hero that my family owes its patronage to him. Without him, our family and most likely a majority of the nobles in the Belfast Kingdom would not be around to see this mighty future of our nation. Before he was exiled by the first king he had given us this book that we carried throughout the generations. My father had given it to me before he left for his expedition. The reason he gave it to us was to find his successor, and I believe you can overcome his trials."

Taking the book from her but not opening it yet I could see the item had orange in its title, meaning it was of legendary rarity. But unfortunately for me, it was bound to me the moment I took it.

"Countess Isabel, may I go out to pursue his trials?" I asked in a humble way.

She looked at me, smiled and nodded. "Yes, I would like you to become as strong as possible and return to me in one month. That is when the army of the Jorgan Principality will return according to the Earls network. I believe we will need every man, and I would feel much more comfortable with you at my side during the event. I wish for you to be my knight."

With her statement, I both finished a quest and started a new one automatically.

I smiled back at Isabel and bowed while holding the book close to my chest as if she would take it back. "Of course my lady I will return with the strength of my name to help you in your time of need"

"Thank you Conquest, now go, become his successor" and without further concern, I turned away and walked towards the edge of the citadel, past all the armorers and smelters, straight towards the walls on the east of the city. Taking a firm step outside the citadel I gazed at the book for the first time since receiving it. Opening the book gave me a menu describing its requirements as well as what it would give me.

Successfully Used <Successor of Grend Amear> Book
Class Successfully Changed to <SwarmLord>
Class requirements Met - Friendly with 2 nobles of Belfast
Defended One City of Belfast
Does not have a Class
Was given the book <Grend Amear>

With that forced class change my status was completely updated and changed. I also received a ton of notifications, as well as a world notification as soon as I used the book.

Title Earned <First Legend>
Plus 40 to all stats
World Message: A Master of Hordes has Returned

This was big news, I apparently have obtained a class no one has, and it was so grandiose that it sent out a world message. Though I don't like how ominous it was to anyone that was paying attention. I do however like the 40 points to all stats, that is the equivalent of 48 levels being gained all at once. Seeing how I have yet to allocate all my previously earned stats from my journey I opened my start menu. Frankly I am still not sure what this class is based around but I don't want to lose my edge as a front line combatant, so I'm going to continue down my path of dexterity. Without thinking any more about it I dumped all of my hard earned stat points into Dexterity, further increasing my attack speed or crafting speed.

Name: Conquest	Class: SwarmLord	Level: 15
Stat points to Allocate:	35	HP: 300 Mana:60
Dexterity:	21	+75
crafting/attack speed		
Strength:	27	+40
physical DMG/ carry weight		
Intelligence:	6	+40
Mana total/regen and spell power		
Charm:	6	+40
Likability with NPC		
Constitution:	31	+40
hp/ stamina total		
Agility:	34	+40
movement speed/ stamina regen		

Moving past the stats I looked towards the skills and abilities the class had given me. To get a better idea of how to master this Legendary class needs to be my top priority. From what it looks like there were a ton of new notifications. . .

Class Abilities Acquired
<Create Monster>
The ability to design and create a monster at the cost of levels and skills. Monsters created this way are Completely Loyal and follow every command. Though when they die, they cannot be revived.
<Grends Swordsmanship>
The swordsmanship of Grend is all about defending and counter attacking strikes from stronger opponents. At the cost of stamina you will be able to defend against strikes that would normally break blocks. As well as sacrificing HP in order to break blocks of opponents that normally cannot be broken.
<Manifest Monster Traits>
At the cost of Mana you can use the unique abilities of a monster you create, the cost relates to the rarity or strength of the skill.
More Class Abilities unlocked when Criteria is met.
<????>
<????>
<????>
<????>
<????>
<????>

Three class abilities and promises for more? Sign me up. It seems to be a mix between summoner and tank class, and for the life of me without the stat boost of the first legend title I don't think I would be able to really do anything with my low level and the cost requirements of these skills. Eager to see how the <Create Monster> skill works I immediately activate it.

This brought up an extravagant menu that takes up almost my entire vision. There are options all over the place with a choice of monsters to create or form and a screen describing modifications for the monster and abilities I could give it. My imagination was running wild at this point and the first option I selected was the frame of a spider, one that was 3 feet tall and had vicious facial features. I then found a praying mantis monster and threw its torso on the spider in place of the face. The abomination of spider and mantis was terrifying, 8 legs and 2 sharp talons that could rend flesh and armor. After dragging that over I noticed the skill list started to highlight and I could give it swordsmanship, I of course selected it and gave it the max skill I could, which apparently was level 4. I could also give it Sneak 1 which was ominous! I then noticed I could choose what level to make it, seeing it could go all the way up to level 14 it was a no-brainer for me.

Once I saw the creation I was satisfied and before hitting accept it prompted me to give it a name. 'Victorum' was my decision and the monster was taking shape in front of me. Though as soon as I hit accept and the menu closed I felt sluggish, looking back at my stats, I had reverted back to level 1, and my swordsmanship and sneak skill had both returned to level 1 as well. If it wasn't for the stat bonuses I had earned from bonuses and the titles I would be fresh as when I first logged in. It seems this summon had a significant cost and I cursed myself for being too eager for not reading all the prompts. Wallowing in regret I failed to notice the evil-looking monster in front of me that is my own creation. The 10-limbed abomination with a silver name above its head as "Victorum" stood at the same height as me, its praying mantis torso making me feel unsettled at its appearance. Not wanting to waste my creation however as I'm not sure how long the summon would last, I looked at it and spoke. "Do you understand me?"

As I asked the question it nodded its giant head at me, making strange clicking noises with its maw. I felt a shiver but slowly accepted my fate as a monster wrangler. Thinking of my first command I spoke to it "Follow me Victorum, we are to hunt in that forest and slay any monster we find" the order was given and moving almost immediately the beast ran into the forest ahead of me. Scared of losing my hard spent resources and my first ever summon I chased after it. Victorum was quick on its feet and ran along all surfaces with her spider legs. Soon however I noticed its approach slowed to the point I could catch up. In the most ominous way, possible Victorum crouched and climbed up a tree, ahead I could see what it saw. Three goblinoid monsters sitting around a campfire, unlucky for them though since before I could draw my weapon my beast lunged from above them, spiraling down from the trees and slicing into the first goblin with its razor-sharp talons. All while spewing silk at another. One goblin beheaded, another goblin stuck in a net of silk while the third terrified of the sudden intruder tried to wring its blade off the belt. It was too slow as by that point I had run up and drove my sword through his back. I was notified of a level up since I'm only level 1 but managed to kill a level 10. It was completely unfair for these goblins however since my stats almost made me as strong as a level 28.

Once we finished off the last goblin I noticed one thing in particular, none of the experiences that Victorum gathered went to me. Normally when someone has a summoned unit they get all the experience their summon has. Though I did notice that there was an experience gauge underneath Victorums health bar. So it seems my summons are unique in the fact they can grow on their own and if I sacrifice levels or skills I can pump them up before summoning them. It also appears that they get the natural abilities of whatever monster they are combined into. I find it annoying that I have to share the valuable experience with this beast, but as long as it is considered my summon I guess that is alright. In the meantime, however, I have to focus on getting my skills and levels back.

Calculating a strategy, both Victorum and I will roam the forest for hostiles, once found Victorum will bind them with her web-shooting ability. Once the monster is bound I will swing at it with my practice sword until It dies or I level up my swordsmanship. Any group of enemies we find we bring them down to the last man and do the same thing. It was a vicious strategy and over the course of 8 hours of tireless fighting, we had a pretty good haul. I regained my levels back up to 15; since this place had higher level enemies than the pesky wolves from stotonely. Even my skills for swordsmanship went back up to 4. Victorum had managed to hit level 23 in her hunting spree. I can easily say that I had doubled my attack power with her at my side. Getting a bright Idea, I talked to Victorum "Victorum, I command you to hunt until you are level 75" not quite confident she would really understand the command, but contrary to my belief she immediately turned around and ran east at full speed. Before I could shout stop she was already out of sight.

Shit. I have no idea when she is getting back, I didn't expect Victorum to immediately run off after the order either. Back to square one, it seemed..

I fired up the monster creation menu and this time had a simpler idea in mind. After slaying the goblin I see it was added to the menu of available monsters to create. Currently, I have 6 available monsters to work with, Ant, Spider, Centipede, Praying Mantis, Wolf and Goblin. It had given me 4 to start with, and the wolf and goblin I had unlocked via killing monsters myself. Trying to see what monster would best suit my needs while also not costing me too many levels and progress I got the idea to make an Ant. Reducing its size and giving it 5 levels and the bandaging skill I made it the same size as a football with legs. I named it unceremoniously "Bug". I hit accept and the small creature landed on the ground standing on its six legs looking up at me with its antennae waggling in different directions. It looked eager for orders and almost cute with its shiny carapace and innocent eyes. It appeared as more of a pet Shih Tzu instead of a scary monster. I tapped my hand on my shoulder and it creepily crawled up my leg and back to mount itself like a parrot on my right pauldron.

"Bug, heal me when I'm hurt and only attack when the enemy is incapacitated," I ordered the little monster and it nodded its antenna at me. Now that Bug was on me I ran a bit slower and used some extra stamina moving around, but it was still faster than having him trail behind me when I ran. His short legs made it hard to keep up. It was a pretty good strategy as well since every time I got in a scuff with goblins I would be able to relax a little knowing that I would be healing mid-combat. Every time I took a hit as long as I kept them off me using <Grends Swordsmanship> I would be back up to full health afterward. The only thing I was losing was stamina over the course of these fights. After another few hours, I hit level 20 and decided to go back and rest. The bug had made it to level 11 but it was hard to share levels with him, every time he struck out with his little mandibles he barely gave any damage. It was a risk I wasn't willing to make, if he died then I would be out of those 5 levels and I am not losing another summon. I took a rest at an inn, gathered some supplies and logged out for the night. It was going to be a long month grinding out levels and getting Bugs up to par.

Habeas

Somewhere in the north of the Empire, a search party was out patrolling, searching for a trained killer. The killer had a newly made reputation for murdering an entire party of adventurers attempting a raid, though they were poorly outclassed by the man. Hiding in a tree above them was Habeas who was wearing a nice suit and wielding two extremely fancy swords. One had red coloring the other blue, both had a yellow-orange hue. After dealing with a pesky raiding party he had felt the best course of action was to leave the country since one was considered a noble of the empire. He figured he had made his point and instead of staying to make a show of force against the Entity Guild, he wanted to look into this new player lord, 'Conquest' he believed his name was. This new lord had apparently walked into an enemy camp and through Habeas network on the dark web, he found that the army had retreated soon after. Either this player was another hidden power like him or he knew someone who was. In either case, Habeas was eager to find a challenge. Leaving the Empire and moving to a small kingdom like Belfast was going to be a new experience for him. Activating a full invisibility spell scroll he eluded the patrol and slipped through the lines of troops searching for him. Throughout the next month, he was either swaying or slaying his way towards the Belfast Kingdom.

Cora

Cora having failed her initial mission and wasted gold on an assassination troupe, then losing her reputation on failing to kill a low-level player was relieved to see that he was in fact noble hiding his level. The fact another player managed to hide their level from her made her more than just mad. Cora was furious. Some people had the skill to hide level and class to other observers and it all made sense to her why the quest she was given was of A rank. It may have been postponed but seeing that it had not failed means that Isabel was still alive and she could still accomplish her mission. Knowing this was a possibility was keeping Cora in the Belfast kingdom, sharpening her blades and striking at opponents in the PVP areas without them even knowing. Cora was hungry for revenge. Formulating a new plan she decided to spend the entire month plotting out the next mission. The assassination of a certain player lord and completing an A-ranked mission.

Theo

I have been hunting in the forest slaying any sorts of vile monsters, other than my own, that I could find. I repeated this process for about a week in real-time and 23 days in the game. I had reached level 45 and Bug had reached level 24. On the 24th day since I separated from Isabel and her posse, I had taken a quest to clear a dungeon in the east of the Citadel. There was one thing missing from my plan to take out this dungeon, however. Numbers. As much as I wanted to rely on my single Bug buddy I knew I would need more to survive there confidently. Luckily my class gave me a semi-reliable, yet costly way to make hopefully loyal allies. I had leveled up my basic swordsmanship to 9 and was just on the cusp of reaching intermediate swordsmanship 1, but I was willing to sacrifice those levels to make a group of swordsmen take some hits for me. Loading up the <Monster Creation> menu I decided to sacrifice most of my levels and skills to create my first official raiding party. Looking at the selection of monsters available and how to splice them together, I noticed it was cheaper XP costs to make them without mutation and mixing species. So the most logical choice was to make 10 Goblins with swordsmanship 1 all at level 3. This cost me 30 levels, but I wasn't done yet. Next, I made 4 more healing ants. I unceremoniously called them "Goblin 1", "Goblin 2", "Goblin 3" etc. The impromptu medics however obtained the names "MediBug 1", "Medibug 2" and the like. It wasn't glorified but as I hit accept and dropped my level back down to 5 I winced at the fleeting strength. Though the troops in front of me made me feel a bit more confident. They were all standing in a five by two-line with the four medibugs standing on the front 4 soldiers' shoulders.

As awe-inspiring as the sight of them was, it was also extremely disappointing. They all spawned in with no weapons and just basic clothing. Ragged pants and shirts among each of them. 'Goblin 1' took a single step forward, made eye contact and flinched but then said as proud as he could muster in extremely broken speech "Goblin Ready for Fight Master Conquest" and threw up a terribly postured salute. I was content with that and raddled through my inventory to find some of the gear I picked up over the past few weeks. I handed out my old training sword to Goblin 1 and then basic gear to the rest of them. It was only semi-pitiful now. I formed a party with the goblins and medical ants, then made my way into the forest again. My goal was to level these guys up to 10 then attempt the dungeon.

With the plan in motion, we started roaming the forest. Every time we located a group of monsters, be it goblins or spiders we would isolate and exterminate them as cordially as possible. There were quite a few close calls at the beginning as these goblins were as green as they were in skin color causing many hits that normally should have been avoided. As the day progressed my soldiers slowly grew in level, I made sure everyone would get a hit in so the experience would be shared among them all. It stung that I barely was gaining any experience myself but the average level of my goblins had reached 7, Goblin 1 had reached 9 however and leveled his swordsmanship to 3. He would be able to take on a level 5 player if he was lucky. The only reason these goblins would survive any of these combats however was because every time they were hit I ordered them to retreat back and begin healing. Every time we got into a fight I would make sure we outnumbered each opponent at least on a 3 to 1 ratio to solidify our advantage as most of their levels was 10 or higher.

Rotating troops to switch the aggro from each enemy onto a full health goblin was the only viable way of farming the enemies. After a few more hours my goal of level 10 for each goblin was achieved, Goblin 1 was level 12 and each of the medibugs was around level 7. Their bandage skills were progressing nicely. I had hit level 10 myself, even though I was barely killing anything. I had however learned the skill <Leadership 1> which boosted all stats of members in my party by 1%, which wasn't much now but imagining what it would be later could not be shrugged off. Curious to see what my goblins stats looked like however I called over Goblin 1 and placed a hand on his head to pull up its stats.

Name: Goblin 1	Class: Swordsman	Level: 12 / 25
Race: Goblin		HP: 250 Mana:60
Dexterity:		10
Strength:		15
Intelligence:		6
Charm:		1
Constitution:		25
Agility:		20
<Basic Swordsmanship 4> Increase damage with swords by 40%		

It was a decent statline for a monster, its charm made sense to be 1 and the intelligence was barely passable as sentient. I did like that the constitution and agility were increased, it fit the bill for a goblin and the strategy of hitting and retreating well. I was curious however that there was a supposed level cap of 25. Does that mean it will not gain any more levels at that point? I am not sure. I was curious so I checked all of my summons levels and sure enough each one had a level cap of 25. My shoulder pet Bug was sitting at 24 still and I really wanted to make him hit level 25 to see what it did. So after a few flush orders we found ourselves a goblin chieftain to slay. It was a whopping level 27 but after taking out its guards we isolated it and took turns taking shots on him. I used my unique style of swordsmanship to block his heavy blows and once he was weakened to a point I felt comfortable risking

Bug I brought him up and over to bite him to death. Sure enough the explosion of experience made him level 25.

Nothing happened. The goblin chieftain dropped a fancy uncommon club that I gave to goblin 2, but for Bug nothing had changed other than leveling up. Or so I thought. After combat had ended and we started to rest again, Bug crawled off my shoulder and cocooned itself on the ground. *Finally,* I thought to myself. After about 15 minutes of guarding the now basketball sized cocoon it started to split apart and Bug crawled itself out. Overwhelmingly curious, I placed my hand on its head and inspected it.

Name: Bug	Class: Medic	Level: 1 / 50
Race: Medical Ant		HP: 350 Mana:60
Dexterity:	20	
Strength:	10	
Intelligence:	15	
Charm:	10	
Constitution:	35	
Agility:	50	
<Healing Spray 1> Heal target for 5% health over 15 seconds		

Bug had evolved! He had transformed into a 'Medical Ant' race which apparently was an offshoot of a regular ant. I do like that his stats got a decent boost and his level reset to 1 again meaning he has to level up all over again as I do. He seems to have evolved his skill as well from bandaging to Healing spray, which seems to be much more efficient. His health surprisingly is significantly higher than I thought, even higher than Goblin 1. Levels really do make a difference. It also seems that every time the monster hits its level cap they evolve automatically and evolve to be more specialized in the way they were created or used. I look forward to seeing all my goblin troops turn into certified swordsmen in the future. I wonder what they will evolve into. . .

Getting back on my warpath I started to farm more experience with my goblin troop. There were 16 of us with the inclusion of each of the medibugs and Bug himself, meaning the experience split was pretty intense. Though the rate we were massacring the mobs in the forest was ever-growing. I stopped to pause for a moment however as I noticed another player in the forest. He did not make any effort to hide at all as he barreled through the brush with a greataxe above his head, barbarian gear head to toe and to my absolute horror was charging straight at Goblin 1. He must have mistaken him for a regular mob in the forest since it was filled with them. I tried shouting as best I could to slow the raging barbarian

"Wait! Wait! That is my summons!" but the barbarian was already mid-swing, Goblin 1 did his best but it was a player he was up against. His heavy swing brought down the sword Goblin 1 tried to block with and cut a clean gash from shoulder to the pelvis. I was already running to intercept with my sword and shield in front of me. Just as the Barbarian was going to bring his axe back into the face of my poor Goblin it instead met my shield, rocking my hands and sending a vibration up my arm rattling my teeth. It was an incredibly strong blow that damn near took me off my feet if it wasn't for my <Grend swordsmanship> sapping my stamina in exchange for blocking the blow. The barbarian looked at me confused as to why I stopped him from slaying the easy experience in front of him.

"Why do you stop me from slaying this goblin? I am here to save you, there is an obvious pack of goblins around us. Let us work together to slay them." He said this with the kindest intentions, but it seemed he didn't know yet these were my summons.

"I appreciate the help here, but these guys are my tames. No need to attack them as they are harmless to players."

"Well if you insist. I have never met a monster tamer, it is a rare class! My name is Sjorn, and as you can see, I am a dwarven barbarian! What is your name?"

"Well met Sjorn the barbarian, I am Conquest."

"Well Conquest, I am going to be hunting in these forests for the time being, would you mind if I tagged along with your merry band of goblins and… are those ants?" Sjorn said this last part with a bit of confusion in his smug mug.

"Yes those are indeed ants, and yeah I don't see why not, feel free to accept the party invite." and he accepted as soon as I sent it.

Sjorn was a level 55 Barbarian Warrior and just as well equipped. I still had my level and class hidden however since I was just not able to trust him enough to share my class yet he tried asking me about it but I always changed the subject, I just didn't want to reveal I had a legendary class yet.

I do not regret bringing this man Sjorn with me through the forest. With his help we made short work of every pack of goblin we saw, even destroying an entire camp together. With him, at our side, we were able to take on 2 to 1 odds with my goblins able to trade-off enemies with more assurance since both Sjorn and I were quick to act in saving them. Once the moon was high in the sky Sjorn came up to me,

"Let us be friends Conquest, you seem to be a skilled player and I don't run into many around here. I plan on joining the expeditionary army rumored to be led by the Duke of the south in a week from now, apparently, he is heading towards Stotonely and I want to gather as much experience as possible. I would assume you would too, and I would feel excited to have you and your goblins at my side." he then looked past me, gave Goblin 1 a thumbs up and a wink then turned back to me.

"Of course I will be going, and of course we can be friends. I could always use a fierce axe like yours taking out my opponents!" and sure enough we became friends. Over the course of those hours of fighting, he had saved not just my life but also all of my monster pets. It was something I knew he didn't have to do and I am also sure he would have gotten more experience going alone. I shook the barbarian's hand and he turned and left my party, heading back to town in the moonlight. I was level 19, all of my goblins had hit at least level 15. It was good training, but before I attacked the dungeon I had to do one more thing. It was time to update the armor and gear on all of my 'troops' if you could call them that. Finding a decent hiding space I told my goblins and medibugs to hide there until I returned. "Hide here until I come back. If a player comes by, block and defend yourself but keep trying to tell them you mean no harm. Otherwise, stay safe" with the order they all stood up straight and Goblin 1 said "Siiir yes siiirr" in an extremely slurred way.

Once the order was given and I felt comfortable enough to leave them out of my sight without losing them like Victorum I left heading into town. The first stop was the adventurers' hall to sell all of the loot gathered over the past month. The biggest seller of those items was goblin ears. I had collected a hefty amount over the past twenty days so I got myself a pretty penny from them. A whopping 150 gold. Though that translates to over 1000 goblins killed it was still a good price seeing how 150 gold is worth $150 real dollars. Making a small dry heave I made my way to the armorer with my newfound wealth-getting ready to spend it all as soon as I had gotten it. Finding leather armor in small size wasn't too hard as there were many shorter players and soldiers but the cost was still an issue. After some bartering and talking, I managed to secure myself an item bag, to increase the number of items I could hold myself. And I also purchased 11 sets of armor. 10 Goblin-sized leather gambesons and a decent set of light chain mail for myself. I managed to purchase an uncommon shield as well to replace this old battered piece of wood I've been using. It had a significant boost in my defence that carried over well with my armor. It cost me 85 gold to secure these goods but I felt it was worth it at the price and I snagged a decent discount from the shopkeep either way.

Afterward, I made my way towards a weaponsmith to obtain some new swords for the goblins. If they were to take advantage of the swordsmanship skill they needed swords. At the moment only 4 of them had swords, the rest were wielding clubs or spears. Entering the forge I was met with a stocky dwarf, the first I had seen up until that point. He was working on a forge with eyes of fire just as hot as the metal slag itself. He hammered metal and smelted a sword before my very eyes, it was entrancing in a way. Once he cooled it off in a barrel of water he set it down and looked at me.

"Thank you for being patient, what can I do ya for? " he asked in a calm tone, clearly glad that I did not interrupt him in his passion for work.

"Yes, hello, I am here to purchase arms for troops. I need 10 shortswords, what do you have?"

The dwarf was in thought for a moment, nodded his head and turned to a rack of weapons. He went up to the rack and pulled a sword that looked clean, shiny and new then held it up towards me.

"I've been getting a lot of these orders recently, seems like the action is a brewin in the citadel yet again. I can get ya yer swords, but I need ya to at least look at this shortsword and tell me what ya think, before buying all the bulk I've got"

And in doing so he passed me the shortsword he was holding. It was a gladius. The hilt was varnished brown and the engraving on the blade itself was intricate and unique. It was a fine blade, inspecting it gave me a bit of a chill however if I were to buy it.

Sharp Lightning Gladius (Rare)
DMG: 40 + 30 Lightning I One Handed Shortsword

Needless to say, it was a beast of a weapon. I was greedy for it, as my sword, as good as it was with its poison property, was just not this. Lightning was a rare damage type in the game that was hard to negate as it did bonus damage to opponents wearing metal armor. Having been convinced I swallowed my eagerness and asked him how much.

"For all 10 blades including this gladius, 70 gold."

"60"

"65"

"Deal"

I had a little bead of sweat over my head when he said 70, I just couldn't afford it. But 65, well it was everything else I had but well worth it if it meant all my goblins would be well equipped. I would give Goblin 1 my old sword as a gift for being number 1.

With a pep in my step, I thanked the dwarf and left the city. It was time to arm my forces.

CHAPTER 9

After a bit of walking, I found my way to the hiding place where I left my troops. All but one of them were sleeping, if I was any other player these guys would have been killed no problem. Spooking Goblin 7 who was keeping guard I woke and scolded all of them. Making a new rule that at least 2 goblins must be awake at all times during sleep time. After the scolding and the mood being low for all of them, I pulled out my gifts. Each one received their very own set of armor and I took the sword away from Goblin 1 and in turn, gave him my *<Sharpened Longsword of Bleeding>*. It was a good trade-off and once I handed him the blade he immediately grinned a toothy smile full of jagged teeth. That charming stat of one was not helping him at all. Regardless, all of them equipped the gear and they all had smiles galore. The armor matched and I made sure to get little patches on each one's shoulder with the picture of the letter C in red and white. I wanted a way to signify they were my troops so if they ever get in bigger altercations they can be pointed out.

Using some paint I put numbers on the backs of each one representing their goblin number as well. It was nice seeing one through ten all lined up, everyone equipped with leather gambesons and shortswords, except Goblin 1, who had my old longsword. Itching to use their new equipment I brought them into the forest for a late-night hunt, hungry for blood we soaked their blades in our enemies and gathered juicy experiences all night. Only in the morning did I take a short break to eat lunch and hop back into the pod. It was a day of grinding as at night we would all be moving into the dungeon. A little afternoon Goblin 1 had hit level 25, a whopping 7 levels are faster than the next of the Goblin squad. To my utter excitement after combat he sat down and started to give off a faint glow, after about fifteen minutes he stood up and stood taller than his peers, not as tall as me still but a solid five feet tall, still a whole foot taller than his other goblin companions. Examining his race it had been changed to 'High Goblin' which meant he had indeed evolved. The stats he gained were respectable, he now has similar stats as me when I was level 10, with the title boost. His sword fighting had also increased to the next stage and became <Intermediate Swordfighting 1> which boosted his attack with swords by 70% and attack speed by 30%. It was a great boon for him. With Goblin 1 reaching this state I was confident we could take on the dungeon. With my forces ready I marched forward with Goblin 1 at my side.

I opened Goblin 1's settings and decided it was time he received a name. He truly earned it after being so far ahead of his peers.

"Goblin 1, from now on you shall be known as- Rango"

Rango caught off guard from the new name change after evolution, was ecstatic at the new rise in status. I am unsure if it was the evolution change or the increase in intelligence but when he spoke next he spoke with a clearer voice, "I thank you, Master Conquest. I will serve as Rango" the voice was a shrill deep one that made me unsettled compared to the higher-pitched garbling he had before. But in either case, he still called me master so that is all that mattered.

After an hour of walking and slaying creatures, we made it to the entrance of the dungeon. It was a cave with an old mausoleum look to it, the building was half encased in the side of a hill as if the mountain behind it caved onto it. The pillars outside looked as if they were made of marble and had been sitting there for centuries. I was both thrilled and nervous at my first ever dungeon but with my goblins and ants at my side, I felt confident we would make it through. Worst case scenario I sacrifice my pets and escape alone. Once we made it to the base of the mausoleum, I looked up the marble stairs that led to two giant doors. The doors themselves were open but not inviting as scrapes and gouges were marked all across it. Upon closer inspection of the stairs, there were scorch marks and cracks littered across them. I trepidatiously made my first step up the imposing walkway but stopped midway as I heard a little rattle ahead. My goblin force was at my back and ahead the source of the rattling continued to get closer. I, not wanting to get stuck on the low ground, started moving forward again, leading my forces. Just as I was about to see over the top of the stairs an arrow flew past my head, following the trajectory I spotted it. A skeleton wielding a bow racking another arrow to fire at us.

Putting my shield up I started pushing as quickly as I could before It could skewer one of my goblins. It was too late as the next arrow wasn't aimed at me but Goblin 3, took the arrow to the chest and was stopped in his tracks. Luckily he didn't die and one of the MediBugs ran to his aid. Before the skeleton could lose another arrow both Rango and myself were upon him. Both slashed and stabbed continuously until the skeleton turned into grey mist and disappeared. The skeleton was luckily alone at the entrance to this dungeon but it was an overwhelming level 25 right off the bat. My goblins, other than Rango, were at most level 18. Being underdeveloped wasn't anything new to us but there was no guarantee once we entered this dungeon that we would be outnumbering them either. Regardless there was not enough time left to put this dungeon raid off again. I only had four more days to go before I had to return to Isabel and head back to Stotonely. Solidifying my resolve I ensured Goblin 3 was back to full health and we made our way into the dungeon. I made sure I was in front and gave Rango my old shield in case more arrows got sent our way.

Once we took a step into the dungeon I was alerted with a new system message.

Entering <Old Mausoleum>
Necrotic Damage Increased 15%
First time Entering Dungeon Applying (25% Bonus XP gain)

It was expected, but some dungeons depending on the difficulty can apply modifiers to both friends and foes. In this case, the dungeon had the effect of increased necrotic type damage, this means that most of these undead type enemies are going to be inflicting much more damage to us. Unluckily for us, we had nothing that could deal necrotic damage to them.

There was also an increased experience since it was my first time entering the dungeon. Once someone enters a dungeon for the first time they are awarded one day of increased experience gain. Not one to shirk such expectations I started marching forward into the dimly lit dungeon.

Every 15 or so feet in every hallway was a torch that barely illuminated enough light between each torch. It was dark and ominous as the only sound was dry wind and rattling bones. The first room we came across was large enough to fit a living room in, and ironically it was completely full of undead. The skeletons were alerted to our presence as soon as we took our first step in the light. They all turned and to my horror, there were seven of them. Our numbers were not enough to keep them all at bay so I had to think fast. I gave out orders as fast as possible otherwise we would collapse under the first fight in the dungeon.

"Rango, play defence and hold off two skeletons, take Medibug 1. Goblins 2, 3 and 4 I need you to each take on a skeleton one on one for as long as you can. Goblins 5, 6, 7 and 8 I need you to take on that skeleton. I will take this one" and pointed at all the targets in the room. Forcing Rango to hold off two skeletons was greedy but I was confident he could hold on long enough for 5, 6, 7 and 8 to defeat one. I was more worried about the regular goblins that were going one on one with the skeletons. Each skeleton in the room was armed with a sword and shield, but the biggest factor here was they were human skeletons, each leaning towards six feet tall. They overwhelmingly beat each of my goblins in size which was imposing but I had confidence. Pulled away from my inner thoughts the skeleton I pointed at for me to fight had made his rambling way towards me. I met it quickly with my lightning gladius, striking as quickly as possible. I immediately felt a wave of relief when the skeleton barely blocked the hits and was instead just taking it, opting to strike at me during each of my swings. Luckily for me, I had a shield in my other hand to swat away the strikes. Taking a glance around the room I started to notice my goblins were faring better than I thought, Rango was in a tight bit of combat but holding his own while the mano e mano fighters were surviving still with minimal damage. The group of four that I sent to take out one skeleton were just about done and moving to the next alone to save them. Just about then I took a gash to the ribs that jarred my thoughts. I was too worried about my goblins to focus on the fight.

I started to press on my attack farther until the skeleton's skull was cracked and turned into dust. I then went around the room and picked off all the skeletons with the help of the others. Rango was last and covered in wounds from the two skeletons he was fighting. It did however come with some good benefits as after the fight he had leveled up and gained a level in swordsmanship. The battle ended at that point and the room was silent again. The only sounds left were the heaving of the goblins as they were getting their wounds patched by the Medibugs. It was interesting to watch as each goblin had wounds even the ones in the quad group, it was a good sign as it meant they kept using my strategy of moving out of aggro letting another goblin take the strikes instead. It was a strategy that would only work on mindless mobs but it was the best one we had at the moment.

I also noticed my leadership skill had leveled up to two in the combat, the extra bits of stats would be valued. Looking over the loot from the skeletons I noticed some dropped shields and silver pieces. I took the silver pieces for myself and handed the two shields to goblins 2 and 3, they deserved it after fighting so hard. Once everyone was in full health again we decided to take on the next room. As we opened the next room it was a mix of 4 skeletons with swords and shields and 3 skeletons with bows and arrows. We handled this much the same except I sent three of my goblins around the back to take the attention of the archers. Forcing them to stop shooting at us while we took out their swordsman. The next fight only took five minutes and dispersing the shields to 3 more of my goblins I felt even more confident as we made our way through the dungeon.

The fighting had continued for quite some time, after 6 more rooms that were about the same, most of my goblins were reaching the 20s and Rango had reached level 7 of the first evolution. The Medibugs were all leveling up quickly as well since my goblins were getting injured much more than they were when we were hunting in the forest. It was both a blessing and a curse to me as most of the durability of the gear we brought in was deteriorating at a fast pace. After a few hours, I started to feel the burn and I could sense that my goblins were feeling the same. After 12 rooms of vigorous combat, we reached a large red door that had engraving across it 'Dead of Haral'. It was a simple engraving but if the red door didn't scream boss chamber I'm not sure what would. I made sure all my goblins rested and that they were at full health then I pushed the door open.

The room opened up into a gymnasium-sized room with coffins on both sides lined up the walls like catacombs. At the end of the room, there was one large coffin and out of it emerged a skeleton wearing red and purple robes. A health bar came over its head and a name to accompany it, the name in a glossy red shined in the darkroom. The Name gave me some fear as its title held most of the weight. As I read the name, the mission that I had picked up before had updated to fit it.

| Conquer the <Old Mausoleum> has been changed to |
| Defeat <Earl Obould Claycoax> |

From what I had researched, Earl Obould Claycoax was the great great grandfather of the current sitting Earl- Jeffery

Claycoax. Being in front of me was undead and standing up, but also showing next to his name was the whopping level 75.

I had only one thought going through my mind when I saw the doors close behind us, locking us in a struggle with this skeletal boss. *We were going to die.*

Bracing myself, as I had the most health out of the party we had, I made my resolve to be the tank- someone who will absorb as much damage as possible and become the target of the boss. Obould was renowned for being an excellent sword fighter but I have hopes that he may not be as strong dead as he was alive, if those other skeletons were to be a baseline of deterioration of skills. Ordering my goblins to begin a crescent shape we made our way down the long room in a wide formation. The skeleton Earl Obould had risen from his casket covered in red robes and once he took one step from his grave he withdrew a sword that had an ornate design on its blade, the golden embroidered hilt shone in the darkness of the room. The moment he placed his second skeletal foot outside the casket he bolted at me with surprising speed. He crossed the 30-foot room in seconds. I was barely able to raise my shield as it struck, instantly taking out one-tenth of my health. As soon as the sound of his strike reverberated around the room, my goblins started to act. Each one began to stab and slash at the skeletal noble, but his health barely shuttered.

"Medibugs onto me!" I called each of the medical bugs to me so they could bandage at the same time that Bugs can spray heal me. The strikes were taking their toll and it was a pure battle for attrition. The undead versus the living damage sponge that was me. I was able to block a lot of the strikes and now that I started abusing the fraudulent abilities of my <Grend Swordsmanship> to block unblockable strikes at the cost of stamina, I was staying alive. Every time I was back at full health I would save stamina by taking the strike regularly then turn it back on again to stop the strikes while the medical bugs did their best to heal me back again. My stamina was draining but my health stayed at the top while fighting the undead Earl. Blow after blow, I started to see his health begin to fade, but just as he hit half things changed.

The Earl, apparently fed up with being hit by the annoying goblins around him, started to swing sporadically at each one. The fight became hectic as he would switch targets every strike towards a different goblin. I did my best to stop him from hitting them but it just wasn't enough. I had to kill him now or we would all die. Readying up my <powerful blow> attack I struck him once, twice, and three times expending almost all my stamina. The strikes combined with my new sword and each strike being placed precisely on his shiny skull, creating a critical strike meant his health was now down to less than a sliver above his head. With all my being and my remaining stamina, I shouted as hard as I could-

"Strike him! Strike him now!"

And like good soldiers, my goblins followed their orders to the letter, abandoning defences and striking the earl with their swords if they could or bashing with their shields if they couldn't. The Earl finally stopped, looked me in the eyes, with his hollow red orbs, and said "Thank you" then turned into a grey mist.

I collapsed on the ground, my stamina was at the absolute lowest. I could barely read the level-up messages and skill increase notifications. I mindlessly grabbed the loot from the earl, patted each of my goblins on the shoulder and smiled as best I could with my tired face.

"You each fought hard, I am proud of you all."

This brought emotion to my simple goblin troops but it was an uplift they highly needed. Most of them had reached level 25 with this fight and I myself leveled up almost 7 times from the battle. I let them start evolving while I went to examine the casket where the Earl was sleeping. Hobbling my way over to the grave I nearly pitched over as I saw the contents. It was the sword! I greedily picked it up and examined it.

Royal Striking Longsword of Leeching (Unique)
DMG: 135 Heals for 30% I Longsword I Level requirement: 75

It was a unique rated weapon at a decently high level! My stamina may be low causing blurry vision but I could see this clearly. It was a weapon I was going to happily sell for profit. This dungeon was worth coming into hands down. Then I collapsed from fatigue.

An unknown amount of time later I awoke from the status effect, my goblins were all around me in a defensive circle. Groggily, I held my head as I sat up in the dungeon, looking around I could see now that all my goblins were the same height as Rango. It was a pleasant sight to say the least. Each one's evolution was accompanied by a hefty stat boost. I now had the equivalent of an adventuring party of 14 level 25 adventurers. Taking a peak, I could see my level had increased as well, I was level 30 again. It was good to see as I had entered the dungeon level 20. The experience boost was definitely the biggest boon of it all. I also noticed that my Leadership and swordsmanship had leveled up as well. <Leadership 4> and <intermediate swordsmanship 1>. I was happy about that change too. I can't afford to create more monsters however since If I was to be a force on the battlefield in a few days I needed all the levels I could muster to fight the stronger opponents. If we fought a smart level 75 player we would have all died without remorse.

With all our new levels we made our way outside the now completed dungeon. I stationed my goblins where I hid them before and went into town to collect my reward.

I alone went into town, the sun was already set and it was night again. I was going to try and run straight into the adventurers' hall to claim my prize but to my dismay, they were closed. I decided to take an inn for the night as I had not used one in a long time and to log out to sell my newly acquired loot.

Logging out I went straight to the computer to put my sword up for auction. It was a spectacular drop, a unique grade item that had decent attributes that made it highly sought after. It was also the perfect time to sell as the average level of players right now was in the 60s-70s. This level 75 weapon would be perfect for anyone playing competitively looking for that edge in combat. Signing into my auction account I placed the sword up for bid to end in three days since that is right before the expedition to Stotonely would be taking place. I based my starting price on existing items that were similar in perceived value. It was a month's rent, starting price. This weapon I had found in my third week of playing the game had already returned its value.

In real life it was about lunchtime, I took some time to get some grub and then went to Rocky to train for an hour or so before going back to Kronos.

————————◆————————

Rocky

Rocky was intrigued by the fighting style Theo had been molding into after every session. It seemed that every day he had adapted slowly to a new form, one that was different than the one taught to him. It was a mix of Rockys style and this new one. Not one to dissuade Theo but instead encourage it, Rocky pointed out the flaws in his footwork, the angle of attacks and timing of strikes to better acclimate to the stance. It was an art to watch him progress and evolve over the course of the month and the one-on-one sessions were extremely beneficial to both Rocky and Theodore's development.

It made Rocky think back on the times where Rocky Senior talked about Theodore during his training sessions with him. The information he was taught was sucked in like a sponge and even though he may not get something instantly, he would train until he did. It was an unquestionable work ethic. It reminded Rocky of himself. In the third week, Rocky had brought Theo to his office and asked him where he was getting this technique he was seeing. Thus began a long conversation about Kronos online, a game Rocky had only heard about on tv or from some of his younger disciples. The progress Theodore was able to make with Kronos online in addition to practicing at the dojo was astounding and seemed to make any knowledge he shared soak into him. This gave Rocky an idea and he opened his checkbook to write out a purchase order for a bulk sale of full immersion machines. If Theo can take advantage of it, why can't all his students?

Not wanting to lose this opportunity and worrying that Theo might disappear again he ordered some of his elder trainees to keep an eye on him. If something happened to Theodore he wanted to be there to help him to avoid what happened the last time he trained here.

Theo

Once I was home, showered and full of food I got back into Kronos. When I logged back in I had my status buff from sleeping in an inn. It was morning in the game so I made my way to the adventurers' hall for my sweet rewards. Waltzing into the hall I noticed a familiar face talking with the man behind the counter. It was Sjorn the barbarian. He spotted me and stopped his tirade with the clerk.

"Conquest! Glad to see you back online, how are your pets? All alive I hope?"

"Yes they are Sjorn and thank you for asking, they saved me behind quite a bit. I am actually here because I completed a quest. Afterward, I was going to grind some more levels out before the expedition with the army. Are you interested?"

"I appreciate the request, but I am going to head deeper into the mountains for some higher-level fights. I will see you in the march!" with that he took a small bag of currency off the counter that he must have been arguing about and left the adventurers hall. Walking up to the same clerk he was dealing with I started by placing the robe of the skeletal Earl on the counter indicating that I had cleared the C+ rated quest he had given me a few weeks ago. But as soon as the clerk opened his mouth I could see why Sjorn was arguing with him.

"Well well well I am surprised you made it out of there alive. I know you are a traveler but even then you must have paid someone to finish this mission for you. Whatever the case you did return the robes as a sign that you did somehow slay the skeleton lord living in the old mausoleum so I will reward you. . ." and as he mentioned the reward my eyes perked up, first a notification saying I had cleared the quest appeared then he left to grab a sack of coins from a back room.

The quest had given me five more levels for being completed technically solo and the gold reward was just as fulfilling. 250 gold, more than making up for the gear I had to spend prior to equipping my troops. I was satisfied and before I could raise a fuss with the stuck-up clerk I left the hall to return to my hopefully still alive goblins.

On my walk, I gave some thought to the mission I was given in relation to the reward. Money in Kronos was always flowing between hands as gold was purchased with real-life currency almost on a one-to-one scale, the mission I had received was one especially difficult as it typically would be split between a party of mid to high-level players. But since I did it alone I did not have to share my rewards with anyone and could profit without concern. The combination of mission reward and the unique item drop was looking to be about 1500 dollars, a hefty amount for someone who just started gaming professionally. My thought of money had ceased as soon as I entered my hiding spot, this time however I was greeted with both Rango and Goblin 2 staring at my approach. This gave me some happiness as they at least were able to register there was someone coming and react appropriately.

All my goblins and medibugs stood up, antennae and swords at their sides as I came near. It was a sign of respect and I was grateful to have such loyal troops, even if they aren't the strongest. Though this put a question in my mind about leadership, if they were to be attacked in my absence I believe they would be torn to shreds fighting mindlessly without leadership. This led me to a sad conclusion, I would need to spend some of my hard-earned levels one more time to create another soldier to lead these men, then power level the shit out of it.

Opening my <Monster Creation> Menu I found what I had been hoping to see, skeletons. There were two sets of skeletons in the menu for me to select, one was just a regular 'Skeleton' with no attributes while the other was 'Noble Skeleton' that had a blue glow around its portrait. It seemed to have indicated that it was a higher form of monster, which I would agree with. Especially if it was pulled from the Earl that we put back to rest. Selecting the 'Noble Skeleton' immediately showed the cost would have been 15 levels and that was before selecting any modifiers or level-ups. This made my heart race as goblins alone were cheap. Trying to level it up more only increased the cost significantly to the point I would not be able to afford it. Instead, I decided to keep it Level 1 and put on <Leadership 3>, bringing my leadership skill down to 1. There was a star next to the *Create* button on the menu however, hovering over it, it showed a description stating:

[This creature will be an Elite level Monster It will gain skills on its own]

[Increase the <Create Monster> skill to increase the number of skills it can learn on its own]

That alone convinced me, as the regular monsters I created like the goblins and ants could only level up skills that I gave it. This meant it was capable of learning unique skills specialized in the way I train it. Perfect for what is going to be my first officer for my troops.

As I eagerly hit *Create*, the option for 'Noble Skeleton' was removed from my options menu. Meaning that once I create an elite monster from a boss mob it removes it from being spammed, there has to be a balance somewhere. After a few more seconds a skeleton began to slowly form in front of me, a purple hue started to form around it and it had clothes on it already. A purple robe adorned his shoulders and the skeleton stood as tall as me. It stared at me with its red orbs, blinked, and its eyes turned a calmer blue. With a rattle, its jaw bone moved and a voice of pure confidence exuded from the skeletal maw.

"My Master has summoned me to Lead. and Lead I shall do. But first, you must give me a name."

This was different. The rest of my summons did not ask anything of me, instead just taking orders without faltering in the slightest. This Monster however requested a name, it must be because he is an elite classed monster. Giving it some thought, as he was going to be my second in command, I decided on a name that would be fitting for a noble skeleton officer.

"From now on you shall be known as Abel. and you will be my ffficer from now on. These-" as I sweep my hand to all of the goblins lined up watching us "-will be your men. I expect you to keep them and yourself alive above all else."

Once I finished my orders the skeleton dropped to one knee, making him just barely taller than the goblins and lowered his head to me.

"It will be an honor to serve you Conquest, as you can see that I have worth as a battle commander. I will not let you down".

"See to it that you don't, my first mission for you is to level yourself up to 20. But not to leave my sight." This last part was added to keep him from skittering off as Victorum did. I was happy it worked out well as he started to rise and turn away as the words were leaving my mouth. I followed him towards the forest, pointing out different spots for enemy spawns and their movement patterns. They were typically different groups of goblins or spiders and I showed him the previous tactics I had utilized to take full advantage of the terrain in combat. He was able to emulate a good amount of my teachings which was great as I was worried he would be stubborn and do things his own way. We made our way through the forest, cleaving through the goblins that used to give us a hard time. Make sure to leave all of the enemies with just low enough health for Abel to finish them off. Over the day he had leveled up to 10 and was able to stand on his own. He eventually gained the <basic swordsmanship 1> skill from watching the other goblins and exclusively using a sword.

In a way, it was a boon but I could see the maximum amount of skills he could learn on his own was 3 at this time. Though swordsmanship was a no-brainer with how we were fighting. I would need to learn archery at some point however so I could make some ranged fighters in my group. The Medibugs and Goblins were handling themselves pretty well under the leadership of Abel, once he started taking in my advice on abusing the terrain against his opponents. Forcing the enemy to march uphill or through the mud to engage us was easier than blindly charging in or waiting for them to hit our line of troops. I made sure to spend all of our remaining time in the forest, killing everything that could give us experience as growth was the biggest problem. I barely reached level 40 again after losing all those levels and Abel had hit level 24. Each of my medibugs had leveled up to Medical Ants like my pet Bugs and Bugs himself had leveled up to 11. It was progress all around. Rango had made it to 15, meaning with both his evolving stats and leveling again meant he was the equivalent to a level 40 player. His swordsmanship had also improved significantly. There was only one day left before meeting Isabel again, and I knew just how to test the mettle of my monsters.

CHAPTER 10

---◆---

I opened my friends' list and found Silvax then sent him a message to meet me outside the gates on the east side of the citadel. I made sure to ask him to bring a squad of his best troops as well. After about an hour he had assembled his men and met me outside the gates. I recognized one of the Denarians, it was Denarian Davis, the blonde talks-a-lot fellow. Accompanying him was a group of 10 other men with swords and shields, fully kitted and ready for battle. Silvax marched up to me first.

"What is the problem? Are you in trouble?"

It warmed my heart a bit to know he was willing to bring his troops.

"No problem here, though I do need your help testing my troops. I know you are a veteran at commanding your men and would like to test mine against yours."

At the mention of 'my troops' Silvaxs eyes started to flutter around the tree line. It only took his trained eyes a moment to spot my hiding forces.

"So you seem to have made quick work of that book it seems. Well if you want to give it a go we can start a group battle, my squad versus yours. I will not participate as I am much higher level than all of you, of that I am certain."

"I appreciate the control. If we can keep my men from dying that would be best"

Silvax was perplexed at my statement and spoke with a tone that showed a bit of excitement

"No need to worry about losing anyone, in group battles they operate like sparring matches, when someone hits 1hp they are incapacitated but not killed and the fight continues until all forces on one side are incapacitated or they surrender."

This made me happier as I was unsure if my goblins would really survive a head-on collision with a trained squad of legionnaires.

I liked the idea, agreed and briefed my Skeleton Captain Abel his mission.

He was listening with passion as his blue orbs were glued to me as I spoke.

"This will be the hardest fight you have ever been in. I need you to do one thing for me to show that you are a good commander of my forces. Survive. We will be on the battlefield soon and I need to know you will all not become a wasted investment. Fight using the strategies I have taught you and be prepared to be on the losing side as this time you will not be fighting odds that are in your favor. Do your best and make me proud."

Abel stood tall in front of me, purple robes draped around him and a clean sword at his hip he brought his hand up in a salute "You will be done, Conquest."

"You have 5 minutes to prepare in the brush, then they will come for you."

As I gave the command Abel immediately started to shout at the goblins to move, their little green legs rushing into the trees and out of sight. It was something to behold as I don't think they have ever moved so fast under my command. Silvax walked up to my side as I watched them run into the forest and asked me "So it will be an attempt at an ambush. . . Not a bad plan on the skeletons' thoughts, but he will be hard-fought against My Denarian Davis. He was my first ward, I have personally trained him to spot ambushes and how to take out hiding opponents."

I was fine with this as my goblins were never going to be at the top of the food chain when it came to combat against trained soldiers- at least for now.

"That is Ok, I want them to feel pressure and possibly defeat."

"Defeat is the only option for them here. But I like the enthusiasm"

"Well you better be careful with that Tongue Silvax, maybe my goblins will surprise you."

"How can they surprise me when I can see that goblins arm sticking out of the bush from here?"

Sure enough, I look where he is pointing and the little green goblin is poking out of the brush just enough that we can spot his elbow. I held myself back from shouting at him to hide better because they need to learn failure on their own. They have to think for themselves if I am going to be fighting my best on the battlefield.

After a painstakingly long five minutes, I could see Davis and his 10 men move forward into the brushes. Their formation was rigid and without flaw as they marched. It was honest to god shield wall, spears poking out the front and the men covering their sides. It was a seemingly flawless push into the trees. They were heading directly towards the goblin that had his elbow showing. I winced, knowing the fate of that poor goblin was to be knocked out right at the start of combat.

Just as the wall of metal and man-made it 5 meters from the goblin in the brush, he jumped up and ran away. Apparently realizing he had been caught. The trained legionnaires broke partial formation and 3 men pursued while the others hastened their pace to keep up without breaking the overall sight of their surroundings. They had made a mistake, as soon as the 3 men made it up to the lone goblin, almost 20 meters ahead of the other forces, the entirety of the goblin squad and Rango jumped them from the brushes and treetops landing above, behind, beside and on top of the three now startled legionnaires. They had used the goblin as bait, purposefully hiding him poorly to lull the enemy into a state of false security. As soon as the guard was dropped however they sprung. All of the goblins focused down on the three men and dropped them to 1hp before the other legionnaires could flank the goblins. Though as soon as the last of the three had fallen the goblins were now in full head-on combat with the line of shields and spears. The head-on collision was not as bad as I had thought and looked over at Silvax he was crossing his arms nodding his head. I believe he was wearing the face of someone impressed by a dog doing a cool trick. And honestly, I could not blame him. As the fight drew on the goblins tried to pull more tricks like flanking and using the medibugs to keep up with the healing, but each of the legionaries was at least level 45, the only one who could fight on equal footing was rango but he was toe to toe with Davis. The fight was a struggle and one by one my goblins were knocked down. The legionnaires were keeping each other covered.

Their movement was precise and they had no wasted motion as they defended each other any chance they could. They may have been outnumbered two to one in the fight but that did not stop them in the slightest. The tides turned for a moment with Abel jumping into combat himself for a brief moment to help out Rango with Denarian Davis, but it was not enough. He was too low level and his skills as a swordfighter was sorely outclassed. After a hard-fought struggle, 4 more of the legionnaires were taken down and all but Rango remained. Rango was pushing Davis back and almost had him if it weren't for the rest of the soldiers coming to his aid. Eventually, after a four against one struggle, Rango too was taken down.

Silvax was impressed and patted me on the shoulder "That Goblin is impressive, his economy of movement was flawless and was sure to keep all his opponents in eyesight at all times, not letting them get behind him. It is hard to do in a warzone and hard to train a soldier how to keep that in mind without taking over. He seems to have it as second nature to him. What was more impressive is he was fighting toe to toe with Davis. He is my strongest soldier hands down and being able to hold his own against him is a good sign."

I was jubilant with the praise and grinning ear to ear, they had fought hard. My goblins might have lost but they had given the squad of trained legionnaires a brief pause in alarm. Though that jubilation was cut short at Silvaxs next words

"One thing you need to work on clearly is your skeleton. As a commander, he needs to stay back and safe. If he drops in combat then the coordination of his soldiers will fall too. The buff he has from leadership was one of the biggest reasons your goblins were able to stay alive so long against my men. As soon as he jumped in to play hero he was knocked out and that is when the formation failed. So you have two options from my experienced opinion. One, train Abel to always stay back, which could be a detriment to morale but will keep your forces from breaking apart in combat. Or Two, make him the powerhouse of the group so he can take on opponents without dying, it will increase his risk factor in fights but the morale boost from a fighting leader is always beneficial. I have had countless fights that were won because I fought on the front with my men. If you take a step first into hell your men will be obligated to follow."

I took his advice with utter seriousness as his level and long-standing command over his men was a clear indicator for success. It was good advice, and since Abel could learn one more skill I had to think of the one that would best suit a frontline commander. Option two was the only real option the way I saw it, the warzone we will be in soon will not give us the option to just run away whenever the fighting gets tough. Abel needs to be able to hold his own in combat.

After a few minutes, all the goblins and legionnaires made their way towards us from the forest, each of them had grins on their faces except for Abel. Rango was walking with Davis, a wide toothy grin was on his face as he approached. His long arm reached up to Davis patting him on the shoulder. Abel walked straight up to me and bowed.

"I have failed you, I am not fit to lead". His spirit was clearly hurt at this. I both wanted to encourage and chastise him for his behavior in combat. "You had a firm grasp on the enemies' plans and you were executing your strategy with ease, keeping your men safe and in command of the battlefield. So Why on earth did you think running up and attempting to fight their strongest man was a wise idea? Were you thinking of glory when you drew your sword? If this was a real battle, all of you would be dead and it would have been your fault."

He lowered his gaze even further to the ground and I continued my criticism.

"You were winning. I have to admit your strategy was fine until you jumped into the fray, so that means you have two choices going forward. One you need to strengthen yourself to be a tide on the battlefield like Rango so you can't be killed so easily, and two you need to wrap your strategies to cover you when you enter the fray, become a true leader. If you jump in as you did here in a real warzone. You will be more than just knocked down."

His eyes looked up at me with a new blue flame of opportunity and asked with glee and excitement for the opportunity "So. . . You are not removing my command?"

"Of course not, I have invested too much into you to strip you of your leadership. You instead will work tirelessly to become the strongest soldier I have. If you are unable to beat Rango In one on one combat then you are not fit to be a leader of my soldiers."

With a goal firmly placed in front of him, he stood straight again, invigorated with most likely ideas of grandeur on the battlefield. "Like a skeleton, I do not tire, at your permission I would like to take the soldiers into the forest to level myself up."

"Permission granted Abel. Return by tomorrow morning so the Goblins can rest."

"Your will be done. Thank you."

As he said this he waved to the goblins and started to turn to leave, Rango gave Davis a firm handshake and turned to walk towards the forest with Abel at his side. I shouted one last thing to Rango before they left eyesight.

"Rango! Be sure to keep everyone alive!" he nodded, gave a toothy grin and threw a thumbs up at me before moving into the forest with the rest of them.

Once my forces were out of sight, Davis came up to me and stuck out his hand for a shake. I of course took it, and he gave me some encouraging words.

"That Rango is good for a goblin, I am earnestly impressed. He was just as good as I with the blade. His footwork was extremely impressive as well. The only thing I could see lacking was when he used his shield it was sloppy. I could see that he would benefit from using two weapons instead of a sword and shield. He has an aggressive fighting style that would appear when using two weapons. You did a good job training him"

It was my turn to be all smiles. Davis was level 55 according to Silvax, and since Rango was able to fight one on one with him for so long was insane, then being told he could be even stronger just by changing his weapon style was a fresh realization.

"Thank you for the advice Denarian Davis, I look forward to having you at my back during the upcoming conflict."

We shook hands once more and he left to the citadel ahead of Silvax and I. Silvax looked at me with some slight concern in his eyes and asked the question that must have been floating in his mind during this entire encounter.

"Why are you so weak? You have had a whole month to level up and gather strength. I can tell you are still at a low level, compared to most of the opponents on the battlefield you will be completely outclassed. Even your humble band of misfits won't be able to shape up the odds if one of the enemies' elites makes an approach. Those Named NPC are no joke and would even give me some trouble."

It was an honest question with real truth in its revelations. I felt weak at that moment but I had to realize I had spent levels to get this strength. I had spent over 40 levels worth of experience on my troops, I could have been level 70+ if I focused on just myself. But that would never be a guarantee without the help of them either. It doesn't help that the XP shared between my soldiers and myself was as if we were a party of players, meaning I get only an equal value of the precious experience. But I was content with strengthening my soldiers, so I solidified my resolve and straightened my back.

"I am plenty strong and will only get stronger as the battle continues. I may not have the level but my stats are still impressive. I can promise I will not be a burden on the battlefield."

Silvax ingested my words and nodded his head in acknowledgment.

"You at least have the drive of a warrior. We leave an hour after dawn tomorrow. Catalina, Countess Isabel and my forces will be at the southern gates, I will see you there."

I nodded to him, then he turned and left.

It was a worthy bout, I needed input on my tactics from someone who had proper experience and Silvax was the best choice. His input made an impact on both myself and my troops who needed to realize the seriousness of the situation they will soon be in. They weren't the smartest but this wake-up call was blunt enough to make it through their little green heads. Abel is who I was most concerned about, but he has to solve that strength problem himself the same way I have. Seeing how it was still relatively early in the day I wanted to go hunting for more levels but I could hear my phone going off outside the capsule. The notification was buzzing in my ears and I decided to log out to answer it.

Once out of the capsule and successfully logged out, I answered the insistent phone ringing. Then a voice that was filled with emotion, and after the first word, I could feel my stomach turn.

"Theo. . ."

It was my mother, and I could tell something was wrong as she was barely able to make the words come through sobbing. It was a sound I was used to hearing when I was younger.

". . . Your father was in an accident. He is in the hospital and won't wake up."

My father and I weren't the closest growing up, with his strict attitude towards anything not work-related or self-betterment, but he was still my dad. He taught me how to become committed to anything I put my mind on, we had our disagreements but he was why I am the way I am. I blinked a few times trying to grasp it in my mind and my chest was tight as if someone reached in and gripped my lungs. I couldn't muster words before my mother continued, her voice still muffled by what must have been her wiping tears from her eyes.

"We. . I don't know if he will get up again. You have to come to see him. . . Will and Maria are already here. We are at the hospital near the house, the one we use to bring Maria. . ."

Finally taking a deep breath I was able to get a response.

"I will be there." and after a few more questions back and forth I hung up the phone and put on my shoes. Practically ran to the door so I could make it to the hospital as quickly as I can.

Getting into my beat-up truck I drove, but to be honest it was a blur to me. During the ride, I had so many thoughts and memories flashing through my head of all the times my dad made me smile, cry, laugh, hate and love him. I could barely concentrate on the road as the tears were already flowing. I was speeding surely but who wouldn't in this situation. I drove with my foot on the gas and made this truck move as fast as it could down the highway, every minute counted to me and I could feel myself counting the seconds every time I was struck by a red light or a slow driver. The temptation to lay down on the horn was evident but I held back, thinking of something my dad once said to me "Haste is the shortcut to failure." attempting to rush the other drivers would only make them slow down more. I had to keep calm.

After driving for what must have been an hour, I made it to the hospital. My little brother James was already at the door waiting for me. My mind, still taking itself through a coaster of memories, just followed silently behind him as we made it to the room. The sickly scent of the hospital cleared in my nose, all the times I was here for Maria flooding back to my mind. The disgusting sterility and monowhite light shining on my mother sobbing on the side of the bed, my sister draping an arm over her, holding a soft sobbing of her own. Being propped up by her wheelchair she could only lean so far but the effort was shown. My eyes were already shrink wrapping over as they moved up the bed.

There he was. The man who helped make me who I am. I can think of all the times he missed an award ceremony I worked hard to earn, my fist was already clenched and released as I saw his eyes. Closed and unmoving. The tubes leading out of him were unnerving, he was unconscious and his face was bruised. His beard was still kept neat like he always had done. His hair, a brown clean-cut but messy and matted in places that must have had dried blood. Everything hit me then, as I saw how vulnerable he was in that bed. He may not be dead, but he may be dying. This man who was shown as a pillar of unmovable might in my life, who always pushed me whether I wanted to be pushed or not, is broken and collapsed in front of me. I wanted to be mad, I wanted to be frustrated, but I couldn't do it. For all the times he stayed out late working, I know he did it because he wanted to provide for us. I won't forgive him for what he did when he lost his job, but those actions don't negate all the things he tried to do for his family.

At that point, my tears started to flow too. I could only get one word out as I came close to taking a knee near him. "Dad. . ." and the tears tried to make their way out. My little brother placed a hand on my back and when I turned to look I could see his young face holding back such a range of emotions.

Those eyes were looking at the wall past us all at nothing in particular. I know that face, as I've seen it so many times before on him. He was holding it in, the sadness, regret, and who knows what else. But I could tell he was hurting and it felt like a knife was jabbed into me again. It felt like when I lived back at home all over again. He was trying to be strong, as he had always been taught to be. As we all were. "Emotions are weakness, and letting them take over will only bring misfortune" It was something my dad always said to me. He had many lessons over the years that I am sure are ingrained in all of us.

Looking at my brother who was holding it in for only himself, I hugged him. I whispered to him then. "Let it out bro. It's okay."

He hugged me back, fists still in balls and finally letting himself go.

And in barely a whisper, taking deep breaths between words as he was choking back the tears - "He. . Wouldn't. . .Want us. . .To Cry."

I held him tighter after hearing him. I *know* I thought to myself. Our dad hated tears, he was hypocritical as when he lost his job it was his emotion that drove the wedge in our family. It was something that hit close to me to hear my brother say it. It showed that he still held to his ways of teaching them. It made me mad, as the last time I talked to him I told him it was the reason I left. This mindless indoctrination of a feudalistic way of thinking. Looking back over my shoulder while still holding my brother, I could see my dad there, unconscious and hooked up to who knows how many machines. His breathing was soft but assisted by the metallic sounds of the ventilator. It gave me. . . chills. In truth I missed him, I missed my sister, my brother and my mother. but I left because of him, and it was years since we last talked. I can't help but still hold a minor amount of animosity towards him. The faint evil thought that it might be better if he didn't wake up.

CHAPTER 11

I decided to stay the night, I wanted to be there to comfort my mother. She had been working so hard recently and I could tell she hadn't slept in a long time with the bags under her eyes. Her hair was messy and she was still in her uniform from work at the accounting firm. It gripped my heart to see her like this again. The last time was when Maria needed surgery for her legs, when she was put under anesthesia mom was stressed just like now. This feeling broke my heart to see her like this. Compared to my dad, my mother was the kindest person I knew. When I was bullied back in middle school, she would be the type to say "If they take your shoes, ask if they need a jacket" because anyone desperate enough to steal shoes would be cold too. Her heart was so forgiving towards anything we did, and we behaved most of the time just so we wouldn't upset her. She had both her hands wrapped around his, head resting on the bed and a red outline around her eyes. I asked the nurses to bring us some extra blankets and pillows, so we stayed the night. In the morning, James turned on the tv in the room.

He was switching from channel to channel trying to find something to get our minds off the constant humming of our dad's ventilator, then I saw a glimpse of the Y.O.K. News network.

"Hey, can you change that back?" I asked him. And with some reluctance he did.

It was showing Chuck Carlson, standing in a field of men that all had the logo of the Jorgan Principality. The men were in formation and marching with an intimidating gait. Listening carefully I had Will turn up the volume. . .

"We have been on the march for a whole week now and soon we will be at the border of the Belfast Kingdom. The duke and his men are set to ransack a city owned by the third player lord that we know of. So far no one has been able to find him for an interview. This Conquest player has evaded our investigations as I march with this formation. If anyone can recognize this man, please do have him give our news station a call for an interview!" and when he finished speaking a picture of me came up on the screen. Since I didn't change much of my character he looked almost identical to myself, just wearing fancy noble clothes from when I was heading to meet the duke for the first time. I could hear some gasps from my brother and sister as what can I assume was them recognizing the figure on the screen.

Then I heard a faint voice.

"Theodore?"

It was a manly voice, though soft almost weak, I recognized it however and whipped my head around so fast I almost hurt myself. And there he was, eyes open and holding a tube in his hand from the ventilator. My dad was awake.

"You're on TV? How long have I been out... what happened?"

The room was full of sudden stillness, everyone was looking at our father starting to sit up from the bed. His damaged face was blinking but his eyes were staring straight at the television. It was true, that was me on the screen but I was too ecstatic to see my dad speaking again. I braced myself, awaiting some sort of scolding that was inevitable from him. Something along the lines of wasting my time playing a game or why I dropped out of college. I couldn't see his eyes any longer.

"Son. Are you still trying to pursue that stupid dream of yours?"

Those words, it was abrupt and shook me to my core. My breathing immediately became hoarse and I managed to look up at him. His eyes met mine and I could see that age-old disappointment I have seen so many times before in those aged brown eyes. They looked so natural like all the times he scolded me or yelled at me for being a failure of a son. His eyes never dropped from my gaze, however, and he continued to talk.

"You proved me wrong. I thought you would have given up by now. How have you gotten by? You even managed to scrape yourself on the television" At the last part he glances at the rest of his family in the room. Mom was at a loss for words that dad was awake but immediately taking it out on me.

She mustered out while drying off the tears

"Theo came here for you, why are you so hostile to him?"

And my dad gently ran the hand not covered in wires and IV's through her hair, a sort of softness he would never show to his kids.

He looked back at me and then at the TV which showed my face in the noble outfit being escorted by knights. And with a sigh as if coming to terms with something started talking again, but softly still as his voice was still barely a rasp.

"You really got yourself on the TV? What did you even do to deserve that sort of recognition?"

With all my being I wanted to brag in his face about all the things that I had accomplished but I had that sinking feeling that it would be left on deaf ears.

"Yea, they think I am some fancy nobleman of the in-game country. I've made some good cash though in the meantime."

He nodded at me. With that same stern look on his face, he gave it some thought, then as I expected he dismissed it with his usual rude tone "So you aren't a noble in the game, and you also haven't made enough to live on your own. You threw away college for this and that is all you have to offer?"

The words stung, and it hurt to hear him be like this again. Some things don't change, but I won't let his opinion of my dream change me. I looked at my siblings who weren't as shocked as our mother about our dad's outburst but they were still embarrassed that I was still a point of attack when he spoke. It was enough for me, my dad is ok and Mom is here to deal with him now that he is awake. I started to get up and find my coat. As I turned away silently not wanting to pursue any more of his attack on me he stopped me again.

"Theodore. Why are they trying to find you?"

The news channel was stating everyone was looking for me among the soldiers and the camera was sifting through the different lines of soldiers.

Then it hit me, the war. It could be starting any time now and I was missing from the field.

"Well yeah, I was going to participate in some big battle today"

My dad's age-old gaze came back, the one that showed disappointment through the years and looked at me with those cold eyes.

"You are missing an opportunity right now. As you can see, I'm fine. Find your success, who knows when you will get this chance again. You know what I say, ``Every missed opportunity is a path blocked forever, so go now son, take it. If you are going to drop everything for this dream of yours, you better attack it with all of your beings." and when he finished speaking, he started coughing fit for a moment. Though the words struck me like a truck. He was encouraging me for my passion in his own way, it may be the cold voice, but his words were anything but cold. It filled me with a form of purpose, and I stood straighter as if all the years I have spent preparing for this and the long nights of thinking were not in vain.

"Thank you, dad. I'll go take this opportunity just how you showed me to"

"Attack it with everything you've got and don't stop until you are the best at what you do" he replied quickly. Then gestured for a handshake, the first one I've gotten from him since I turned thirteen. I grasped the hand back, then went around hugging everyone, my mom, brother and little sister. Just as I was about to leave the room, Marie shouted to me

"We will be watching! Go team!"

It was a small gesture but one that hit home right where it needed to be. My dad was a stern man, when it came to encouragement so when he mustered that little bit, it was more than he had given me in years. Besides, I want to become successful in Kronos for my brother and sister, Marie and James. If I can make the money I will get them through college so they don't have to drop out as I did. I was in a rush, full of emotions and red-faced as I ran out of the hospital.

Knowing I wouldn't make it home in time to get in a pod I ran as quickly as possible to the nearest POD rental, like a PC cafe but for the Kronos Immersion Pods. I was filled with a purpose to make a name for myself during this conflict.

———————◆———————

Habeas

If someone were to pay attention over the course of the week, they would see a straight path from the Empire to the Belfast Kingdom in which there were no monster spawns. There was even a dungeon outbreak that was quelled during the straight line that was almost drawn onto the world map. It was the course of Habeas. His goal was clear, to encounter the strongest player in the game. Currently, the player 'Conquest' was on his radar as someone who had accomplished becoming a Noble of a country something only two other players have accomplished. The network he was using to spy on him was unable to find him in Stotonely- the supposed town he was a noble of, which was doing nothing but excite Habeas more. The fact he was evading the watchful eyes of the darknet spies, he was impressed. Habeas had no information on the build Conquest used but he was confident that regardless of the skill set it would be an amazing duel.

There was one small hiccup in Habeas plan, however. As he started to cross the border he was hearing of two famous NPC that was going to be on the battlefield soon, a battlefield that will contain Conquest as a participant. Habeas had a set of rules in his own mind, killing NPCs would be avoided if possible, and only harm those who are 'bullies'. To him, Kronos Online was a place to have fun regardless of what level you were. If you were to ruin someone else's experience then you are to garner his wrath. The problem with this rule is that when those two NPCs enter the field, he would most likely be forced to encounter one of them. Now Habeas has to decide which side he wants to take in the conflict so he at least has an excuse to meet Conquest on the field. He has heard the rumors about the duke in the south of Belfast, his elite troops called the Red were always something of interest to him and sparking a little conflict with them is sure to inspire some excitement. Though if they were as strong as the net projects then he was not willing to lose any of his gear in an accidental fight.

That is when Habeas came to the new conclusion, be on no one's side. Once he reaches conquest, tell him his purpose and challenge him to a duel right there on the battlefield. No one would be able to refuse a challenge there without taking the loss in honor or morale. This thought made Habeas happy, so he cleaned his blade of Elder Lich's tattered robes and patted off the skeletal dust from his suit and continued his march towards the battlefield that was not far off.

*****

Cora

Amongst the lines of troops carrying a flag with a snake's head were disguised assassins marching in formation in perfect cover. The seven assassins were all united in one hired mission by a player named Cora, the newest scheme to take down the player lord and capture the now Countess Isabel. The plan had multiple steps and all revolved around immersing themselves in the battlefield under the cover of the opponents' forces. If they hid well enough, then their goals would be hidden in the eyes of their enemies. To them, they would be regular soldiers who fight abnormally well. But when push comes to shove their skills will be revealed and a sneak attack will pincer straight at the leaders before anyone can react. A high-level player like Cora was sure of this plan, especially since she had 6 level 90 assassins with her to follow along. Each with the <Meld Shadow> ability. It was a rare ability that lets the assassin sneak through the shadows. It was a common misconception that the assassin class could only be used in cloak and dagger tactics. That just is not true. The battlefield is when assassins truly get to show their colors as a point and kill type of soldier, the <Meld Shadow> ability doubles down on this trait that gets pulled to its full potential on large scale battlefields like this where the chaos of the field is like a ripe field of fruits waiting to bear their yields. Cora had spent a majority of her remaining gold on these assassins, including a good amount of her reputation to recruit them. They were the best available and all of them together could take on Glass in her mind. The best player in the world couldn't stop them if they didn't see her coming. The march was relentless and in only an hour would their forces meet the armies of the Belfast kingdom composed of The Earl Claycoax and Duke of the South's forces. As long as she kept the Duke's gaze from her and her assassins she would be safe.

◆

Theodore

The blood was rushing to my head as I made my way to the pod rental shop, luckily there was a slot left and I was able to log in quickly enough.

Logging into Kronos Online was quick and the machine was the same model I had at home which was good since that meant there wasn't any difference in feeling. After what felt like forever in loading into the game for the first time at this location I was rewarded with being placed outside the walls at the Citadel. Looking around I couldn't see any of my summons, I didn't tell them any specific orders so my concern started to grow. I only knew one place I could find them. Running as quickly as I could towards the old hiding spot I found them taking a lookout. Abel was looking over the rest of the goblins and going over strategy talks as I approached. They all stopped and stood up in salute at my approach. It was nice to see. I was happy to see them all still safe and ready for combat. Taking a quick glance at Abel I was glad to see he had accomplished my task before and managed to evolve. He was no longer a "Noble Skeleton" but instead "Skeleton Baron" His class was "Captain" which was fitting, checking through his class abilities they were all revolving around the leadership skill I had given him. He seems to have gained another skill as well, filling up the last available skill slot.

<Light Group Heal> it must have been a skill he picked up from Medibug who was sitting on his shoulder.

I nodded my head and looked at all of them, solidifying my resolve that I could lose some or maybe all of them in this upcoming conflict. Standing straight and putting on a serious tone, the cheery atmosphere left quickly as I started talking.

"It's wartime, all of you have been training for this moment. Do not let me down, do not die and waste the resources I have put into each and every one of you. Do not let anyone kill you or your companions."

With it said and done I told them to pick up the pace as we started running towards Stotonely. I was firing off messages to Silvax letting him know I was catching up and on my way.

"Took you long enough, Isabel was upset that her hope didn't keep his word"

"I know I know, family emergency. I will try and meet up with you all, where are your forces posted in the lineup?"

"We are marching in the center-right of the formation next to the Duke of the south, Isabel is currently having a conversation with him."

"Ok, just hold tight with your men as best you can before I get there. I don't want to miss the action"

"Sounds good to me Conquest, Get here quickly, you should experience warfare from the front with us."

I closed the chat after that and kept up the pace, all my goblins, medibugs and Abel were keeping up as we marched quickly to catch up to the moving army. Luckily a group of 17 is faster than a group of 10,000.

After about 3 hours of vigorous marching, we saw the clouds of dust in the distance caused by the army's footsteps. I could feel my blood pressure rise exponentially as my goblins and I approached. I was given questions by a few men who were set up as guards around the marching forces, but after throwing around names such as Countess Isabel and Centurian Silvax. I was let in reluctantly with a minor escort to the center of the moving camp. When I made it to the center of the formation there were two large contingents of knights I could see, one in the distance was a large formation of men on horseback with purple robes or armor pieces that must signify the house Claycoax. While the one I was being led to was adorned with the color red on every bit of livery possible. The mages all wore red and had a fiery symbol embalming all of their backs that signified they served the Duke of the South and were part of his elite forces, 'The Red'. It was impressive as I could easily tell each of them was high level just by their equipment. In the center of this formation was a stationary tent that must have been hastily put up for a meeting.

Outside the tent, I saw Catalina and Silvax who were mustering his troops' information in front of him. He has one cohort of troops, a solid 100 men under his command, and in turn 100 men that serve Countess Isabel.

The men that were guards at the city of Stotonely were to stay behind and hold off the enemy should the army fail to defend against the invaders. Silvax was quick to wave me over, so I quickly made my way forward with all of my men in tow behind me.

"Conquest, I see you finally made it. This is shaping up to be one of the largest conflicts Belfast has faced in a decade. It seems many people have forgotten the rumors of the southern Duke."

I was still in the dark on why everyone always talked with a reverie about the duke of the south, he had met one duke already but was not impressed.

"What is so special about this Duke? I had met the duke of the Jorgan Principality and he did not show much strength compared to the rest of his elites-"

Silvax then looked at me with a bit of alarm, rushing up to me and stopping me from talking by putting a hand up quickly.

"You can't compare them like that, especially when the Red are all around us. The duke of the south, the warden, is an immensely powerful man. I personally have not seen him in action, but reputation in Kronos is a very useful thing. If someone's reputation is spreading everywhere then their abilities are typically proportional. The Duke of the south in Belfast has been heard about in almost every neighboring country. He is even renowned amongst those in the Empire. His elite troops, The Red, were personally trained by him to take down all that opposed him. They apparently earned their name by being able to cut off a bit of his bright red hair. Which is all they could do, all of them, together."

This caught me off guard, looking back at all of those elite troops and doing the math in my head, I was almost spinning with the possibilities. I placed a little note in my mind to never piss off the Duke of the South. . .

Before I was able to respond to Silvax, I heard a booming voice from the tent.

"Who is the bastard who left my Niece Isabel without a guard?" Soon a huge man built from head to toe came out of the tent, his outfit seeming almost casual on this battlefield full of knights. If it weren't for the giant hammer on his back that is. His red hair and blue eyes scanned the men around when countess Isabel came rushing out behind him, her face flushed red and a major sign of annoyance on it. "He did not leave Uncle! He was just late. See he did come here!" and to my absolute dread, pointed straight at me.

The giant of a man came storming forward, and at his march, all of his elites took notice and were swarming behind him surrounding me.

I thought to myself as calmly as possible. *Shit.* I could see out of the corner of my eyes Silvax back up a few feet. *Double shit.* I stood up as straight as I could and bowed to the Duke of the south. His booming voice was right above me as I could see his shoes from the way I was bowed.

"You have the audacity to bow in front of me? What, you could leave my Niece, a Countess, standing vacantly when she gave you a mission but a duke, that is where you draw the line? What is your name."

I was almost shaking at this point, his presence made me want to run away with everything in my being. I was full of fright at the monstrous man in front of me. "I am Conquest my Liege" not daring to lift my gaze from the bow.

"Conquest. . . Not a bad name and you have certainly had some decent feats to go along with that label. Lift your gaze Conquest." at his request I finally lifted my bowing form to stare up at him.

"You did not cower like I thought you would, instead you arrived and even brought men of your own. . ." he glanced at the goblins and skeleton, then shook his head and looked back at me ". . . Well, sort of men. Either way, you did arrive and I am going to give a task to you and Silvax there, the only forces that my Niece commands. You are to defend her with your life. I know you are a traveler and to me, that makes your life expendable. So spend it if you have to keep Isabel alive."

It was a clear order that I was going to follow regardless if he gave it or not, so I nodded my head and the quest notification disappeared into my menus.

"Well looks like you got some balls, Conquest. When this is all over, we will have a little chat. Isabel, your knight is here and fine. See I didn't even hit him once"

Isabel was completely red-faced and punched the duke on her way past him. It was a sweet scene that Isabel definitely needed as a break from all this tragedy. I made sure to bow to her as well when she arrived.

"Enough of that Conquest, we have work to do. Have you become stronger?" I looked her in the eyes and nodded confidently, looking back at my troops, specifically Rango and Abel. I felt ready for whatever conflict awaited us.

"Good. Then we will be setting up our fortifications here, the enemy will be upon us in the next hour. It is time for war."

CHAPTER 12

---◆◆---

I was doing final checks with my goblins, ensuring their armor was secure and they were using the optimized gear for this warfare. I was not sure how long the combat could last, so preparing for a battle of attrition I made sure they used weapons that used less stamina and inflicted damage over time. Rango was happily swinging two swords now instead of a shield and sword combo. The defence stat was key as well on them as their levels meant they would be vulnerable to strikes from much higher leveled opponents. As much as I wanted to rely on Silvaxs men I knew I couldn't because of the circumstances. It was war, anything could happen.

Once I did my basic checks and had my squad line up in formation, Abel and rango came to stand on my left and right respectively while Bug sat on my shoulder. We were as prepared as best we could be for this, at least I hoped we were. Glancing around I could see the lines of troops digging up trenches and building mounds as well as temporary fortifications as we awaited the enemy forces. One of these such buildings was a tower that was 30 feet tall, it was nothing fancy and just wooden logs tied together with rope hastily constructed to provide a better vantage point over the battlefield. Wanting to have a better view myself I started climbing up said tower. Once at the top there were two guards already there holding bows and standing next to a large horn. One of them looked at me once I finished climbing up and scowled at me saying

"Why are you up here? We are busy."

"I just want a better look at what is coming"

"Make it quick, we have not made the sight of the enemy yet"

"Thank you"

And with that, I was able to gaze upon the Forces of Belfast, easily 10,000 men from two great houses. The Earl Claycoax and the Duke of the South, all their men were busy at work below stretched over a kilometer. The men were hastily building defences and preparing for the enemy forces that were coming. It was the most impressive sight I have seen, it doesn't do it justice when watching on the television as it never captures the sound of it all. Scattered among the men you could tell there was an occasional player, I even saw some familiar armor glinting in the distance, Horus from Stotonely and the man with a giant piece of steel stood near the front, helping the soldiers dig a trench. A lot was on the line for the players of Belfast, if leadership changed then so would their way of life here. The effects of the war were not lost on this game world, especially to the players that were forced to become a part of it during times like these.

After some time of analyzing the battlefield, I was able to get a grasp of what formations were just levies drafted by the country and which ones were trained army soldiers. Not only was the gear they wore different but so was how they marched. The trained soldiers always moved with distinction on the battlefield, a line moving all at the same speed while the levies were more of a force, higher in number and like ants swarming in a direction. The levies were hastily trained and drafted for the purpose of defending their towns, it was a sad thing to see but necessary for them to keep their families or friends safe. The life of NPCs was precious, they only had one life and once they died they could not be revived, unlike players. The craziest thought to me is the fact these wars happen often in the world of Kronos, countries rise and others get chunks ripped out of them by sieges like this.

While I was lost in that train of thought the two guards were busy scanning the horizon for movement. The south would soon be covered in the banners of the Jorgan Principality, an invader that has been openly hostile in recent months and now escalated a border skirmish into an all-out war. Then they both stopped, staring at a single moving post in the distance. Over the course of the next few seconds, it was like time had stopped for them as the singular post turned into ten, forty, two hundred, a thousand. The horizon was becoming covered with the forces of the enemy. One finally snapped out of his shock and grabbed the horn blowing the alert that the enemy was here. I too gazed at the oncoming army. There were no levies to be seen, they all marched in distinction and their numbers were identical to ours. The green color of their shields and banners littered the lines of their forces giving me an ache to see. They were all organized and trained soldiers, their formation was impeccable and they marched with certainty towards us. It was soon going to be time to fight.

My ears were soon filled with drums, deep bellowing drums from all over our forces. I drew my eyes towards the sources and sure enough, there were at least a hundred giant drums that were being banged, the men were shouting and hyping themselves up for the enemy. The drums of war had begun. I quickly slid down the ladder to regroup with my force. I noticed a buff had been applied when the music had started, a decent five percent buff to attack speed, spread across an entire army would be beneficial indeed. The levies in the distance I could see coming to grips with the soon-to-be fight, making sidelong glances at the approaching army with fear and regret. But it was too late now. They were on the battlefield and would have to fight.

I was proud to see my goblins were unwavering. They really were loyal and it made me happy to see, though they were a bit too short to see the true number of enemies coming. Their height was still short but the armor and weapons gave them a decent stature. Almost like young teens on the battlefield if it weren't for their pointy ears and green skin to differentiate them from the rest. Seeing the C on their shoulder as well as the numbers on their back was also fitting and nice to see. I walked towards Abel who was busy examining Silvax and his men's formation. He must have noticed my approach as he was unphased when I placed my hand on his shoulder and started talking.

"Abel, I hope you are prepared for the coming conflict. I have a lot of hope for your performance today and I want you to learn as much as you can from those around you."

Abel and his glowing blue orbs took a moment to process this as he stared intently at the movement of the legionnaires, then finally turned to me and nodded.

"My master, I will not fail you. The sparring match against them was beneficial to me, and I do look forward to learning more this day. I will take their bones as trophies and show any who target my master what it feels like to be hopeless."

It was dark, fitting for a skeleton, but I was pleased with it nonetheless. He was ready, I was worried he was still distraught about losing but he seems to have gotten over it.

"Good, Our goal during this is simple: Keep Countess Isabel safe, keep you and your forces alive and fight as unfairly as possible to win. There is no honor in war, only the victors and the dead."

"Spoken like a true leader. You will be done, Conquest"

He bowed slightly to me and turned back towards the goblins lined up. He began giving them orders, mimicking the formation of Silvax and his legionnaires, making sure the shields were equipped well and their blades sharpened.

The drums grew louder and more intense and the shouts of the soldiers were beginning to deafen us from their enthusiasm. Then above I could see the first strike being launched, huge fireballs being flung from the opponent's side of the field, but they were met quickly by mages shields throughout the encampment. It had begun.

One of my favorite things about Kronos online is how the Heads up display or HUD is for the player, the menus that display health or hotbars for skills and such are not nearly as populated as other games since the field of view is so much larger. Instead the only form of menu that is displayed at all times is health, stamina and mana. Other than those you have to think about the menu you wish to see and they will show in the corner of your vision. When it comes to other players, monsters and NPCs however, there is a rule in Kronos to prevent screen clutter, when more than a certain amount of entities during events like these it will leave names or hp bars off everyone except the person you are currently targeting with an attack. This provides the maximum amount of immersion during large-scale events, and It was something I thought I would be prepared for.

I really did think I was ready for combat and this war, but when the combat hud kicked in, removing all names of everyone and leaving just the gritty sounds and visuals of war it made my knees weak for a moment. The heat from fireballs being launched above could be felt from the mages and the shouts of soldiers and war drums being blasted at all times were starting to set it. The horizon was covered with enemy soldiers and the banners were beginning to get close enough that the archers were beginning to open up. The sky became covered in a cloud of arrows that even the magical shielding couldn't prevent on either side. Luckily for us, we were in the center of the formation, meaning most of these first volleys were striking those at the front lines. But the grey pixels rising up from the frontlines was a testament to the power behind those volleys and expressed that many people had already perished in this war when only minutes had passed.

Glancing over at Silvax and his men, I could see him staring at the lines of troops being destroyed. He was restless and I could see he wanted to act. Hundreds of levies were being killed and he felt like he could save some. He tightened the grip on his shield and sword and the calculations were being made in his mind, it was a conflict of interest as right now he and I were the only ones defending countess Isabel. Talking to no one in particular Silvax started a rant "They are using the levies to reduce the stamina of the enemies. It's cold, and so many are dying. I can't sit back and watch this. The Earl really is tricky in his tactics."

Looking back at everyone around us, the Countess was still with the Duke in the back, surrounded by the elite forces of the Red. I was confident she would be safe at least at the beginning of this. It seems Silvax was thinking the same thing since when I went to look back at him he was also looking at the countess. After a moment of self deliberation, he must have come to his conclusion. Making eye contact with me and then to all his men he started his orders.

"We came to this battlefield to save the lives of our countrymen and we cannot do it from the backlines. For our Falanx and prepare to march forward men. The east side of the battlefield is the worst and that is where we will go! MARCH" The energy he invigorated in his soldiers was impressive. They switched to a perfect formation with Silvax at the head of it and started wading their way through the soldiers and soon levies to the front. Not wanting to be left behind I made my way through the path his men made, my little band following close behind me roughly mimicking Silvaxs formation. We did not have nearly the same numbers in our formation but the compact nature of the goblin's formation from the past month of conflict has helped their form as we marched behind.

I wanted to place ourselves behind Silvax and catch any straggling enemies that attempt to flank him or get past and rush the Countess. I thought I was ready for it.

The ground was stomped down and the grass was destroyed by thousands of soldiers' footsteps. As soon as I caught up to Silvax at the front of the line I saw the enemy, they were only 100 meters away and closing quickly on us, The levies on the left and right of Silvax were terrified as so many of them already died to countless arrows shredding their friends apart and now they see a wall of armored, trained and bloodthirsty soldiers aiming to take their heads. It was a lot for anyone, including me. I made my way next to Silvaxs formation on the left. I want to help the levies in any way I can now that I see the residual grey pixels of who knows how many men have already died. Once I finally broke through the line of petrified levies the march was even closer, Silvax was shouting commands but I could not hear them over the constant war drums. Soon a horn blew on the opponent's side and the horde of enemy soldiers broke into a full sprint the final 30 meters to us. My goblins readied their shields and swords, Rango opting to stand at my side with two swords instead of the shield and sword combo.

The pure amount of mass collided with our lines and it showed there that goblins were not meant to hold a full charge of man. The enemy immediately broke through the side of us. It was not without cost, them breaking through meant their sides and bellies were exposed to the counter-attacks of the goblins. Luckily these soldiers were not high leveled and just regular foot soldiers, possibly around 20 - 30. Rango, Abel and I worked quickly to close the gap that was opened from the initial charge. The rest of the goblins worked hard at keeping the enemy soldiers at bay, the Medibugs working diligently to keep them healed. Taking a cautionary glance at my surroundings I could see the levies on my left were being broken quickly, while Silvax on my right was tearing the enemy apart. I could see the rage on all their soldiers' faces during this. The senseless slaughter of their countrymen clearly got to them. I do not blame them in the slightest. My focus was pulled back to my line as the sound of a goblin screaming caught my ears. It was Goblin 5 according to the number on his back, he was being attacked by an enemy soldier that had a green helm with shinier armor clearly indicating he wasn't a regular soldier.

Thinking quickly I rushed forward at the Man attempting to kill my goblin. Brandishing my sword and coming from the side I started quickly with a <Heavy Strike>. The blow caught the green helmed man off guard and finally as I struck the Hud identified him as my target. It was a player, with the name of SlapShift. He was quick to react as it seemed he was an officer of the enemy troops. His counter strike was efficient but my shield was up and blocked before it could connect. I made a glancing blow on him and the extra effects of my sword kicked in damaging him because of his armor. The blows we exchanged were quick and bloody, my goblins would take strikes at his back when they got a chance but most were too focused on the oncoming enemy forces. After a minute of exchanging blows, I finally eliminated the player. I kept minimizing the pop-ups for experience gain and leveling up as there just wasn't time to look at them.

As soon as I took down that player I could see a group of heavier armored troops in the distance on the enemies' side making their way towards Silvaxs group. They clearly spotted the rut holding this side of the line-up and are here to dig it out. Silvax spotted the oncoming forces and came to a quick conclusion.

"Forces! Tactical Withdrawal, head back to the trench and wall line, we will hold them there."

The order was given and I could see that his men started to walk backward, shields and swords still pointed at the enemy, never giving them an opportunity to strike at their rear. I was going to attempt to mimic the motion but Abel beat me to it. In his deep aristocratic voice, he boomed out commands to my men.

"We must pull back, Keep your swords at the enemy and let the Medibugs guide your path, Rango, Pull up any stragglers!"

After his words, we too made our way back, but instead of splitting and taking our own line, we were able to group up with Silvax behind the temporary fortifications. It was only a retreat of 100 meters but the march was treacherous as dozens of enemy soldiers kept on assaulting us as we made our way back. Looking at the sides I could see Levies were not as lucky and attempted a breaking run towards the walls but were cut down by the oncoming soldiers. Awaiting at the temporary fortification were the first sets of real soldiers of the Belfast Kingdom. If I were to estimate we lost at least half of all the Levies in that initial wave and maybe killed half that in enemy soldiers. The price was high for those 100 meters of ground.

When I caught myself looking around the makeshift battlements I was shocked to see not a single man from Silvaxs force had lost a member yet. Their hundred man formation made extremely effective use of swapping techniques and the help of a few cleric class healers. The levies on the sides however did not make it as lucky. The enemy made short work of any who were caught with their back turned and did not pursue us in our new defensive positions. I was worried that their morale would break, but soon actual trained soldiers with spears made their way changing positions with the levies allowing them a break as they took the line in their stead and filled in the ranks on the front. I saw one was a player, a barbarian class with a club that seemed just too large to be functional. The name hovering above his head was Roadkill and he marched up to my little posse of goblins with a huge grin on his face. His character was easily two feet taller than I was and was towering over my goblins like they were the bugs on their shoulders. With a booming voice that everyone could hear, even over the sounds of the war around us, he shouted "CONQUEST! I saw you on the NEWS! Not often do you see a Noble fighting the good Fight!" and with his giant hands pats me on the back almost knocking me off my feet. He had some strength that was impressive, to say the least. His speech had different parts louder than others, almost as if he wanted to hear himself over the combat as well.

"Would you be Offended if I FOUGHT at your Side!"

There was a large amount of me that wanted this behemoth to get twenty feet away from me, but the added strength that will keep my goblins alive was too tempting of an offer to put away. I nodded my head and sent him a party invite. As usual, I kept my level and class hidden, he was willing to share and I was surprised to see he was level 86, before I could comment or say anything he started talking again in that strange loud voice.

"I am sure you would not MIND if my other Friend joined us?"

I was hesitant at first then sure enough from the distance I could see a short stocky man that I recognized, and before Roadkill could introduce us, Sjorn burst through the line of soldiers in our line, hands out wide shouting "CONQUEST! It's you! Glad to see you already met Roadkill, he is a barbarian like I am"

I immediately sent him a request as well to the party and I felt much safer on the battlefield.

"Of course It is good to have both of you in my party, Let us win this war!" We all passed around fist bumps, I introduced them to the silent but noble skeleton Abel and Roadkill immediately began nudging his shoulder and annoying him with his loud voice. I could see his blue orbs wincing every time he spoke just a bit too loud in his non-existent ears.

They each took an edge of my forces, Roadkill on the right flank between my group and Silvaxs, and Sjorn on the left side between us and the spearmen. This left Rango, Abel and myself spread throughout the formation in the center to keep the ranks and save any goblin in over their head.

The enemy forces started eyeballing us and glancing behind them, it made me a bit freaked out since they weren't staring at anyone else. Soon I realized it wasn't my goblins they were looking at but me. Eyes glinting with hatred and greed overtook their warlike demeanor. That is when I could see them muttering to each other, nodding heads and pointing. Maybe Roadkill said my name just a bit too loudly. As one face in the enemy ranks seemed to melt away behind the rest's shadow.

Cora

The lines of Jorgan Principality soldiers were ruthlessly led by the Duke, Stanely Freneferd. He made his men run ragged day and night to get to the enemy encampment, enraged at his betrayal and deceit from the enemy lord, Conquest. Cora saw this through the rushed action of his commanders. The knights were scrambling to push the lines and even against normal levies they were taking losses. In her eyes, it was pathetic. The waste of life for revenge was unnecessary but she couldn't criticize too much as she was there for the same reason. Her judgment for the duke and his strategies was cut short during the first interaction, any poor soldiers who were unlucky enough to encounter her or her assassins were cut down without even knowing they were fighting someone skilled. Usually, a blade to the legs or back of the head causes critical strikes.

Her assassin band was spread loosely through the front lines, trying their best to get a sight on one of their targets. Conquest, or the countess Isabel. After the Belfast kingdom performed a tactical retreat, spreading the lines between the two, the Duke finally came to his senses and halted the pursuit. Leaving the gap between the two armies. She messaged her assassins to scout the lines in search of their prey. It wasn't long until a booming voice could be heard across the battlefield. At her distance it was unintelligible but soon enough a shadow moved near her and out emerged an assassin, instead of reflexively striking at it she waited to hear what it had to say, as he was an assassin she hired.

In a face that looked as innocent as the soldiers around them but a voice that was full of gravel and evil it said slowly almost as if there was a knife in the words spoken "Conquest, has been found"

Finally, she could have her revenge. She started to gather her assassins and group up on the side of the battlefield near Conquest. But before she made her way there, the not-so-innocent assassin spoke "There are very powerful travelers with him, what is your command?"

Without even skipping a beat she responded in the coldest tone possible

"Kill them all."

Theo

The enemy began again, their lines began shouting and the forces moved quickly across the open ground between us. I could feel the shaking of the dirt beneath my feet as the thousands of soldiers ran at full speed. Abel was quick to get our goblins into formation again and with Roadkill and Sjorn at our flanks, we felt quite secure compared to the last time. I was taking deep breaths and thinking back on what Rocky had told me about composure in the eyes of my enemy. 'Never lose focus, keep calm and solutions will be found to win' he was, of course, talking about one on one duels but I feel that knowledge could be used here as well. I may not be in command of the field but this little corner of it is mine. I have complete trust that Silvax on the west of me will hold my right flank. His soldiers are trained and veterans to large combat.

I shook away the last of my jitters and loosened the white knuckles that I had formed around my sword. The enemy collided with my line. The goblins this time were able to hold their stance right and brace the enemy soldiers. One unlucky fellow met the twin blades of Rango and almost died because of it. I was quick to act as well and pushed the goblins that were struggling most to the side to fight their attackers. Most of the enemy soldiers were in the levels of 30s while my level might be in the 40s. The stat buffs I have gotten from the titles make me almost as strong as a level 80. It was complete overkill and only two or three hits were enough to kill most soldiers. Sjorn and his axe was a brutal sight to see as he kept a spinning form cleaving with a forward stroke and then a backhand constantly hitting his opponent. Sometimes he would strike two or three at a time causing bleed effects. Roadkill was insane with his club, absolutely nailing people into the ground who got too close. The club had so much mass behind the swings that it would knock soldiers back, up and behind the enemy lines. The strikes could be felt from 15 feet away with the shock of them.

I was optimistic, to say the least. Looking at Silvaxs line I could see his phalanx was operating perfectly, spears and swords would cut down any enemy that made it in close and the shields above would prevent any strikes from arrows that were launched above. I couldn't see Silvax as I assumed he was further to the west of his line covering the flank himself.

Occasionally an enemy player soldier would make their way into the lines, pushing back Rango, but with Abels help, they would make short work of them and push them to grey dust. It was a rinse and repeat the action that seemed almost repetitive, but the stamina drain was costly especially with the medibugs healing most of our wounds as they occurred. Levels were flowing constantly to my goblins as player kills must give much more experience to them. I didn't have time to see their growth but I was excited to see their strength.

Then I heard it. From behind us, there was a terrifying clicking. Like a ticking noise that overcame the combat. It was a form that was almost ten feet tall and its legs towered over the soldiers beneath it. The blades on its body were sharp and the face was that of a praying mantis. The eight hairy legs were fast, full of sharp hairs and marching quickly over the gawking soldiers. They recognized it as an ally not a monster thankfully because of the system and I was in complete shock as I saw the behemoth monster approach me with the glowing name 'Victorum' above its head. I was entranced at the absolute strength of the beast, so much so I failed to see Silvax get launched into the air to my right.

CHAPTER 13

———◆◆———

Habeas

The glittering blades shining on the sides of Habeas did little to counteract the shotty armor he was wearing. In comparison the only gear of value he was equipped with was the swords, the armor was as simple as a decent suit and dress pants. Common gear with almost no stats to them except a buff in charisma. He wore these because at this rank and with the soldiers that are around him he does not have to worry about anyone except the other highest-ranking players or the dukes. So he kept a low profile as he weeded his way through the ranks of soldiers. Occasionally he would be mistaken as an enemy to both sides of the war and just knock out any soldier who attempted to strike him. They didn't deserve to die for fighting in this war against him.

The A.I. only have one life and to Habeas that was a noble thing, they had lived in this world and he wasn't about to ruin that just to satisfy his ego. That's what the other players were for. It took a bit of finagling to make his way through the soldiers but since he was approaching from the western flank of the Belfast Kingdom it wasn't nearly as inconvenient. He would sometimes step into the foray of battle since the middle ground between the armies had the cleanest route into the lines. Habeas saw a monster then, easily an elite class monster he had never seen before making its way through the Belfast army, it had eight legs and was marching tenaciously towards the frontlines. It put an interesting feeling in Habeas stomach that made him want to pursue it. With that goal in mind, he started moving in the direction it was heading.

After knocking down a few Belfast soldiers Habeas noticed a phalanx that was blocking his way, it was an impressive formation but nothing that could stop a skill use. Raising the new red sword that he took from Glass he activated a simple CC skill, or crowd control skill, called <Earthshake> that destabilizes the formations of anyone around them and makes the ground shake to the point that everyone loses their balance. Habeas was obviously not affected by it and proceeded to push through the shielded soldiers that were looking on in horror at the man dressed in a suit waltzing through their line. Luckily for them, the soldiers on the Jorgan Principality were equally affected by the skill.

"Oh no you don't" a voice called out in front of him as a man wearing the armor of a centurion with a frilled helmet, wielding a shortsword and shield stood between him and the Spider Mantis's goal.

Habeas basing his years of experience playing MMO games could gauge the level of his opponents usually off of their armor and weapons, this player 'Silvax' his name was had a decently high level so far that he had seen in the 90s. It was strong enough that he would humor him with a fight.

Silvax was looking at him and behind Habeas at his men that were starting to get up again. Then, concerned that Habeas would strike them while they were getting up, lunged at Habeas with a skill that lit up his blade. Intrigued by it, Habeas chose to block it with his blue sword, the gleam was intense as it struck. The moment the shining blade connected with the blue sword, it exploded. Shaking Habeas and momentarily giving a glint of a smile as his health bar lowered, not much, but that it moved at all was impressive to him.

"I will award your effort, Silvax"

The smoke had cleared to show Habeas clearly unharmed and Silvax rounding his shield up to prepare for the counter-attack.

Silvax shouted at the unflinching Habeas "I see the Jorgan Principality is sending their Aces to deal with me!"

But Habeas was quick to put that fire out "I don't even know who you are, I just want to fight Conquest"

At the mention of Conquest, Silvax made a mistake. He glanced over his shoulder to his left, looking at the front lines across from his soldiers' formation, in the direction that the giant spider was marching.

In a now happy tone, full of condescension Habeas was quick to pick up on the glance "So that is where the New Lord is hiding!" And turned to start moving in that direction. Silvax was quick to stand in the path, "We aren't done here!"

"Oh, we are." and with that Habeas powered another skill through his blade and smashed into Silvax like a batter smacking a home run launching him through the air in the direction he was marching.

"Here I come little lord," Habeas muttered, marching unphased by the soldiers scrambling to get back into formation around him.

Theo

I was aghast to see Silvax on the ground in front of me, his shield was dented and a half was completely cracked off. He was gulping in the air trying to catch his breath, luckily he landed behind the goblins and not in front where the combat lies. I reached out a hand to pull him to his feet, and between labored breaths, he tried speaking but nothing was coming out.

"What's the matter, Silvax? How did you get launched over here?"

Seeing the events unfold and the giant spider Mantis that was approaching, Sjorn and Roadkill both pulled back from the line to regroup and see what was going on.

Both readied their weapons at Victorum that was approaching at an unsettling speed.

I quickly stopped their hasty defence "No not her, that is my summon like the goblins"

They both looked at each other, confused and perplexed but after Sjorn muttered some things to Roadkill they were calm again. Now all of us were looking at Silvax who had regained his composure and was able to breathe again, whatever the strike was it took out his entire stamina bar. He finally spoke.

"Run"

One word through labored breathing, sent a chill down my spine as I looked over to his line, it seemed relatively fine, his soldiers were still information but. . . There was a man. He was wearing a black suit and dress pants, but in either of his hands were extremely illustrious swords. One was a shining crystal-like Red, it looked surprisingly familiar, while the other was a cool sea-colored blue. The name above his head was Habeas, and the smooth features were chilling as he did not once blink or take his eyes off me. He approached at a steady pace and both Sjorn and Roadkill looked at each other and nodded. Some unspoken words that the two must have shared after months of playing together.

Just as they were about to make a charge at him, I noticed the shadows move beneath us all. An unsettling sound emerged from Habeas, a twisted laugh followed by him swinging his sword at the shadow beneath his feet.

"Impressive! No wonder you were able to avoid my spies! To have such elites working under you must mean you live up to your name! I hope you understand however, I must kill them because they got in the way of our duel, nothing personal."

Then I mimicked his action and swung at the shadow near my feet, striking a semi-solid form that soon sprouted from the ground. Each shadow then popped up from everyone's backs bringing shape assassins that were hiding in wait. Since I acted quickly the player assassin named Cora narrowly missed my throat with her dagger. She then backed up a step between Habeas and myself. Sjorn and Roadkill were both hit by the surprise attacks but their endurance was higher than the assassins must have expected, as Roadkill just clubbed one on the side and Sjorn completely ignored the strike and swung at the same one Roadkill had hit.

Cora looked at me, exasperatedly and shouted "You were waiting for us! Do you know how much gold I have wasted getting these assassins to kill you! Just be a good puppet and die!" and took another stab at me. I wasn't able to block it even with my enhanced speed and light armor, the strike was too quick and I wasn't able to trigger <Grends Swordsmanship> to force the block. The dagger bit into me and I could feel its poison seep into my body. The giant spider mantis saw this, however, and Victorum, enraged at finally reuniting with its master, barreling its way towards Cora. The giant blades lash out to strike at the high-level human assassin. She was faster, I have to give her that. Lunging backward she was able to avoid the praying mantis forelegs. Victorum brought her giant spider legs in front of me as a sort of shield between myself and Cora. using the moment to look at her stats, I was able to see she had indeed accomplished her mission of being level 75. That includes the evolutions which must have made her this gigantic size. I wasn't sure what her true stats were since the shadows below her legs started to move unnaturally. Cora had used a shadow walk skill to move below to strike against me causing the defense that Victorum had made me become a detriment instead.

The blade caught me again and my health was dropping faster with the effect of the poison stacking. My shoulder pet Bug was quick at work to keep my healing during all of this but it was severely lacking. Just as I began my counter-attack, Cora vanished yet again in front of me. Thinking back on the first encounter we had in Stotonely I brought my sword pointed to my side that I thought she would approach from. Sure enough, the blade actually caught her black garments and cut deep into her skin. The added effect against armor was useless towards her since the clothes she was wearing were meant for light strikes and hidden fights. Though the level gap was not nearly as far apart since the last time we fought, and this time her health moved visibly. It was not some insurmountable wall and I was filled with hope again. Shouting at the behemoth above me, knowing as powerful as she was would be no help for me in this fight, "Victorum! Help your juniors! Help the Goblins!"

And much in Victorum fashion did shirk in grumbling sounds and charged towards the line of soldiers the goblins were holding back. In the distance, I could hear the shouts and terrified screams of enemy soldiers as the monster approached them. I was unable to afford to turn to look however as the strikes of Cora were ceaseless and I was constantly looking for any flutter of shadow or movement to predict her next strike. My training with Rocky was invaluable at times like these. I could feel my stance had improved significantly compared to the last time I fought her and my senses were at their peak. It helped that my stats were much higher than before, allowing me to act on my instincts when she came at me from angles that were normally unblockable. For the briefest of moments, she stopped and I could see her eyes roaming me, scanning me in a way. It gave me chills for a moment and her facial features twisted in a confusing way, so much so she asked me a question. "What the hell is a swarm lord?"

I was completely stunned, she did in fact scan my class and possibly my level too. To stop her from leaking my secret I charged her first while she was trying to dialogue with me.

"Stop struggling Conquest, let me take your head and steal that little countess you have been hiding!" she taunted me as she disappeared from in front of me and reappeared from behind and I could hear the whispers accompanied by a feigning jab at my gut with her knife. I was constantly on the defensive now. Suddenly I could feel her attention fade from our fight at the loud Crunching sound behind me.

"Come now Conquest, Let us have our duel, stop playing with that assassin!" Turning around I could see the grey mist form around the feet of Habeas. He had just finished killing the assassins that were attacking Roadkill and Sjorn. Cora shouted at him then "You bastard! Do you know how much reputation they cost to recruit! Not to mention the gold! Who are you!"

Like a cat playing with its food, Habeas looked at the last assassin and spoke with such an annoyed tone I felt offended for her, "The fact that you paid anything for these is a joke of its own. You should always expect a mission to fail when you put in an investment. Now Leave so I can fight him" and pointed towards me.

Cora, looking between both Habeas, myself and the grey dust that were her old comrades shouted and fluttered into the shadows out of sight.

All that was left in this gap of space on the battlefield were Sjorn, Roadkill, a wounded Silvax, myself and Habeas. Behind us were soldiers not wanting to intervene in this high-level fight and in front were the frontlines that had my goblins and Victorum holding off the enemy.

Sjorn, Roadkill and Silvax all regrouped at my side. Silvax whispered to us "Does anyone know this guy? Why does he have a death wish for you?"

I honestly had no idea so I told him as much. "He said his name was Habeas, he wants to duel me apparently."

"But why all this trouble" commented Sjorn

"I know I always want to fight strong people, I could understand to an extent," said Roadkill.

It left me in a bind. This player was obviously strong, strong enough to knock Silvax over 100 feet was enough to leave me a grey mist with a swing if I let it. I don't know why he was so fascinated with me.

Then it hit me, I remembered where his sword was from. The red crystalline sword was from the number one player in the game, Glass. I saw he lost it in a raid on the news.

I had to know for sure, so I spoke to Habeas "Where did you get that blade? The red one looks familiar"

"I am glad you recognize it! Glass donated it to me through blood. He wasn't as strong as I had hoped."

"Glass, as in the player from the Entity guild?"

"Who else?" shrugging as if it was a matter of fact not some extreme feat to take the supposed number one player's sword.

I looked back at my companions, a bit of horror on my face. Silvax was equally concerned at this revelation. There was a public ranking for players who revealed their levels to show everyone and boost their levels. Some people wanted to hide their ranks for who knows how many reasons. Glass was the number one publicly ranked player in Kronos, but clearly not the strongest. In Kronos Rank did not always mean everything, even with myself getting titles that gave stats it meant that anyone could become a powerhouse. Habeas was clearly one such power. We all came to grips with what was to come and Habeas was keen on fighting me. I didn't want the rest of my friends to die here on the battlefield if it meant I could stop it. I grabbed Silvaxs shoulder who was getting into a combat stance again.

"Take care of my men, let me handle this. There is no need for you guys to die for his kicks. He just wants to fight me."

Silvax had a look on his face. One of concern and newfound respect at the offered sacrifice. But his face soon switched to resignation as he looked at the ongoing battle in the background full of enemy soldiers beating on the line. Victorum standing majestically above them crushing and slashing enemy soldiers with reckless abandon. He came to a conclusion then, If he was to make an impact on the battlefield he had to be alive to see it to its end. He understood the sacrifice I wanted to make and accepted it, then began walking backward through the crowd of onlookers. Roadkill and Sjorn however, were not on board with this plan.

Sjorn in a stocky dwarvish accent, even though it was unnecessary, spoke proudly

"I said I would fight at your shoulder during this, if this guy wants a piece of you, then I will make him take a bite of my axe first."

Roadkill was quick to agree by readying his club for combat. Silvax backed up and stood with the line of onlooking Belfast Soldiers.

Habeas was looking at our three-man team nodding his head and said "Well you are welcome to have some additions. Come at me"

Roadkill reacted instantly, a berserker's rage carrying him forward with the weight of his club being lifted above his head, overhead swing brought down with extra weight as he shouted the skills name "Hammer Of Valhalla!" narrowly missing Habeas who glanced the blow into the ground next to him with his sword causing the floor to crack apart like splintered wood. The reverberation was impressive but the swing that connected with Roadkills jaw was blinding. The red sword struck a critical blow on Roadkills face giving him the blind status effect, but much like a barbarian he didn't stop there and retreat. Instead, he brought his club swinging up from the ground at Habeas. Habeas saw this coming however and blocked with his blue sword. And finally silenced the raging barbarian with a quick double thrust in the chest.

Roadkill turned to a quick grey mist and Sjorn burst his way through it with a raging shout.

"Roadkill!" and swung his axe sidelong into the parrying Habeas. He was prepared for the blow but it still pushed him back, which is the most anyone has done so far.

"Impressive" Habeas said, almost intrigued. But the flurry of blows afterward struck Sjorn so many times he couldn't raise his axe in time to block them all.

"But in the end, a disappointment." finally stating as if a known fact as Sjorn too turned into a grey fog.

"It is your turn Conquest, prove your name"

It was too quick, my allies were cut down in less than a minute of fighting. Luckily they were players and could log back in once an hour had passed. But by that point, this battle would be over. I gripped my shield and readied my sword. Habeas gave me a lookup and down, looking at my equipment with disdain and curiosity then asked me the first question since all this began.

"Are you really not going to put on your good equipment for this? I'm going to kill you if you don't"

I had no idea what he was talking about. This is the best gear I own by far, even using my ring of regeneration to keep my health topped off. I set Bug on the ground and told him to go heal Rango while I did this fight, I didn't want him dying during this duel.

Almost like my dad he sighed and said "So be it, don't disappoint me" then lunged at me with the red sword above his head. The crystal shape glowed intensely, and the shine reached into the sky with a gleam that almost blinded me. I at least saw the strike coming so prepared my <Grends Swordsmanship> to block the blow with my shield. The strike hit my shield with a thunderously loud crack in the air, my teeth felt like they would fall out and my arm felt numb, but it held. My HP was still full and my stamina was reduced by a tenth from just one strike blocked. Then, as quickly as I could muster, I stabbed forward at the gaping maw of Habeas and jabbed at his chest with the tip of my sword. I made sure to trigger <Grends Swordsmanship> here as well to force the strike to get through the block he made.

For the first time, Habeas's health went down. I was dealt more damage from the backlash of penetrating his defense than I dealt with him. But after the strike, he stood back a step nodding his head as he did so.

"You are exactly what I expected, not a scratch on you from my skill! Damn impressive, no wonder you didn't switch to your good gear if I didn't either. Lets both get serious then"

My heart sank as his equipment all changed. His suit was swapped out with a full plate chest piece, magical iron leggings, and a helmet that screamed demon on it. His back sprouted a set of black wings that seemed to suck the light out of the air as they showed behind them. His face was all that was visible of his skin and it showed a glistening white smile that had devilicious intentions.

"I shouldn't be using these weak weapons either when fighting you" and put away both of the swords he had been using, instead of pulling out a greatsword with both hands. The sword took my breath away with how majestic it looked, a vibrant black blade that was shimmering with white dots. The sword was clearly Legendary in rating and I could only imagine what the stats on it were, the rest of his gear was at minimum unique in rating as well.

"I started first the last time, this time you go!" Habeas said, conceding the initiative to me this time around, his smile was genuine and the stance he had was serious. I was honestly terrified but I solidified my resolve and charged him. Combining my swordsmanship training, <Grend Swordsmanship> and my only true attack skill <Heavy Blow> I struck an overhead swing at Habeas. He blocked with his legendary black blade, but the Grend swordsmanship caused my attack to still deal damage. However the armor he wore almost completely negated it. Habeas's face fell to a frown then at the little damage he took and spoke "I thought you would get serious, I told you I did and you can even see I put on my Player vs Player gear. Fight me Right!"

And a dull whistle started to grow, soon growing to a roar as the wind was being pulled into his blade as he charged it back for a swing that looked like it would cut the battlefield apart. I prepared my shield and even my sword behind it in an attempt to block it. Once he swung, however, a hammer stopped the blade in its tracks in front of me. A deep voice that I had heard before spoke then, "Hey now I can't have you killing my Niece's only Knight like that." A red war hammer stopped the striking cold and following the hammer's hilt back to a strong arm and a man with no sleeves stood the Duke of the South, his red hair and beard a clear indicator of his title. The Red Duke. "You really got yourself into a pickle here huh Conquest " Said the Duke, with a mischievous grin on his face. That face then looked at Habeas who was wearing a deep frown full of annoyance.

"Conquest, this was supposed to be a duel between us, why get an A.I. to intervene?"

I was at a loss for words, but I tried to satiate the man's urge for my blood.

"I am in the middle of a war, why now?"

Habeas looked around, as if oblivious to the battlefield he was intruding upon.

And with a perplexed look on his face asked "So?"

The duke, as if amused by the whole interaction looked at Habeas and said in his firm voice with just a hint of sarcasm to it "You've got some fancy gear, clearly not hired by the Jorgan Principality, if you have a score to settle here with Conquest, how about we make a bet."

This caught Habeas attention, forcing him to respond "What kind of bet are you thinking? I don't want to fight you here"

This filled the Duke with a belly-filling laugh, and he started to shake his head with his hammer at the hip. Then I noticed the little ballpoint hammer in his other hand, he pointed it at Habeas and then the field of Jorgan Principality Soldiers "I wouldn't want to fight me either. Instead, let us make a bet on who can slay the most enemy soldiers. If I can kill more than you, you must shake hands and be friends with Conquest, if you win, then you can have your duel to the death with him."

I was stunned. A bet for my life. The duke looked back at me and winked, then turned back to Habeas, "What do you say?"

After a moment of self deliberation, Habeas looked at me, then the duke. "I will take you up on that bet."

The duke smiled a toothy grin and shouted "I am Duke Michael! Fear Me!" and literally Jumped into the air towards the enemy soldiers.

Habeas, not one wanting to fall behind, and having his competitive spirit inflamed, flew after him.

I didn't want to miss out on the action so I whistled at Victorum to come back to me, it lowered its giant 8 legged body and I climbed atop its spiny back. Standing 10 feet above the battlefield I was able to get a good view of the onslaught that the Duke and Habeas were committing on the enemy.

The ground that the Duke struck first was turned into a crater, easily leveling dozens of soldiers. Soon he was swinging his hammer left and right, each swing killing two or more enemies at a time. Habeas was not far behind, his demon-like sword sucking in the air and cutting laterally across the battlefield. Each swing lacerating a dozen foes. It was a sickening sight and the enemy was coming to the same conclusion. Rushing by me were the elite forces of the duke trying to catch up with his highness. The Red was a combination of knights and wizards that were trained for over a decade directly by the duke and they were rushing full force to catch up to him on the field. I was in utter disbelief that an individual had this much power. Though the enemy knights started to intervene, and their onslaught began to slow down as stronger and stronger opponents showed themselves.

Not wanting to miss out on the opportunity for the extra experience I ordered my forces to move forward and nip out any enemy soldiers branching into the gap made by Duke Michael and Habeas. Victorum made quick work of any opponents my goblins could not handle alone. The sheer speed of her strikes with those powerful talons made me shudder. Each strike was like lightning, the scariest part was the fact that her forelimbs made no sound when lashing out at the poor soldiers below. If any soldier came too close and began to strike at her legs, they would be met with a flick of those powerful, spike-covered legs. The damage she was able to inflict on the enemies even when fully surrounded kept a grin on my face as we effortlessly slaughtered the enemy in the path of the others.

After about 30 minutes of cutting down Jorgan soldiers, my goblins were finally exhausted from the combat. It was all bloody and there were quite a few close calls in the mix. On the occasion I would catch myself watching them cut the ranks of enemies, a horn was blown and the Jorgan Principality soldiers started to retreat. Silvax had regrouped with his men and all my goblins were crowding around the legs of Victorum. After a moment I lowered myself down, and as I did so Silvax made his way towards me.

"I'm sorry I wasn't fast enough, It took some convincing to get the Duke to come," he said, clearly full of apology.

"What do you mean Silvax? You saved my life." and patted him on the arm.

"But Roadkill and Sjorn?"

"I am sure they had a great time fighting a truly strong opponent, besides we can grind those levels back after we win this battle. The war just started amirite?"

The mention of the war was a bit of a sore spot on Silvax, but the sight of victory around him filled the centurion with pride and hope.

It was one battle. But the war had just begun.

CHAPTER 14

Looking at the fleeing enemies I noticed two figures approaching from the distance. They were distinct in their form. One was wearing a suit and wielding a red sword, clearly switching off of the insane gear he was wearing before, and the other was the Duke of the south. Following at their sides were almost 200 of the duke's elite force, The Red. It was an indomitable force that made its way towards us. The air above the field was filled with dust and grey mist from defeated soldiers. On our side were thousands of men who were licking their wounds from the combat, medics running up and down the lines in an attempt to heal as best they could while their mana and stamina let them. The clerics were earning their pay today elevenfold.

Even the Medibugs that I created were working hastily on my goblins and then Silvaxs soldiers. His unit only suffered a few losses throughout the battle which was spectacular considering the damage dealt with other parts of the line.

"Conquest!" I heard a booming voice from almost a hundred meters away, it was the Duke making his way towards me at a fast walking pace. His armor is still pristine and his arms bare to the wind as it was a unique set that seemed to be seamless. He noticed my eyes glancing at the lack of wounds on his bare arms and commented on it

"It lets me swing this hammer-" Lifting his hammer and making practice swings back and forth in front of him while he comes closer. "- The ease of the swings becomes even more powerful as I see it. And besides, look at these bad boys and patted his muscle with the arm not holding the huge hammer. I wanted to be impressed but I was too anxious about the result of his and Habeas's bet about my life. But looking at Habeas who was walking a few paces behind, hand on the hilt of his sword as he marched alongside the group. It was impossible to discern the result as his face was still that of complete neutrality as when I first saw him. The only difference was that his long black hair was disheveled in front of his face instead of neatly paired behind his head. When the pair finally made their way up to us I was itching to hear what the verdict would be. Practical sentencing. The Duke could sense this tension that I had on my shoulders it seemed as he came closer and placed a hand on my back.

"Don't be shy, he will be a good friend to an upcoming knight, Conquest"

And with those words, I was immediately put at ease with his comment. I looked at Habeas and he nodded his head to affirm what the Duke had said. I smiled and walked forward towards Habeas, and out of the corner of my eye behind me, I could see Victorum come closer as if protective of her master. She could sense the danger in the man in front of me and it gave me a new respect for the first monster I ever created. Habeas finally spoke, "It was hard to figure out, but you have a special class don't you? You have a posse of monsters as followers and seeing how they aren't unsummoned like normal summoners you must have at least a rare rated class." It was an unexpected remark but the observation skills of Habeas cannot be overlooked. He was completely right about the summons not being de-summoned. Typically the longest a summoner class can keep their summon out would be for 10 minutes.

"I can confirm it is higher than rare."

This confirmation made Habeas's eyes light up, "So it is a unique rated class then?"

I smirked at him and didn't say yes or no, not wanting to reveal yet that I had a Legendary rarity class. This set a wildfire in Habeas's eyes. He outstretched his right hand for a handshake.

"I lost to the duke fair and share, his area of effect attacks was just unmatched on the battlefield. And as promised, I will shake your hand and give you a token of our friendship."

This was interesting to me as He was just told to be my friend, but as I brought my hand back from the handshake and before I could ask what he meant he handed me a red crystalline sword. Glass's old sword.

"This trinket was fun for a while but its modifiers don't suit me. Give it to one of your summons and I'm sure you will have better use for it."

I was at a loss for words.

"Thank you Habeas! What can I do to pay you back"

"Don't, it was a token of friendship. Become stronger so we can duel in the future, maybe not to the death next time." and that creepy smile loaded with vile intention was flashed before me. I would have said more but he put a hand up to stop me, then started to turn away.

I couldn't let things go like that so I shouted towards him "Hey, at least add me as a friend before you leave", and sent him a friend request. He didn't say anything and just kept going. Leaving my friend request sitting as pending.

With that taken care of, I turned away from the leaving figure and looked back at the Duke who was grinning from ear to ear at me.

"I could see you have inherited Grends techniques. You will be a true asset to this country in the future. My niece did well to choose you as her knight. Just don't pick fights you can't win, I won't be there to save you next time."

It was true, I was extremely lucky Silvax had the foresight to get the dukes to help with Habeas. Next time I would have just died. Hell, Sjorn and Roadkill both did.

"Thank you, Duke Michael, you truly did save my life and I appreciate the praise you have given me."

"I can tell you worked hard for it. I heard what had happened in the mountains with Count Von Torrez. It was a shame that he died, he was a close friend to me as well as my brother. Isabel is a good girl, she has a fighting spirit so does well to serve her at Stotonely. If you need advice on being a knight feel free to take some time to learn from mine, The Red. They have all learned from a young age what it really means to have the honor of a knight. Just whatever you do, stay far away from the Earl when you can. He is a lecherous man who grabs at power whenever he can."

The duke gave me very good advice along with the reminder of his brother, the late count Von Torrez. I have to get back to Isabel, the Countess who had given me a chance to become a knight.

"I should go check on countess Isabel"

With a hearty laugh and a hard slap on my back, he pushed me in the direction of his camp.

I started moving towards it with some happiness in my bones and all my troops at my back. Even Victorum was towering above the other soldiers as I made my way to the commander's tent that Isabel was waiting in. As I approached I noticed something wrong. There were no guards outside the tent. No soldiers standing at attention at my approach to check me in either. My skin began to crawl as my walk turned into a flat-out sprint into the tent, sword drawn and shield at my front as I shoved through the tent's flaps.

All I heard was a scream from Isabel shouting "Conquest!"

And a knife bounced off my shield that was covering my face as I burst into the room. Isabel was on the other side of the war table in the room with a familiar-looking assassin holding a blade to her throat. It was Cora. looking at the hard-faced countess on death's door with a blade at her neck she was not scared or crying but instead absolutely infuriated. If it wasn't for the dire situation I would laugh at the personality Isabel had even in these circumstances.

Cora tensed her arm closer and used Isabel as a cover between us and shouted with desperation in her tone "Drop your weapon Conquest! If you don't I will kill the Countess right here and now."

I had no choice, my goblins were outside behind me and I could tell they heard the situation outside as they stayed on the other side of the tent entrance. I unequipped my sword and shield and raised my hands in the air.

"Good, now walk slowly over here and bind yourself with the rope on the table."

Sure enough, there was a bundle of rope on the war table that seemed to be the same stuff used on Isabel. I was desperate. Thinking quickly on most of my skills to find a way out of it there was only one skill I hadn't used until now. <Manifest Monster Traits> It let me manifest any skill one of my monsters had that I did not. Activating the skill as I approached I selected the only skill I could think of that could help me. It was Victorums and called <Web Bind>. Activating it, I felt my stomach lurch as something came up my throat- I shot a ball of webbing from my mouth at Cora. She was completely entangled by the webbing from the unexpected attack and separated from Isabel who quickly ran behind me with her arms still bound. Before I could re-equip my gear the top of the tent was ripped apart as Victorum slashed it apart, apparently sensing her skill was used in the tent. I shouted as quickly as I could at Victorum "Kill that assassin!" and pointed at the struggling Cora. But as Victorum went to strike her she broke free and threw the dagger at Isabel, thinking quickly I dove in front of the blade and took the strike in the stomach. Cora was turned into a fine gray mist by Victorum and I lost half my health from the blade and the rest of it was plummeting from the poison on it.

Seconds later my goblins were rushing around the now open-topped tent and helping untangle Isabel from the bindings and huddling around me. The Medibugs were quick at work to try and keep my health going up but it was useless. My health was going down too quickly from the poison effect. Once the countess was unbound she rushed to my side as well saying quickly and quietly

"No no no no, not you too. Why must you sacrifice yourself for me."

It was sweet, the countess had sorrow on her face again for me. This was going to be my first death in this world, but I would come back as it is just a game for me. It was their lives that could not be brought back.

Through struggling breaths from the poison filling my lungs I was able to get a few words out before I too was turned into a grey mist.

"I will be back for you Countess. Victorum, Abel, Keep Isabel safe until I return. Do not leave her side." With that, Abel and Rango both stood straight and saluted. It was the last thing I saw before my screen turned red and the notification came up in front of me.

```
You have Died

<Lost 2 levels>

<Lost (Iron Shield)>

You can log in again in 1 hour and 59 minutes
```

It was a bad end, I closed out the notification of my death and got out of the pod. Then before I could even leave the rental room I noticed seven burly men sitting in the waiting chairs, and in the middle of them was Rocky.

It freaked me out to a point I didn't speak, like a deer caught in headlights. Instead, Rocky spoke first.

"I heard what happened to your dad. I wanted to make sure my disciple was ok."

And he came to the pod placing the callused hand on my shoulder.

"I just wanted to make sure you were going to be ok. We saw that you didn't go home and were worried you would have taken other measures."

I could see the emotion in Rockys eyes, that of true concern and it slowed the unsettling feeling I had towards him. The others in the room were still stoic but all familiar faces that I had trained with over the past month. It was more comfortable in ten seconds than in any that I received from my father earlier. One of the faces looked more familiar like I had seen them shopping for groceries or other times when I was out of the house. This practically forced me to ask him a question I felt I already knew the answer to.

"Thank you Rocky. It means a lot to have you comfort me like this. But how did you find me?"

At the mention of finding me, he became squeamish. Which was unlike him. He looked down at his feet which were fidgeting back and forth and he muttered "Well we had seen you leave your apartment like a bat out of hell and just happened to see you go to a hospital and leave afterward. . ." So he was actually following me. The fact I never noticed was unsettling, to say the least. His grasp on my shoulder was still there and I wasn't quite ready to give him a firm reprimand when they were towering around the room with me.

He smiled after I didn't comment on his behavior and tightened the grip on my shoulder.

"Let's escort you home Conquest and hit the gym early in the morning for a good session. How about it?"

By the time I got home, the two-hour log-out penalty would be over and I could log in again. *Yeah, I guess it was time to go home*, I thought to myself. But I needed a real reason that he was following me, no one trails someone like this if it was just to take care of a disciple. I stood up and removed the hand from my shoulder then as bravely as I could say to him with a hint of shakiness in my voice "I won't be going anywhere until you tell me; Why did you follow me?" I braced myself and had a semi-stance ready in case I had to defend myself. I was tense and I could feel my heart palpitating in my chest as if it too wanted to run away from this situation. The seconds moved so slowly as Rocky digested my question, his face however did not turn to anger or any other hostile look but instead turned to a deep forlorn gaze. His eyes that were hovering over the ground for the most part finally made their way up to greet my eyes as well. After a deep sigh, he took a step back after seeing my stance- one full of tension. And instead of taking a stance of his own, he brought both hands up, palms facing up in the calming gesture he uses at the end of sparring matches then started to explain himself. The emotion he carried in his voice was different from any I had heard him give me in the past, normally the man had a solid attitude full of vigor and enthusiasm. This time it was full of what could be seen as regret.

"Theo. I will be honest with you, the reason I took you in as a disciple is that it was at the request of my sensei, the late Rocky Senior. Before he passed, he told me that you were the best disciple he had ever trained, and to not lose you. The only times he had so much praise for someone else was with me. And when you finally came back to our dojo I vowed to keep you there and make sure you became stronger under my tutelage. And over the past month, I could see exactly what my father told me about you, your veracity and a tenacious attitude to learning everything thrown at you are inspiring and the fact you are willing to work until you pass out is mind boggling. It is not a trait found easily. I learned the last time you left was because your sister was hospitalized and you were forced to pay the loan sharks for her medical bills. So when I heard you were rushing to the same hospital I assumed the worst and refused to sit back and watch as you got plummeted into debt and had to leave my gym"

It was a lot of information and praise that I was not expecting, but it had a warm sound to it as he went on. Rocky genuinely cared about my well-being and it was a nice change of pace. In the past month I hadn't talked to my family at all other than the hospital visit, not once did they ask me how I was or if I was okay. And over this past month, Rocky had made sure I was healthy and eating right, even when I told him how much I gamed he set me up with a meal plan that didn't take away from my time in Kronos. It all makes sense to me now, all the things he had been doing for me were more than just a typical disciple at his gym. I gave it a few more hard thoughts, but seeing how I wasn't packed into a bag by everyone here I could safely assume they weren't here to harm me in any way.

"Thank you Rocky. I appreciate the honesty and I am thankful that I have you in my corner. I luckily don't have any medical bills this time around, those are worries of the past and my dad can face his own problems on his own. With that said, I don't want to be stalked like this anymore. Instead, just take my number. Then if something goes wrong I can just call you."

The offer to give my number to him was a good middle ground for me, I don't want to be followed by people from the gym, I like my privacy. He smiled and nodded. We then exchanged numbers and he flagged his men to walk me to the truck.

I was basically escorted to my truck at the complete shock of all those in the store. And before I got in my car for the long drive home I said one last time to Rocky "Thanks again for being there, I'll see you at the dojo tomorrow morning" and bowed to him.

He smiled and went back to his car that he had one of the other disciples drive for him.

The drive home had me thinking for a long time about the events of the day. My dad, his audacity to still hate me pursuing my dream and my siblings who were still stuck with him. It sucked that I couldn't get them out, but that is why I am going to keep trying at Kronos. Thinking of Kronos made me think about the war, it was brutal all around, nothing really prepared me to have arrows thrown from every direction and in all instances, the enemy is out to kill you no matter what. Then there was Habeas. He was a walking force of nature as his dark blade cut through my friends. Luckily they were players and could respawn, he had so much power in all of his strikes and the gear he flashed at the end still sends chills down my spine. My summon Victorum returned gave me some pride but even she would die to that strike charged by that sword. I at least would not want to put them in a fight against each other.

Like lightning struck me I thought about the gift Habeas gave me, It was the crystalline red sword. The sword is owned by the public number one player in all of Kronos, Glass. If I sold that sword I would make a decent fortune for sure. With the thought of money on my mind, the rest of the trip was a smooth journey in the dark.

Habeas

Hours after the battle Habeas looked at the sitting friend notification on his screen. It was the first time he truly considered accepting it. If Conquest was to become a true opponent in the future it would be good to keep track of him with the friend list. But, it didn't have to be rushed. He minimized the notification but didn't accept or decline it. As Habeas made his way off of the battlefield he made sure to keep out of sight of the notorious reporter Chuck Carlson. He was foolish and sure to have been seen when fighting earlier. Now he has to make an escape from the country else he may be pursued by the Empire's soldiers and the Entity Guilds men. But to him, the fighting was worth it. Now he just has to pursue his class quest to get even stronger, not wanting to be left behind by Conquest if he too has a Unique grade class.

Cora

Cora respawned in the Jorgan Principality as it was the closest respawn point that was non-hostile to her. The failed assassination was weighing on her mind and during the two-hour waiting period, she was at her wit's end watching the news. It infuriated her to be so badly defeated by an opponent. That beast Conquest called 'Victorum' especially enraged her as its speed was far higher than what she was capable of at this point and even after taking the 2 levels lost the penalty which made her level 97. She was one of the top players in the game and one of the highest-level assassins in Kronos. That Mantis Spider monster was faster than her, and with a quick cleave was able to rent her in two. Looking back she realized she lost her dagger during the death as well, incredibly unlucky. Though she failed her quest now, she did however spawn in a country that will be in open war with the Belfast kingdom. Work would be easy to find and she could exact revenge at a later date. This time however she had something that was going to be key for that revenge, knowledge of her targets class.

And with that Cora's mind started to turn gears as she started heading towards the capital of the Jorgan Principality in search of the closest library, she needed to find out more about this 'SwarmLord'.

⬥

Theo

After a long drive full of introspection, I was full of desire to sleep. I knew I couldn't rest however since I needed to make sure my summons was okay. Practically barging into my apartment I ignored everything else and hopped straight into the immersion pod and entered Kronos.

Since it was the first time I had died I was respawned at the closest respawn point to my death that was in friendly territory. Luckily for me, this was in Stotonely, the place where it all started for me. I appeared in front of the church of Grisia, the god of creation in Kronos. Looking around the city I was happy to see it wasn't in flames. I started quickly to run towards the south. I needed to see my summons again. But before I could make it outside the city a familiar voice called out to me from the top of the walls.

"Conquest! Where are you going?"

To my surprise, it was Knight Captain Randall. The man in command of all the guards in Stotonely. Figuring he must have a lot of questions I didn't want to stay and chat for long.

"I am heading out to check on the war front, I have to find Countess Isabel. Please open the gate for me"

Looking up at the all-powerful gatekeeper Randall I implored him to open the gate for me.

"You won't find her out there, she returned to the keep about an hour ago. She had a whole entourage in tow including Duke Michael as well. I'm sure you can head that way to try and see them"

Relief flushed over me at the news, "Thank you, Captain Randall!" I waved and turned to run. The last thing I saw was that happy grin on his face and his wife Teresa at his side.

Thinking of the last order I gave Victorum and my followers, they should be near Isabel.

Pushing my character to its limits I ran at full speed towards the keep, the closer I came the more soldiers I saw littering the streets. And when I came into the training grounds that were littered with scorch marks and battle scars I could see the Red standing guard scattered and patrolling the grounds. Some noticed me but recognized who I was and pointed at the gate I did not use during the escape a month ago. Heading in through the front gate of the keeps inner sanctum I was met with an irritated Earl Claycoax who was pacing back and forth with a hand on his head and a plump man with an abacus next to him.

I could hear their conversation as they were being anything but quiet.

The plump man was trying to reason with the Earl but clearly to no avail "Sire, I do not see any logistical capabilities that we could muster to completely man the Drandall Mountain ranges. At most, we could occupy 5% and begin a skeleton crew of soldiers to patrol the mining encampments. But with the war coming into full force there are no guarantees we could keep it safe during any prolonged sieges. If we were to lose production in the first few months of establishing our-"

The Earl was impatient and refused to listen to more, sticking out the hand that was busy running through his long hair in the face of the plump man.

"I don't Care! It has to be done, this woman took advantage of us, the contract she signed to us was just for the mining rights, none of the equipment or the manpower to handle such a venture. She has completely pulled out everything of value. Leaving us with a bare monster-infested mountain range. But the diamonds and gems that could be pulled from it are worth the investment.-"

The Earl was about to continue but he noticed me and it was like a bucket of cold water was poured on his fuming visage. It flickered a face of calm until he recognized me, then his rage returned and was pointed in another direction, me.

"Oh here comes the talk of the town. How audacious of you to act like royalty, peasant. The countess and Duke may look kindly to you, but I see through you. You just want the glory and gold. Take my advice, stay where you belong" that he pointed his nose back up at the sky and walked into another side passage out of my sight. I already did not like this Earl but that attitude really pisses me off. He made sure to shout something before completely going out of sight, however.

"You better go talk with those barbaric war masters in the meeting hall, I refuse to trouble myself with other household affairs."

I shook my head and ignored it as I continued further into the keep towards the main hall, following the signs.

Occasionally there would be men from the Red marching throughout the halls, with scattered bits of battle damage amongst the walls and their armor. They must have had to recapture the keep from the infiltrators that attacked before. Continuing my march I came upon a set of large doors that led into the large room that the guards pointed me to. The place the Countess was supposedly waiting for me, with the Duke. I pushed the doors open slowly and with nervousness quaking my bones. It was an unnecessary fear that I realize now as once the doors were fully open I could see an ornate war table in the center with chairs of high-ranking army officials and the nobles I was looking for. The duke of the south, Michael, was leading the meeting pointing at different locations on the map. The table had a topographical map of the southern half of the Belfast Kingdom, complete with mountain ranges, forests, cities and towns that occupy its vast land. It was a beautiful table with little flaws. But as I approached the table I noticed the conversation was cut off as everyone's eyes turned to me.

I froze under the cumulative stares, it was natural, I could see Silvax wasn't at the table and instead was waiting on the side of the room with other Centurian ranked military officers, I did not notice this until now that all of the ones at the table were at least of Tribune rank. Tribune was the rank equivalent to a Colonel in real military affairs. The rest were ranks that were even higher, the true big wigs of the Belfast military were here, all at the call of the Duke. And all of them were looking at me.

The Duke decided to cut the tension then and introduce me "Conquest I see you finally made it. I see you travelers are as durable as ever. Now as I was saying to you all earlier, Conquest here has made direct contact with the enemy's commander, the Duke of the Jorgan Principality- Stanely Freneferd." With the announcement of the name, the military officers all gasped. This name carries weight amongst the older officers it seemed. The Duke continued - "Yes, it is true. He was at the back of the formation testing our lines during this first battle. He did not get involved even when I showed myself on the field. None of his elite soldiers made an appearance either which worries me. Using the authority of my name, Duke Michael, I hereby declare an official state of war with the Jorgan Principality. It is no longer at the stage of a border skirmish as we have also confirmed he conspired and succeeded in assassinating my brother-in-law, the late Count Rodriguez Von Torrez. This act of war cannot be ignored, and with the help of our ally the Raynor Kingdom we will teach those Principality dogs what it means to be at war with us." The crowd all threw applause and cheers at the speech, the war had been declared but the confidence everyone in the room had for the Duke was unshakable. For the next hour or so they discussed strategies and other tactics that involved troop formations and placements throughout the southern half of the kingdom to be able to best react to any strikes made by the Jorgan Principality.

Much of the conversation was ideas and strategies on how to react when Duke Stanely Freneferd makes an appearance. According to their measurements, he was as great a strategist as the Duke of the south. They paid special attention to their special forces as well, apparently consisting of extremely talented mages that could counter the Duke of the south in a direct confrontation. All of these conversations however did not involve me so I slowly started to slink back into the crowd at the sides of the room.

That is when I noticed between two tribunes at the table was the countess, I could barely recognize her as she was in full plate battle dress armor. The only reason I recognized her was that Catalina was standing behind her in her signature full plate armor as well. It was good to know she was by her side at all times.

Soon enough the meeting calmed down and everyone started to leave the room to give orders. Thousands of men were to be mobilized for a war effort that spanned three countries. Most of the other big wig officers ignored me on their way out since I did not even hold a formal rank and was just a traveler in their eyes. That was not the case with the countess however, she stopped in front of me before leaving, "You died for me Conquest, I can't think of a more loyal thing a knight can do. I want you to know that all of your troops are safe, and if you want I can get you to become an official knight with the Duke's blessing. Do you accept it?"

I knew this would happen eventually as everyone was already calling me a knight of the countess, but now that the notification finally appeared in front of me I was unsure if I wanted to commit to this job.

Class change available <Royal Knight>
If you change class you will lose <SwarmLord> and all of its
abilities and instead become a <Royal Knight>
[Warning: You cannot become a SwarmLord again if you change
classes]

What finally solidified me to refuse it was that it would change my class from <Swarmlord> to <Royal Knight> and I did not want to lose those benefits. So I shook my head.

"I cannot become your knight, my lady, It is not the way of Grend Amear. If I am to truly become an asset to this country I need to be free. But If you ever need my help, I am never going to be far away."

The refusal hit Isabel with a shock, but she nodded at it anyway, accepting it. No reputation or favor was lost with her which was a nice touch.

"I understand, then instead I want you to take this." as she reached into her armor to grab something, the Duke who was watching nearby saw this and stopped what he was doing to put his hand on the Countesses' shoulder.

"Are you sure?"

Isabel nodded her head and continued to grab something from her armor. Soon she pulled out a vibrantly deep blue-colored necklace.

"This necklace is something my father gave to me, it was so he could find me If I ever became lost. It has two halves, I have one, you can have this half. Now you will know If I am ever in trouble."

I cupped my hands in front of me and she gently placed them in them. I understood immediately the significance of this gift. She could have given it to the duke, the strongest man in the kingdom according to the rumors. But instead, she entrusted it with me, leaving the duke to focus on the war effort.

"I will always care for it. Thank you for having such trust in me Countess Isabel"

Her cheeks flushed for a moment and she stood straight again to speak.

"You may not be my knight but you can still serve me well. Your soldiers are being brought to the training ground as we speak and I am sure there will be plenty of opportunities for them to act in the war effort, right?" as if I would say no to fighting in the war.

I gave it some thought but only for a second, fighting in a war was too good of an opportunity for me. So I kneeled in front of her, still gently holding the necklace away from me.

"I will fight during this war and make the enemies of you the enemies of myself. May Victorums blades run red with the blood of our enemies."

"Good, I look forward to your results, and please stay safe."

Her face flushed again and she hurriedly walked away. The duke then came closer to me after I stood back up from the kneel.

"She trusts you, you know that. I see that. But you really have to make an effort in this war, you have to prove that you are what she thinks you are. I do not see that hero yet, just someone who has gotten lucky. Prove me wrong." and with a huge grin, he slapped me on the shoulder and walked out of the war room, leaving just a few guards and myself left.

Letting the information sink into me I turned and left as well towards the training grounds, eager to see my summons again.

As soon as I made it to the training grounds where I spent my first days in Kronos, I spotted the impossible-to-miss Spider Mantis monster I had created named Victorum. She was towering over the goblins and watching as Abel put them through training strikes with each other. It was blissful to see them again. I made it a few more steps when Victorum spotted me and charged headlong in my direction. A few soldiers were caught completely off guard at the sprinting monster moving at an unnatural amount of speed that Victorum moved at. Many let out gasps and shouts of fright for a moment before realizing it was a friendly beast.

Once Victorum made it to me it lowered its bulbous head that had eight eyes and spider-like mandibles as well as the two large eyes that looked like a mantis. Its head was easily the size of my torso and its antennae stuck out in various directions. Off the top of its head dropped Bug, my little Medibug I made for myself. It was great to see he was okay too. The rest of the goblin crew and Abel spotted what made Victorum rush across the field and they too came close, all happy to see me again. Abel proudly pronounced to everyone,

"As I said to you all, the master is immortal, he is a traveler and does not fear death!" The goblins ate this up and all cheered at their leader's return. Though some still seemed to lose balance when throwing their swords in the air. I had a lot of work to do to get these guys into better fighting conditions when we entered this war as active participants.

It made me excited and I no longer wanted to wait. It was time to grind these guys up and buff up their numbers. But first, now that I knew they were safe, it was time to rest. I gave them the command to hunt in the forest for the night and for Victorum to keep an eye on them, then logged out.

I put my new red crystalline sword on sale on the marketplace for Kronos and went to bed knowing I had so many more adventures to go on tomorrow. After Rockys of course.

Name: Conquest	Class: SwarmLord	Level: 42
Stat points to Allocate:		HP: 1250 Mana:160
Dexterity:	96	
crafting/attack speed		
Strength:	67	
physical DMG/ carry weight		
Intelligence:	46	
Mana total/regen and spell power		
Charm:	46	
Likability with NPC		
Constitution:	98	
hp/ stamina total		
Agility:	95	
movement speed/ stamina regen		

PROLOGUE

---◆---

Unknown

"The preparations are complete," said a gravel-like voice.

"Then it is time for the first phase, unleash the dungeons." hissed a voice that was full of malice and evil.

"Yes, my prince" responded the gravel-sounding man.

"Soon the sides of the Drandall Mountain range would begin to open up and all of the dungeons would have an outbreak, unleashing hordes of monsters upon the Belfast Kingdom." cackled the one referred to as the Prince.

"Your plan is flawless my Prince! Those Belfast dogs will not know what struck them"

"It only cost the souls of nobles, the Raynor kingdom provided plenty."

Then in the middle of the night, a kingdom-wide message appeared for everyone in the Belfast Kingdom –

<S> Defend the Belfast Kingdom
Dungeon outbreaks have opened up all across the kingdom's mountains, you must help in defending your town or city from the coming monster assault.   Rewards depend on Contribution: Reputation   Gold   Items   Failure: The loss of each city/ town is permanent

It was an S-grade quest, one of only three that have ever been given in the world of Kronos online. The connotations of it were clear and the mission seemed simple in its description but everyone who received it knew the situation must be dire for it to have been given such a ranking. Everyone, including the non-combat classes were forcefully given this quest. And all throughout the night any player logged in would be forced to prepare for the attack.

It was a dark situation that triggered the start of the war between Belfast and the Jorgan Principality.

To Be Continued

Made in United States
Orlando, FL
07 April 2022